A PLAYER FOR A PRINCESS

By Tia Louise

A Player for A Princess
Copyright © Tia Louise, 2016
www.AuthorTiaLouise.com
Printed in the United States of America.

Cover design by Steven Novak.

For Mr. TL, my prince.

ALSO BY TIA LOUISE

THE DIRTY PLAYERS

The Prince & The Player (Book 1), 2016

A Player for a Princess (Book 2), 2016

Dirty Dealers, 2017

Dirty Thief, 2017

* * *

THE ONE TO HOLD SERIES

One to Hold, One to Protect, One to Save (Derek & Melissa)

One to Keep (Patrick & Elaine)

One to Love (Kenny & Slayde)

One to Leave, One to Take (Stuart & Mariska)

One to Chase (Marcus & Amy)

* * *

PARANORMAL ROMANCES

One Immortal (Derek & Melissa)

One Insatiable (Koa "Stitch" & Mercy)

CONTENTS

Chapter 1: Old Habits

Zelda Wilder

My heart is beating too fast. Glancing down, I see my hands tremble, and I take a few measured breaths to try and make them stop.

I've never been this anxious on a job, but everything has changed in the last six weeks. Looking over my shoulder has become a nonstop addiction it seems.

For the first time, I'm alone with Seth, just the two of us. Unknown hit men took out our longtime partner Helen, and we don't even know how long ago it was. The radio report simply said her body was found in a bathtub in a cheap hotel in Miami. A plastic bag was over her head.

Clutching my black purse, again I look over my shoulder. Through the neon lights and arcade noises of the Divi casino in St. Croix, I see men in black blazers dotted among the gamblers. Men with curly earpieces in their ears, men with dark brows lowered over steely eyes, men sweeping the room for any signs of criminal activity.

I do another quick sweep, and I realize I'm looking for Ava. *Stop that, Zee.* My little sister is far away from this life, and it's because I chose to distance us. I decided her safety is more important than keeping our family together.

The last time I saw her, she was wounded and pale, unconscious in a hospital bed. It tore at my heart to leave her, but at least I know she's okay. Thanks to the Internet, I've been able to keep up with the "developing story" of the assassination attempt on the future king of Monagasco and the shooting of his fiancée, a.k.a., my sister. Rowan has taken Ava from the hospital to the palace, where she's recuperating under the watchful eyes of his royal guards.

With a steady exhale, I release the nerves, reminding myself it's for the best. She's with the man who loves her, who promised to take care of her. If a crown prince can't do that, I don't stand a chance.

Still… it isn't me.

I'm not watching out for her.

As the oldest, I've always had that job. I've taken care of us since our parents died, leaving us at the mercy of the foster system. I've protected her ever since that last asshole thought he'd try relieving his sexual frustrations on a little girl entrusted to his "care." It was me who'd bashed him over the head with the lamp, grabbed her hand, and run us out of there.

We'd hidden all night in the pouring rain in a concrete culvert, and I came up with a plan to keep us out of that life for good. Passing the baton to someone else—even a future king—hits me harder than I thought it would. My throat aches at her absence, my chest heavy. *Stay safe, Ava-bug.*

Tonight is the first time I've ever entered a place like this without her. Ava is the only person I can count on in any situation. Every security guard in this room reminds me of how we've always been a team. If anything goes wrong, I grab her hand and we run, just like always. We stay alive.

Only, I made the deal that changed everything. I shook hands with the devil.

I could argue I didn't have a choice. We were facing jail time, felony convictions in Florida for grand theft, and while I'd be willing to take my chances in jail, there's no way in hell I'm letting Ava go to prison. So yeah. Agreeing to work with Reginald Winchester might make me a "bad guy," but I'd do it again in heartbeat.

A heartbeat...

Squaring my shoulders, I slide a lock of jet-brown hair behind my ear and force confidence into my stride. I make my way through the glittering, noisy casino to my target—a shiny brass roulette wheel—and prepare to start the show.

The last time we worked this con in Miami, Helen had been waiting at the table when I got there. I can still hear her gravelly voice and see her "May Contain Alcohol" sweatshirt. Sadness followed closely by fear ricochets through my insides. Whoever killed her is looking for me.

We were on our way to Tortola to hide when Seth said we should stop in here and bank extra cash. As Americans, we don't need passports in St. Croix, and we can catch a cheap ferry and slip away in the night to our ultimate destination.

Keeping off the radar is the goal—as always. We'll pocket a few thousand and disappear unnoticed. At least that's the plan.

"No more bets!" The dealer passes his hand over the wheel just as I arrive, and I quickly assess the table rules. Minimum ten dollar bet. *Decent.*

Opening my clutch, I remove two hundreds and pass them to the dealer. He quickly exchanges them for twenty pale blue chips. I'll join the fray next spin.

Tonight the transmitter is hidden in my shoe as opposed to my cuff bracelet. I'm wearing a strappy black dress that stops mid-thigh, and my black heels show off my legs while hiding the device facilitating our winning streak.

I have to sit with my legs crossed and point my toe to activate it. One dainty point, one shiny silver ball drops right in the tray, predictable at ninety percent accuracy. So far the odds have been in our favor.

We'll play until Seth gives me the signal they're onto us. Then I'll calmly cash out, walk away, and meet him at the pier on Grapetree Point. From there we'll make the forty-mile cruise to Tortola.

An elegantly dressed woman shakes her head and gives me a bitter smile as I sit. "Don't stay longer than three spins," she grumbles.

I smile in response. "That's the rule, isn't it?"

"That's the rule." Her expression tells me she lost a lot tonight.

As a student of casinos, I know how steeply the odds in roulette are stacked in favor of the House — they're the worst of any game. The longer you sit, the greater your chances of losing, times a million. If I were giving advice to a rookie, I'd say stick to blackjack. At least there you can use strategy and possibly win a little. Walking away is something I learned early on. You can never be afraid to walk away — even when you're certain you're lucky. Luck is the biggest liar of all.

I place half my chips on the black rectangle and watch as the wheel begins to spin. The dealer snakes his hand to the side and releases the ball. It flies around the shining wood with a sharp rasp. I need to lose this round. The job doesn't start until Seth arrives, and I can't win for longer than a few spins or it'll look suspicious.

Another glance over my shoulder. He's still not here. Casting my eyes down, I watch the wheel spinning, *black-red, black-red, black-red, flashing brass.*

"Have you been here long?" A man in an elegant suit steps into the space beside me and fishes out his wallet as we wait for the ball to drop.

"I just sat down," I say without making eye contact. I'm not here to make friends.

He passes a crisp one hundred dollar bill to the dealer. "Then we have no way of knowing if it's a good table."

"Sorry," I shake my head. "I play red or black."

"Not much of a gambler?"

A glance, and I see he's tall and thick with dark brown hair and a cocky expression like he already knows the answer to his question.

"No," I say in a discouraging tone.

No, thank you. Even if I hadn't left my heart in Monagasco, I never let romance interfere with a job. Well, almost never.

"Logan Thomas." Mr. Persistent sticks a hand at me.

He waits, and I hesitate. *Two first names.*

"Regina Lampert," I lie only barely touching his fingers.

"Regina," he gives me a nod, but that twinkle of knowledge is in his eyes.

A knot forms in my throat. I don't like this. The ball drops on black seventeen, and a lady at the other end of the table emits a little cheer.

"You won," Logan's voice ripples toward me.

The dealer adds more chips to my pile, and I'm ready to hop up and intercept Seth.

11

A swirl of warmth at my side tells me I'm too late.

"Roo-lette!" Seth exclaims in the exaggerated southern accent he reserves for our cons. "Well, I'm as happy as a tornado in a trailer park at this turn of events!" He turns to a man at the table. "You know, I'm a student of roolette. Only three spins and you're out."

Tilting my head so Logan can't see, I level my blue eyes on Seth's green ones. As usual, he's wearing black horn-rimmed glasses.

He ignores my pointed glare, his smile as overblown as his accent. "I hope you don't mind if I stand right here beside you, Miss — ?"

"Lampert," I say, tightening my jaw. *Abort, Seth. Abort!*

"Lampert?" He looks up behind me at the big guy getting too close. "I don't believe I've ever heard that name before. And you are?"

"Logan Thomas."

The men shake hands, and Seth shakes his head. "It's sure nice to meet you. I tell you, I've met the nicest people in Saint Crow — Ah, Dealer? I need a hundred in tens."

The dealer doesn't even look up as he exchanges Seth's money, and as soon as the chips are distributed, my partner in crime splits his money on two corner bets. I rotate in my chair so I can cross my legs. He's sticking to the plan, and my insides are quaking.

Logan Thomas is onto us. Somehow we've been detected. I've been in this situation before, and it cost us a partner, two if you count Ava.

I can only guess the man to my right is another of Wade Paxton's thugs — or worse. Law enforcement. Perhaps Reggie made good on his promise to expose Ava and me to every casino boss this side of the Atlantic.

"No more bets!" The dealer's hand passes over the table, and the ball shoots around the spinning wheel.

I sense Seth's body tense. It's time for me to do my part. Logan Thomas is probably waiting for this exact moment to arrest me. Five years and a felony conviction.

My breath is coming in short pants. Perhaps I should let it happen. *Would I be safer in prison?* Seth clears his throat, and I swallow my terror. The slightest twitch of my ankle, the slightest point. The ball stutters and drops...

Twenty-nine black.

"WOO HOO!!!!! Well, I'll be Johnny Mack Brown!!!" Seth explodes with excitement. "I WON! And on a corner bet to boot!"

He grasps the table edge and does a little jig. I can't breathe waiting to see what our ominous table mate will do. Will he whip out a badge? Detain us? At least with the device in my shoe they won't find anything in a pat down.

"Congratulations," Logan says. "That's two and oh for me, so I'll be saying goodnight, Miss Lampert." He does a little nod in my direction, still with that knowing smile.

I don't make eye contact, and Seth is busy distracting the dealer. I haven't touched my chips on black, yet again they've doubled in number. One more turn is all I can stay.

"Now *this* is the hard part," Seth says loudly, pinching his top lip between two fingers. "Should I leave them there or move them?"

He glances down at me again, a twinkle in his eyes. "What do you suggest, Miss Lampert?"

Shaking my head, I again feign ignorance. "I don't know. I only play by color."

He nods looking again at the table. "You know what they say. If everything's headed your way, you might need to change lanes."

I move my pile of chips to the red field just as the dealer starts the wheel. Final bets are going around, and Seth stares at the green felt, appearing to be deep in thought. At the very last minute, he reaches out and moves his chips to opposite ends of the grid.

"No more bets!" The dealer snaps just as Seth's hands leave the area.

He straightens, still doing his very best acting job. His lip is again pinched between his fingers, and now he's bouncing on the balls of his feet.

"I tell you, Miss Lampert, I'm as nervous as a long-tailed cat in a room full of rockers."

My jaw tightens. *That makes two of us...* I can't shake this tension, even with Logan Thomas out of sight. For all I know he's waiting outside the door.

The ball starts to slow, and I shift on my stool, pointing my toe as I do so. In that instant, the silver ball drops quickly into the tray.

Red five.

"HOLEE SHIT!!!! I can't believe it!" Seth shouts, slapping the rubber table-guard. "I can't believe it, I WON AGAIN!" He turns to me, and I glance up, giving him a little smile. "And look at there! So did you, Miss Lampert!"

"I should probably quit while I'm ahead," I say, rising from my chair.

Warmth at my back, and a familiar voice clenches my insides. "You shouldn't break a winning streak."

Jumping away as if I were electrocuted, I turn to face the owner of that sexy voice. Our eyes lock, and standing here, right at this table, a knowing smile curling his lips, is MacCallum Lockwood Tate, my playboy prince. The one I left behind when I ran.

If I couldn't breathe before, now I'm about to faint.

"Cal!" It's a startled whisper, my fingers tightening.

His smoky hazel eyes won't release me, and all the desire I feel is reflected back at me. At the same time, something new is in his—an edge I've never seen before.

"I'm sorry..." His voice is slow, measured. "Have we met? You seem familiar..."

Glancing down, I relax my grip on the chair. I focus on calm, stay in character. I straighten the enormous ring on my hand. It's costume jewelry—fake yellow topaz set in fake yellow gold. How fitting, considering everything about me is fake.

Still, even in this remote location, wearing this silly dark-brown wig, I feel exposed, laid bare. I can't do this in front of him. Even if he knows what I am, I'm ashamed for him to see me doing it.

Seth only pauses a hiccup before resuming the act. "He's right, Miss Lampert. You can't walk out when you're winning."

I want to kill Seth. "I can't..." I start, but it's too late.

The dealer only pauses a moment before starting the wheel again. My heart beats too fast. It shoots a pain between my shoulder blades, and I haven't moved my chips. I haven't moved anything. I have to sit down if I'm going to activate the switch, but if I sit, I'll be right beside Cal. Our arms will touch. I'm not sure I can handle that.

"No more bets!" The dealer's hand passes over my stationary chips.

Seth had moved his a few rows to the left, and I feel his eyes on me watching, waiting to see if I'll choke. The wheel is slowing. I can hear the noise of the ball decelerating on its track.

Cal's hazel eyes are like heat against my skin, never moving away, not letting me escape this time. I hear his voice the last time we spoke: *I love you, Zelda...*

My chest rises and falls quickly. I'm still standing.

"It's slowing down!" Seth's voice is eager, but it's directed at me. He's trying to snap me out of it.

If I blow this spin, we'll lose everything. I'm on my own now. I left Cal behind, and even if he followed me, it changes nothing. I have to be able to take care of myself.

"Slower..." Seth says again.

With a blink I break Cal's spell over me and lean down as if to adjust my ankle strap. A flick of my wrist and a curl of my toe, and the silver ball clatters into red seven.

"OH!" Seth bellows. "I DON'T BELIEVE IT!!!"

He slaps my shoulder, but I haven't regained my footing. Pulling up quick, I'm slammed into Cal's chest. My palms are flat against his jacket, and his warm breath skirts across my cheek. Strong hands grip my waist, and his warm-cedar and citrus scent floods my brain.

My insides clench. Whatever made him come after me, it's certainly over now—unless now he wants to make me pay for what I did in Monagasco, my role in his brother's assassination attempt. I might not have known what Reggie and Wade were planning, but I helped them get into the country all the same. I lied to all of them.

"Zee," he says softly, his fingers grazing the skin of my lower back. The tiny hairs on my body rise, and my stomach flips the way it always does when Cal touches me. All the places and all the ways we've been together flood my mind.

"I'm sorry," I manage, pulling away.

I can't be here with him like this. It hurts so much knowing he knows everything. Everything we had, those moments with him were all stolen. It's what I am. A thief.

And now he knows.

Seth grabs my upper arm, pulling me to his side. "I say, Miss Lampert, you must be my lucky charm." The accent is still there, but ice is in his tone.

The muscle in Cal's jaw moves, and I see his anger flash at my partner in crime.

"Cash me out." I swipe my black clutch off the table, twisting from Seth's grip.

My hands shake as I collect my winnings. I don't even bother to count them. I take the money and run. Seth will meet me at the dock like we planned. Noises are behind me, but I don't stop. I practically sprint to the doors and out to the line of cabs. It only takes a moment for me to dive into one.

"Grapetree Point," I say, slamming the door.

I fall back against the cracked vinyl seat as we speed off into the night, tears lurking in the corners of my eyes.

17

CHAPTER 2: TRACKING

Prince MacCallum Lockwood Tate

She's in St. Croix.

In a casino, no less.

I'm standing in the shadows of the run-down resort, watching the dim-lit area fill with gamblers, waiting in the wings for her to appear.

Logan discovered the Divi on the largest of the U.S. Virgin Islands and decided to check it out. It was a long shot, but it paid off. We'd spent a day on Tortola, doing our best covert investigation, trying to adjust to "island time" despite our sense of urgency. We waited and waited, and neither Zelda nor Seth ever appeared.

Visions of Helen Regis dead in a Miami bathtub flickered in my mind, and my fists came out. I took a few chances asking questions around Road Town.

Harbor guards insisted no one matching her description had passed through any of the docks they monitor. I was on the verge of searching boat to boat when Logan suggested we try this place.

The resort needs renovations. It's nothing like the Royal Casino back home, but I suppose I grew up in the gold standard. It's not an entirely fair comparison.

A few green-felt tables for poker and blackjack are surrounded by brown leather high chairs. A wall of slots glows like a carnival, filling the air with their tinny music. In the center of the room is a roulette station.

Zelda is a shark at blackjack. I remember the night I watched her turn one hundred euros into eight hundred without batting an eye, and I was such a love-struck fool, I accepted her "Daddy taught me" excuse. It won't happen again. I'm wise to Zelda Wilder. According to Ava, she'll head for that shiny brass wheel if Seth decides they need money.

As much as I don't want it, my stomach tightens at the thought of her with Seth. I'm simultaneously furious and over-protective. The first night I met him at the yacht party, I could see he made Zee uncomfortable. The way she flinched when he danced with her, the annoyance touched with fear in her eyes is on my mind.

She belongs at my side. I'll deal with her lies and her role in what happened to Rowan, but when the reckoning is over, Zelda is leaving with me.

A thump pings my wrist, and I look down at the text on my smart watch. It's from Logan: *Target spotted. Making my move.*

Every nerve in my body sparks to life, and I sweep the room again searching for her pale blonde hair. A man in a dark blazer approaches the table just behind the wheel. I see Logan's tall, beefy form casually approaching from the left. My brow furrows, and I don't understand why I can't find her. I watch as he walks around the group. His eyes are fixed on a woman with her back to me. She's wearing a black dress with straps of fabric crisscrossed over her back. Her hair is a severe, dark bob like the woman in *Pulp Fiction*.

Then it hits me — it's her.

I watch as Logan speaks to her, and I recognize the movement of her shoulders, the way she pulls away defensively. I hold the brass rail in front of me to keep from storming out there and grabbing her, throwing her over my shoulder and carrying her out of here like some ridiculous cave man.

Lingering in the shadows, I watch her sit on the tall barstool at the table. She crosses her legs, and I allow my eyes to glide down them to the black heels she's wearing. Zelda Wilder isn't tall, but she makes up for it by wearing shoes that accentuate her gorgeous legs.

I'm furious and relieved, and as much as I have to keep this part of me on a leash, I want those luscious legs wrapped around my waist. She won't run away from me again.

Seth strolls up to her other side, and my anger is back. I've researched this guy since learning how much influence he has over my girl, and I've learned several things—for starters, he is not a Kentucky colonel.

He's a con artist from Kansas. He's been arrested a few times for petty crime, nothing major. Still, I can tell from his track record he's smart. The only thing keeping him from real jail time is his brain. He's a tricky bastard with no clear motivation, which makes him dangerous. He's helping Zelda in order to get something in return. But what?

Commotion at the table draws me from my reflection, and I see Logan pulling back. He does a little nod and walks away from her. We agreed to verify and walk away, hang around outside then follow them to wherever they're hiding.

It's what we agreed to do, but I can't stay away from her. As if pulled by invisible chains, I take the

21

short flight of steps down to the main floor. I cross the room to where she sits, her back to me as she faces the wheel.

I want to touch her, inhale her sweet scent. I want to hear her voice. I want her to know I'm here and come to me. I want her to say she's sorry for all of it.

At the very moment I reach her, she steps back and makes a comment about leaving. I look at her stack of chips on the table, and while I don't know what they're doing, I know it's something illegal. No one wins that much at roulette.

"You shouldn't break a winning streak," I say near her dark head.

Her entire body tenses as if I've shocked her, and she spins around. Crystal-blue eyes lock on mine, and my chest squeezes. Everything between us floods my brain. She can see it in my eyes. I can see it in hers, until she blinks away, pulling closer to Seth as if for protection.

No, beautiful. I'm the one who protects you. I step into the gap left by Logan, closer to my girl. She's cowering like a puppy who knows she's done wrong. I'll deal with her, but I won't have her turning to a snake to escape me.

"Have we met?" I say softly, letting my warmth pass over her bare shoulder. Her little shiver makes me smile. "You seem familiar." *Very familiar.*

She twists her hands, not looking at me, and that asshole Seth gives her some order about staying. I want to pop him in the mouth. Instead I watch Zelda, waiting to see what she'll do.

I know my Zee, and she's strong. She's smart as a whip, and she's loyal. What will she do now that she's cornered? I almost laugh as the answer springs to the front of my mind—she'll slide open a window, jump into the ocean, and swim away.

And I'll swim right after her.

"No more bets!" The dealer passes his hand over the table.

Her internal struggle is plain on her face, from the tiny line piercing her forehead to the way her blue eyes dart around the grid like little birds. She's flustered by my presence, and I love that I throw her off balance. I love that as strong as she is and as much as I've given her, I still have the upper hand.

She leans down as if to adjust her shoe, and the roulette ball wobbles. My eyes dart to the table, and I watch as the silver ball shimmies and then drops straight into red seven. *So that's their game.*

It's a clever scam, and one our security has dealt with before in Monagasco. Ours was a three-person job—one man placed the bets, a second distracted the dealer, and the third activated a radio transmitter from the next table over. It was actually a woman with the small transmitter hidden in her cigarette case. She pressed the button, and the metal ball dropped like clockwork into the corresponding space on the wheel.

Seth lets out a yell and slaps Zee on the shoulder. It sends her straight into my arms. I scoop her up, reveling in this familiar position. Her blue eyes blink up at me, round and full of... something very new. Is it shame?

"Zee," I say, a crack forming in my wall of anger.

That bastard Seth jerks her away, and I'm ready to take care of him when she whips her arm out of his grasp.

23

"Cash me out," she says to the dealer, and as soon as she's handed her winnings, she practically bolts for the door.

I'm right behind her, but at that moment, a wad of garishly dressed tourists spreads out into the path blocking me.

"Excuse me," I growl, trying to get around them, but we launch into a game of back and forth and by the time I'm away, so is Zee, speeding off into the night.

"Dammit!" I shout, but my irritation is cut short by a black SUV pulling into the circular drive and stopping in front of me.

The locks click open, and I see Logan in the driver's seat. I'm in the vehicle at once, and we're heading down the dark, two-lane road after her.

"I've been watching the door for her to come out," he says, increasing our speed. "She was moving fast, but I at least caught their direction."

"Good work—any idea where she's headed?"

"None. They could be staying on the island, or…"

The way his voice trails off causes me to look up. "Or?" I demand.

"Or there are several piers hidden along this cove. They could have a charter at any one of them."

I know how to contact her. I still have her cell number, but after the way she ran from me, after her not showing up in Tortola like she said, I'm not sure I want to alert her.

"I think it's best if we head back to the airport." Touching my fingers to my upper lip, I look out the window into the night.

"It's probably the right call. We don't know who might be watching us."

"Right."

We're not the only ones looking for Zelda Wilder. My pulse ticks a little faster. I know the truth of that statement too well.

What are you thinking, Zee? Why are you running from me?

CHAPTER 3: CAPTURED

Zelda

Grapetree Point is a secluded beach with a curved bay and deep water close to shore. It's hidden from the road and difficult to find, making it perfect for our needs. I follow the very narrow path full of brambles from where I paid the cabby out to the soft beige sand. A small charter is waiting in the low ripples just a few feet out.

I don't want to board without Seth. I don't even want to be seen out here alone, so I walk deeper into the grape trees rising above the foliage. Although it's still twilight, the gnarled trunks and low-hanging branches increase the shadows and darkness. I run my fingers along the strange, knobby limbs dotted all over with deep purple fruit.

Reaching up to my forehead, I pull the silly wig off my head along with several of the pins used to keep it in place. Blonde tendrils fall around my cheeks and temples, and I lean my forehead against a bare spot on the tree. I exhale a shuddering breath as Cal floods my thoughts. I remember his eyes — the heat *and* the anger in them. I wasn't prepared to see him, especially not on a job.

A harsh, shushing noise in the brambles changes my moment of shame to fear, and my eyes go wide, straining into the darkness. Someone is coming down the path fast, headed this way. I step back, further into the shadows, rounding my shoulders and hoping to disappear in the trees. Good thing I'm wearing black, although I have too much skin showing to be completely camouflaged.

Another step back, and a dry limb cracks like a gunshot. The shadowy figure stops. "Zelda? Is that you?"

Seth! Exhaling loudly, I step out of the trees toward him. "What took you so long? We've got to get out of here."

"Don't tell me what we have to do." His voice is sharp, and he grabs my arm, jerking me toward the open shore. "Your boyfriend almost blew our cover."

"He's *not* my boyfriend." My reply is emphatic. MacCallum Lockwood Tate cannot be my boyfriend in this realm of possibilities.

Seth is still fuming. "How did he find us, anyway? You're in disguise. There must be a hundred islands here we could have gone to—"

"I honestly don't know. I haven't communicated with him since we left Miami." It's the truth. The last time I messaged Cal, I told him we were headed to Tortola, which was true at the time.

He waves a small LED light over his head back and forth, and a dark head pops up in the center of the boat, waving a similar light back at us.

"That is not fucking encouraging," he says.

I watch as he rolls up his pants. "What do you mean?"

Green eyes flash at me. "I mean if he found us that fast, other people can find us just as easy. Come on."

My blood runs cold at the thought, and I look over my shoulder for the thousandth time. In the dark, the gnarled trunks and twisted branches all look like men crouching forward, coming to kill us. I shake away my fear. The people looking for me don't have to hide in the bushes. They can pull out guns and shoot me from hundreds of feet away.

"Just like they did to Ava," I whisper.

"Zee!" Seth shouts. "Get on the boat!"

Snapping out of my trance, I look up to see him already across the narrow strip of water and pulling up on the bow of the small yacht. I wade into the warm waters, not even caring that the bottom of my dress is getting soaked. My clutch and shoes are high over my head, and when I arrive at the boat, I toss them onboard before pulling myself out of the water.

"Patch has clothes you can change into," Seth says, handing me a towel. "Once we're on Tortola, we can shop for something better."

I think about the eight hundred dollars in my purse. Seth should have the same amount or more on him. He couldn't have played roulette longer, as I have the transmitter in my shoe; however, he could have stopped off for a round of blackjack to beef up his winnings. I'm pretty good at the game, but Seth is better. He taught me to count cards when we first started working together in South Beach.

The roar of the boat engine fills the quiet night, and it takes only moments before we're shooting out, away from St. Croix. We most likely won't even use the sails tonight.

"Get comfortable," Seth says, handing me a small stack of clothes. "It's a five-hour voyage."

Taking the clothes, I do a quick calculation in my head. "We'll arrive after midnight?"

"Thereabouts."

Turning, I go down the silver ladder to the small space below deck to change. "So you have a plan?" I call up, sliding the zipper down my side and quickly shrugging out of my wet dress.

I step into the boxers and jerk them over my hips, whipping the tee on just as fast. The entire time, I fight the memory of Cal, of catching his eyes on me in Occitan as I changed into his clothes the night I hurt my ankle. A hollow ache spreads through my chest, and in spite of everything, I miss him so much.

I wasn't supposed to fall in love with Cal. I was hired to do one job—seduce his brother Rowan, expose him as irresponsible and unfit to rule—and then Ava and I would disappear, walk away and live the rest of our lives on easy street.

The only problem is Rowan is not irresponsible. He's very focused and serious about his country, and his uncle is a bigger con artist than me. Reggie had us fooled from the start, and all he'd wanted was to get back inside Monagasco, where he and Wade Paxton could take over the small nation-state. They sabotaged Rowan's Formula One car, nearly killing him, and shot Ava to silence us. They would have killed me if I hadn't escaped.

"Oh, god," I whisper, leaning my head against the corner of the small room.

When I reemerge above deck, Seth is sitting against the stern, watching Patch operate the large, silver wheel.

"We have to split up," he says, and a splinter of fear clenches my chest.

My involuntary response frustrates me more. I hate being dependent on Seth. I don't like being dependent on anyone, but least of all him. Still, without Ava, I don't have much choice. On my own,

I'm a sitting duck—or more like a fish in a barrel, an easy mark.

"Why?" I ask, working hard not to sound afraid.

He does a shrug. "Together, we're easier to find. All anyone has to say is a new American couple just moved to the island, and they'll head straight for us."

"Then what made you think we'd be safer in Tortola?"

"You got a better idea?" he shouts at me, and I walk away.

"No," I mutter, leaving him for the front of the boat.

The last thing I'm in the mood for is a Seth Hines poor-anger-management moment. I'll stay in the bow until we get there.

When we ran from the killers in Monagasco, he said he had friends on Tortola who could hide us. Now we're splitting up. Whatever, I'll figure it out. It's not like I believe for a moment it means Seth will leave me alone. I have the black American Express card with our shared money on it.

Like a joint-custody arrangement, it ties us together no matter how much I never want to see him again. I promised him five thousand dollars in Monagasco, and he's not going anywhere until he gets it.

The boat rocks, moving fast, bouncing over the waves. It's a dark night, and we're the only ones on these waters as far as I can see. We'll likely pass a cruise ship or two before we reach our destination, but they'll take no notice of us.

I lean back against the bow, using the plastic bag containing my clutch, dress, and wig for a pillow. Closing my eyes, my thoughts go where they always do at night—to Cal's smoky hazel eyes. I remember his warm hands cupping my cheeks and lifting my mouth to his. I picture his broad shoulders, his six-foot-two frame towering over me. I think of the way his golden-brown hair goes all sexy-messy when he pulls his shirt over his head just before he climbs into bed. I remember his lined torso and his strong arms. I feel his hard body pressed against mine, urgent and demanding as he takes what he wants, what we both want...

A large hand shakes me roughly, and I jump awake with a gasp, throwing my arms out. "What?!"

"Get up," Seth snaps. "We're here."

I stretch my neck to the side, trying to orient myself. "I'm must've fallen asleep." My voice is scratchy, and I rub my shoulder. "I slept in a weird position."

"I'm surprised you slept at all with what's hanging over us."

Seth has no clue how Ava and I grew up, how many nights I barely slept listening for anyone creeping up on us. They might not have been men with guns, but some wounds go deeper than bullets. I follow him, walking low to the back of the boat to the long pier. It's dark and deserted at this time of night.

Seth climbs up the wooden ladder then reaches back for me. "Like I said, we'll split up," he says. "I know a few guys from South Beach here. Blix is pretty connected. He'll let me know if anybody's snooping around, asking questions."

We're walking toward a deserted shopping area. A large clock mounted on an iron post tells me it's after two in the morning.

"What kind of a name is Blix? Is that German?"

"Short for Blixen. He was a baron or something. Lost all his money and spent some time in Miami before moving further south."

Sounds like a Nazi. My nose wrinkles at the thought. I know what kind of shit Seth was involved with in South Beach. "More like he's on the lam."

"Things were different ten years ago."

I don't believe that, but at this point, all I care about is a bed. "Do we at least have rooms?"

"You're at Frenchman's Hotel. I'll be at Maria's." We're through the small mall in an alley where the road diverges in opposite directions, and he stops. "I'm taking off. Here's your address and info."

He shoves a piece of paper in my hand, and a charge of panic hits me. "You're leaving me here? In the middle of the night?"

"You'll be okay. Tortola is relatively safe."

"I'm sure it is—for the average tourist."

He exhales a loud breath. "Look, my hotel is five blocks that way," he points behind him, then he turns me roughly in the opposite direction. "Yours is two that way. Walk straight, don't act suspicious, and no one will suspect anything."

"You're a jerk," I say, shoving his hands off me.

"A jerk who saved your life." His voice is impatient. "Look, I don't have a gun. I'm not a fighter. If somebody jumped us, we're better separated. Then I can get help."

I notice he doesn't say *he'll* help me.

"You realize if something happens to me, you get nothing. No money."

He's already walking away from me toward his hotel. "You're a survivor, Zee. Survive. I'll call you tomorrow."

33

Seconds tick past, and before long, I'm alone in the night. Seth is gone, and the only sound is cicadas screeching loud in the background. I take a step toward a hotel I've never seen. A knot tightens my throat, but I fight it. *I will not cry.* My jaw clenches. *I stopped crying in Tampa years ago.*

"Asshole," I mutter instead, sucking up my fear and walking faster. "A purposeful, determined stride," I say.

Everything in me wants to run, but I won't do it. I'm taking back control. Seth is right—I'm a survivor. I'll survive this, and I'll be stronger for it. They can't break me. If I let them scare me, they win.

A sign up ahead glows in the night like a beacon. It's wood painted white with a golden fleur de lis and the word *Frenchman* painted in precise black lettering. I feel a small victory over the bad guys. I found my hotel on my own.

I'm just at the path leading to the door when a loud *BANG!* makes me jump a foot into the air. An involuntary scream flies from my throat, and I run the final steps into the hotel, shoving through the door and hiding around the corner.

Several seconds pass where the only noise is my rapid breathing. Gripping the doorjamb, I lean forward to peek, at the shadows lining my path, searching for the source of that noise. A black and white cat stands beside the trashcans, looking my way.

My stomach is in my throat, and I exhale a swear. "Fucking cat."

No one is behind the counter. "What now?" I say to myself.

Lifting the sheet of paper Seth shoved into my hand, I see a room number and a combination for the door lock written on it.

"Convenient." I skip the rickety old elevator and take the stairs to Room 213.

I'm so tired, I don't even care that the stairwell smells like piss and the hotel is probably the seediest place I've stayed since leaving Tampa. A concrete balcony leads to my door, and I pause to tap out the combination on the lock. A buzz and it's open.

The doorknob flies in my hand, jerking me into the room. "Jesus!" I squeal, my heart galloping in my chest.

Someone has left the balcony door open, and the suction of the wind makes it nearly impossible for me to shove the room door closed. Falling against it, I use my entire body weight to force it shut and twist the deadbolt locked.

I drop the plastic bag on the small table without even switching on the lights. Stopping at a small mirror hanging on the wall, I reach up to pull the remaining bobby pins out of my hair. It falls in smooth waves around my face and over my shoulders. I lift the thin tee over my head and toss it to the side when the skin on my arms prickles.

I'm not alone. In my peripheral vision, I can just make out the silhouette of a man sitting in the darkness on the edge of the sofa. He's watching me, and my stomach is in my throat.

"Who are you?" My voice is calm, level, and totally fake. I'm terrified.

He rises fast, closing the space between us.

"Stay BACK!" I shout, scrambling away until my bare back hits the wall.

He catches both my hands in a tight grip, pinning them beside my face, and my body is trapped beneath his hard frame. "I've been waiting for you."

I recognize the deep voice, but my fears aren't eased. "Cal?" I've never seen him like this, so forceful and furious. The swell of my breasts rises and falls with my gasps. "How did you find me?"

He speaks through clenched teeth. "Were you hiding from me again?"

"No..." My voice trembles. Still, as frightened as I am, I can't stop the desire unfurling low in my stomach.

Pale light from outside the balcony illuminates his face, and I see his square jaw dusted with light scruff. His hazel eyes blaze. "So the con was on me? You make me fall for you then walk away? Humiliate me?"

"NO!" I shake my head fast. "I would never—"

"Save it." He pushes off of me turning his back and walking across the room. Tension ripples off him in waves, and I want to touch him. At the same time I'm afraid he won't let me. "Pretty sick joke calling yourself Regina Lampert. You'd make a better Charles."

"You've seen *Charade*?" Of course he has. Movies were the one true thing we shared.

"How many passports do *you* have, Mrs. Lampert?" His eyes flash.

"It's Miss, and none. I've never had a passport. Not even one. In my real name, at least."

The muscle in his jaw moves, and he's across the room again, grabbing my face in his hand, causing me to whimper.

"Stop lying to me."

Pain collapses my insides. Cal's anger is so much worse than I could possibly have imagined, and still I want him so badly, my heart is breaking.

"I'm not!"

"You fucking conned me from the start."

A hot tear hits my cheek—I can't deny it. I did.

"I'm so sorry," I whisper.

Gripping my face, his rough mouth covers mine, shoving my lips apart. My knees go liquid, but he jerks me up firmly against his chest. Gripping his shoulders, my fingers curl against his hard muscles as his tongue claims mine.

He lifts his head, and our mouths break apart with a gasping smack. My lips throb with the force of it.

"Is that a lie, too?" His eyes are dark.

"N-no," I gasp. The fine hairs dusting his chest tease the skin above my bra, and I'm so wet.

His large hand slides between my thighs, over those thin boxers. I'm bare underneath, but he's not invading, he's teasing. I ache for him so much, I can barely stand it. Still holding my cheeks, he forces me to meet his angry eyes a moment before he kisses me again. Again, it's hard, passionate, demanding, and all the sensations overwhelm me.

Jerking my head back hazel eyes burn into mine. "Every time you moaned for me, every time you begged... Were you lying then?"

"No!" I cling to him as his hand snakes around to cup my ass through the thin cotton material. "I never saw you coming. Even if I had, I never could have been prepared for you. Not in a million years."

His eyes narrow slightly, and he places both hands on my cheeks, moving his thumbs over my mouth. The muscle in his jaw moves, and I can see so much anger in his eyes.

"Cal—"

"Don't." A thumb stills on my lips, stopping my speech.

He slides his thumb over my slightly fuller top lip. His eyes follow his movements, and I remember our night on the boat, him telling me all the things he sees when he looks at me. Just as fast, I remember the way he fucked me that night, the way we were both wild and passionate.

Our eyes meet, and I have no idea what he sees now when he looks at me. I don't know if the love he felt for me has been snuffed out by the truth of who I am. I don't know what he'll do next now that he's caught me.

I only know as much as I don't deserve him, he's my prince. I gave my heart to him, and no matter how far I run, I'll never stop wanting him.

Chapter 4: Reunion

Cal

Our small plane touches down on the airstrip just outside Road Town. Logan easily found the hotel where Regina Lampert is staying on the short flight from St. Croix, and he shows me the shitty dump in the middle of the tourist district.

"We're at least an hour ahead of them," my tall, muscular guard says as we descend from the aircraft. "Should we return to the villa?"

"No." My jaw is clenched, and I'm having a hard time keeping my anger at bay. "I'm going to her room."

An SUV is waiting for us, and Logan gives him the address for her hotel. It takes less than five minutes for us to be there, and I slip down the alley to the back of the building. The utter lack of security coupled with how easily I climb the short fire escape, cross over to her balcony, and enter through the unlocked patio door angers me in a whole new way. Anyone could do this. She could be dead before dawn at this rate.

"Yet you run from me," I grumble, sitting on the uncomfortable couch as I wait for her to appear.

My mind travels across the miles in the darkness. I remember the first night I saw her in Monagasco at the charity ball. I remember her strapless black dress and the way she wobbled on those too-tall stilettoes. She looked up at me, blue eyes flashing with humor and determination, and I couldn't resist. I'd never seen anything like her.

I didn't understand why she was so focused on my brother. It was an entirely new experience, but it didn't matter. After our first night, I knew she was mine. Unfortunately, it seems I am completely hers as well. My fists tighten, and the noise at the door tells me she's here.

Tightness fills my chest at the sound of her voice. I left the patio door slightly ajar, and she struggles against the wind tunnel created. The sea breeze surrounds us, overwhelming us both. My breathing is heavy, barely audible as I watch her, alone in this dark room. She stops in front of the mirror and takes the pins out of her long, blonde hair. It falls in silky curls around her shoulders. I can still see the tips curling at her nipples the last time I fucked her.

She pulls off her shirt, and she's my kryptonite.

I flew half a continent to Tortola then hopped a puddle jumper to St. Croix then did it again. She has jerked me all over the god damned western hemisphere—I would never put up with shit like this—yet here I am, aching to hold her, wanting to slide my thumb across those full lips I long to kiss.

I came here desperate to find her, and now I want to turn her over my knee and spank her. I'm mad because she lied, but even more, I'm livid at her recklessness.

She's like a child running into the path of oncoming traffic. She ran from me when men with guns were chasing her. She left with her sister lying wounded, nearly dead in a hospital bed. I told her I loved her, and she ran even further.

I fucking love this woman.

I fucking want to strangle her.

Fury heats my blood and I cross the room, pulling her trembling body into my arms.

"Cal?" she gasps, and I hear the fear in her voice.

She's wearing boxers and a thin bra. I can just see the tips of her succulent breasts, and I can feel her heat through the fabric of her shorts. Memories of our last night flood my mind — the two of us in her bed, our bodies entwined like contortionists.

Stepping back, I pull the shirt I'm wearing over my head. Her eyes change as they move from my hair down my neck to my chest. Her lust is stronger than her fear. My lust is stronger than my fury.

"Take it off." My voice is anger mixed with desire.

I watch as she reaches around her back to unfasten that bra. It falls away, and her creamy breasts, her dark nipples are highlighted by the streetlamp outside. My fingers ache to touch her.

Not yet…

"All of it," I say, waiting as she bends to slide the boxers over her hips to the floor.

She's bare in front of me, and a little shiver moves through her. I watch her breath swirling in and out in little pants. She's the sexiest thing I've ever seen.

Moving forward, I gather her to me, feeling the soft press of her body against my bare chest. We both groan. It's so good. My chin drops, and our mouths meet. Her tongue touches mine, but I'm holding back. She strains into me, trying to get her arms free, but I hold her tighter, imprisoning her, turning my face.

41

"You helped the assholes who tried to kill Ro," I say as much to myself as to her.

"No — NO!" The break in her voice claws at my chest. "I didn't know, Cal. I never would have hurt him like that — "

"You have degrees of how you hurt people?"

Her face drops, and her body goes limp in my arms.

Clenching my fist in the back of her hair, I want to pull it. I want to shake her but instead, I kiss her. I cover her mouth with mine tasting her sweetness. I taste the salt of her tears as I kiss her cheeks. I'm so fucking mixed up inside.

Loosening my hold, I step back. I need to get my head straight. I'm not ready to forgive her this easily.

She only hesitates a moment before lowering to her knees in front of me. Lifting her chin, she looks up, blue eyes round and glistening with tears. Her palms are flat on the front of my slacks, and she slides them up and down before lifting them to my waistband. Every cell in my body is focused on her movements as she unfastens my pants.

"I'm so sorry, Cal," she whispers as her delicate fingers lower my trousers, my boxer briefs, until my aching cock springs free.

My emotions might be conflicted, but my dick knows exactly what it wants. She touches me lightly with her fingers, wrapping them around my length, and I lean my forehead on my arm against the wall, breathing hard as I watch her guide the mushroom tip between her lips, past that full upper lip I want to bite.

My eyes slide closed, and a low groan scrapes from my throat as her hot mouth closes around my cock. She teases me, running her tongue along the edge, down the base. She opens and pulls me in again, but I'm too big for her. I only hear the sweet sucking sound around my tip as her fingers go the rest of the way down my shaft, pumping fast.

"Fuck," I hiss. This feels too good.

She's on her knees, submissive pose, appeasing my anger. *Get it together, Cal.* Reaching down, I catch her under the arms and lift her fast. She comes off my dick with a soft *Pop!* Her back is again to the wall. Those satin lips are swollen, her eyes rimmed in red.

My teeth clench. "I won't let you play me."

"Never—" her head shakes.

"Say it," I order, cutting her off. Her blue eyes widen, and it takes all my strength to keep my wall of anger firmly in place.

She blinks quickly, and I remind myself she's most likely trying to decide what version of the truth she's willing to give me. I still can't trust her, especially now that she knows my heart's involved.

"I-I'm sorry?" Her voice is soft.

"Are you asking me?" Mine is hard.

"No." It's a firm reply laced with sadness. "I never meant to hurt you, Cal."

"Too late." My hand slides into the back of her hair, and I pull it, forcing those eyes to stay on mine. "What else?"

Her brow lines. "I've told you everything."

"No, you haven't."

Our bare chests are together. Her fingers rest on my shoulders, and I loosen my grip, threading my fingers in her soft hair, waiting. My erection is straining for her bare pussy. I want to be inside her. I want to spend this night like all our other nights—

fucking and teasing, talking and holding each other, napping and then doing it all again.

But not yet. Right now I want her to admit it. I want to know she ripped out her heart and left it behind when she ran from me—just like she tore mine out and took it with her.

"What's left?" she says in that quiet voice, so different from our usual, feisty banter.

"I think you know."

The moment she realizes, a startled light hits her eye. *Yes, beautiful, I know your secret. Now say it.* She tries to turn away, but my fingers tighten in her hair, holding her steady.

"Say it." My voice is lower.

"I can't," she whispers, pools forming in her eyes.

"I won't let you go until you do."

"Cal—please."

"Save the begging for when I make you come. Now tell me."

She does a little sniff and closes her eyes. "I love you. You know I love you. Why are you torturing me?"

Boom. Her confession hits me harder than I expected. It's a mini-explosion in my chest, and that fucking wall is down. Me, the "playboy prince," slayed by this hustler, this grifter…

This woman I love.

My jaw flexes and I focus on the mission.

"Now open your eyes and tell me." I want her to hear the words from her own lips. I want her to know I'm not the only one with a weakness.

Her blue eyes open, and she shakes her head, conquered at last. "I love you, Cal."

Leaning forward, I kiss her slowly at first, gently. I pull that top lip between mine and give it a little nip. I sweep my tongue against the seam of her mouth and take a little dip inside, tasting her sweetness. I feel the heat rising in her torso solidly pressed against mine, and I know she's wet.

Meeting her gaze, I don't smile. We still have work to do, but before all of that... "Now I'm going to fuck you."

I take her mouth again, but this time it's more urgent. Our previous feelings are shoved aside, and raw need and blazing heat are between us. Her lips chase mine. Her tongue is in my mouth, and I lift her, holding her up against the wall as her thighs part, her gorgeous legs go around my waist.

"Oh, god, Cal!" she gasps.

Her chin rises, and I kiss her beautiful neck. I bring my face down to catch a beaded nipple in my teeth, and I'm rewarded with a little squeal. My dick is so hard it aches as I fumble to find her entrance.

In one swift drop, I'm inside her, wrapped in the clenching warmth of her body.

"Fuck, yes," I groan, moving my hands to her ass so I can hold her, grind her against my pelvis.

"Cal!" she moans, moving her hips around, accommodating my size filling her, stretching her.

She's clenching and wet and the only place I want to be. Holding back is about to kill me. "Okay?" I groan against her cheek, my eyes closed as I focus.

"Fuck me, Cal," she begs, and it's all I need to hear.

I let loose, pounding and grasping. Her thighs squeeze my waist, and I feel the slight pinch of her nails cutting into the skin of my shoulders.

"Oh, god… Oh!" She cries as her orgasm starts to rise. I feel her inner muscles tight around me as she grinds her clit against my shaft. "Right there!" she says.

My fingers bite into her soft ass, moving her faster over me until she's bucking and coming, crying out and straining. My brow lines and I let go as well, pulsing deep into her, filling her, leaving this planet momentarily as we shoot through the stars together in a blaze of orgasm.

Knees bent, I grip her harder, holding on as we drift down together. My heart beats wildly in my chest, but I'm anchored to this place by her luscious body. A bead of sweat rolls down my cheek, and I feel her lick it away. She kisses my jaw then touches her tongue to the side of my neck just before she gives me a little bite, drawing another pulse from me deep inside her.

"Fucking amazing," I manage, and she makes a noise like a purr.

Slim hands move to my cheeks, and she holds my eyes. "I love you, MacCallum Lockwood Tate," she says, and my grip on resistance falters.

Chapter 5: Simplicity

Zelda

Light streams through the cheap plastic blinds, and Cal's arm is draped across my waist. I blink at the ceiling, dying just a little and loving every second of his body against mine.

"What have I done?" I whisper.

He breathes and moves, turning onto his side. His hair is messy bedhead, and that irresistible dimple appears briefly at the corner of his mouth. Every time he almost smiles, he stops himself, and my chest squeezes.

He's still angry.

He has every right to be angry.

"This is possibly the shittiest bed I've ever slept in, and I spent six months in the desert with our military."

"Spoiled," I say, sitting up. "This is hardly the worst place I've stayed. It's not even in the Top 10."

"Those days are behind you."

He places his warm palm against my bare back as I hug my bent knees against my breasts. My chest aches, and my body is sore like it always is after a night with Cal. We didn't just make love against the wall. We moved to the bed and did it several more times. Rough, angry makeup sex. Only, I'm not sure we're entirely "made up" yet, even though I told him I loved him so many times. An involuntary wince causes me to cover my eyes with my hands. *What have I done?*

"I suppose those other, better places leave scuff marks on your skin?" he says.

"What?" I look over my shoulder and telltale red abrasions cover my upper back. "That's never happened before."

Our eyes meet briefly before I look away again.

"I suppose that's some distinction. I'm the first lover to fuck you senseless against a cheap motel wall." Those words from him make my stomach flip. *Damn irresistible MacCallum Lockwood Tate.*

"It might surprise you to know I've had very few lovers before you." I run my fingers over my face, suddenly conscious of crusty eyes and morning breath. "I've intentionally avoided such things."

He sits up, and I hear him rubbing his hands over his face behind me. "Time to go. Collect your things. Logan is waiting for us with a car."

"What are you talking about?" I snap, looking over my shoulder at him.

His brow lowers. "I'm taking you back to Monagasco with me."

"I'm not going back to Monagasco." Exasperation is in my tone, but he is undeterred.

"Yes, you are. It's where you belong."

Slapping the mattress, I push out of the bed, stomping around the room looking for anything to pull over my naked body. "It's not where I belong! It was a job, MacCallum. Everything you saw in Monagasco was a job. It wasn't me!"

The white button-up shirt he discarded last night is on the floor. I snatch it up and pull it over my head. It's still buttoned halfway, and I fumble with the top buttons. He stands and crosses the room to me, large hands covering mine, heat radiating off him in luscious waves.

"You love me. You want to be with me. I'm taking you home."

I shake my head. "I'm not a puppy you can rescue off the street. I'm a petty thief and a con artist. Ask Ava—she'll tell you. I'm no Cinderella. I never even dreamed of being Cinderella."

"We'll deal with your checkered past once I know you're safe."

"Ugh!" I let out a little scream. "You can't keep me safe in Monagasco! I was almost killed there before the race!"

Protective anger flashes in his eyes. "I didn't know what was going on before the race. I had no idea all the shit you were hiding from me. Everything is different now, and I *will* keep you safe in Monagasco."

He's so fucking sexy, I almost cave. *Almost.*

Shaking my head, I argue, "Even if that were the case, it won't work. We're from different worlds, Cal. Worlds that don't mesh—they collide."

His lips press together, and I watch his hazel eyes move around the room as he thinks. The truth aches in my chest. I hate my truth, but at least I know it.

"I could never fit into your world. I wouldn't even know where to begin." My voice is quiet, and even I can hear my lack of conviction. I'd do anything to be with him.

A few more seconds pass. A beat where I watch him process what I've just said. Finally, he speaks. "I don't suppose we have to leave Tortola right this minute."

Turning away, he goes to his abandoned slacks on the floor, that damn tight ass flexing as he walks. I give up and sit down on the bed. He makes my knees weak anyway.

"You know I'm right." I say with an internal swoon as he pulls the black pants over his naked body.

He picks up the tee Patch loaned me last night and holds it up. "Interesting..." he says, turning it to me. Grey text on a grey tee reads *My penis is huge*.

"Oh my god." I exhale a laugh, covering my face. "It was too dark. I couldn't read it last night."

With a shrug he pulls it over his head. "At least it's truth in advertising." My eyes narrow, and he tosses me the boxer shorts. "Either way, we're not staying here another night. Get dressed."

With a sigh, I pull the shorts over my hips. "Where are we going?"

"Freddie leased a house when we arrived. I'm sure we can extend our time there a day or two."

Picking up the plastic bag containing my still-damp dress and small clutch, I think about meeting Seth today. As far as I know, he doesn't have any plans beyond getting his five thousand dollars. How we're supposed to make that transaction on this small island is anybody's guess. At least after our con last night, he's not so tied to me for immediate cash.

I sigh, turning the bag over in my hands. "I need to buy clothes."

Cal steps in front of me, holding my hands to stop my movements. "We'll get set up in the house, get the car, and I'll drive you to one of the shopping malls. It's an island, but I'm sure it has a few boutiques."

I study our hands, his larger ones holding my slim ones. "I don't shop in boutiques. I shop at Wal-Mart... or Target if I'm feeling fancy."

That tone I love is in his voice. "You'll have to make do, I guess. Tortola has neither a Wal-Mart nor a Target."

"You know what I mean."

"I know you're being difficult. Now come on. Is that all you have?"

With a nod from me, he leads me out of the small room.

The "house" Freddie leased is a freaking villa situated on a cliff overlooking the bay separating Tortola from St. John, the smallest of the U.S. Virgin Islands. It has five bedrooms and five and a half bathrooms. The entire thing is at least ten thousand square feet.

Stepping out onto the wooden balcony surrounding the second floor, I clasp my hands at my chest releasing a little "Oh!" at the panoramic view of the shimmering turquoise waters with the green, rolling hills of St. John in the distance.

While I would never take back my statement that our worlds are vastly different, I could very, *very* easily get used to this part of Cal's life — the ability to run away to a villa on an island far from the trappings of royalty.

He joins me on the balcony, and I long for the days when I could melt into his embrace. "I'd say this is better than the other place."

"It's so beautiful," I confess. I'd be an idiot to say otherwise, and I won't lie to him again.

"We can stay here a day or two, but then we have to get back. It's not secure here, and Rowan

51

needs me at home." I study the buttons of his shirt until he ducks down to catch my eyes. "Are you listening?"

"Are you?" My voice is soft, not attacking, but he's not listening to me. "I can't go back with you, Cal."

"And I'm not leaving you here, so you've got forty-eight hours to figure it out." He reaches out to lift my chin, and our eyes meet—his still flinty. "Don't make me have to arrest you."

Jerking my chin away, I stomp inside the gorgeous home. The floors are covered in wide Spanish tiles and the walls are a mixture of white plaster and huge French doors, half of which are open to allow the sea breeze to fill the room. An enormous king-sized bed is against one wall, and assorted pieces of leather furniture are positioned in front of it in a small sitting area. Two ceiling fans hang from the ceiling — *two!*

With a little frown, I shake my head. "Look at this place," I mutter.

"I'm thinking of buying it," he says, following me. "It's for sale, and you won't always be in danger. At least I hope not."

His voice has changed, his anger diminished, and I use the one argument I think might work. "Your *people* won't approve of me."

"I think the citizens of Monagasco will be more accepting than you believe. I'm not as much of a figurehead as Ro, and you're actually quite charming when you're not robbing casinos."

My chest burns with shame. "That's exactly what I mean." I walk to a wooden armchair and run my finger over the bright yellow pillow positioned on it. "I've met your mother. I've met Lara

Westingroot. I've seen the disgusted glares from the nobility. They'll never approve of me."

"They've never approved of me." He walks slowly to the bed and leans against it. He's listening to me, and I kind of love him more for it. "I've done things that would make your little casino heist look like catechism—and it's all been captured on film and plastered across social media."

That makes me grin. "Yes, but they're stuck with you."

When I look up, he's allowed the tiniest smile. "Thanks."

I still need clothes, and it gives me an idea. "Tell you what. I'll show you what my life is like, and then you can decide how it fits into your pampered existence."

"I'm not so pampered, but I'm not staying at that shit hole again."

A little eye roll, and I exhale heavily. "Other than where we stay, everything else is my call. I set the agenda, and that way you can see what I'm really like."

"Does it include eating pizza, drinking champagne, and criticizing bad movies?"

I can't help a grin. "Substitute cheap beer for champagne, and yes. That part of my life was pretty authentic. Outside of the sex marathons."

A naughty light is in his eyes. "Don't peasants have sex marathons?"

"Peasants are typically too busy trying to stay alive." I walk past him into the hallway and down the expansive stairway.

He's right behind me. "I plan to correct that part of the equation."

Stopping in the ginormous kitchen, I examine two sets of keys waiting on the bar. "Jeep or Mercedes?" he asks.

Shaking my head, I take the keys to the Jeep off the counter and start for the door. Looks like we're headed to Waterfront Drive.

I'm wearing faded cutoffs and a white shirt with navy horizontal stripes across it as I drive us to lunch at Smuggler's Cove. I could never afford a car, but a Jeep is far closer to what I might drive than a Mercedes.

Cal changed into longish cargo shorts and a light blue V-neck shirt. I can tell it's designer, but I don't say anything. As much as I can't jump immediately into the life of a princess, I can't expect him to embrace the life of a beach bum in one day.

Pulling up at the surfer bar, I shove the stick into park and kill the engine. A colorful shack consisting of sand floors and a thatched roof is in front of us, and just beyond that is the sea. The water is so brilliant turquoise it actually glows.

I lean back in the driver's seat and exhale. "Look familiar at all?"

His eyebrow quirks and he quickly scans the area. "Should it?"

"They filmed the movie version of Hemingway's *The Old Man and the Sea* here."

He nods. "Ahh... Never saw it." As I sit staring at paradise, he hops out, rounding the vehicle to my side.

Taking his hand, I climb out of the Jeep. "I always hated that story. It's depressing."

"It is pretty bleak," he says in that clipped accent I love. "He catches the biggest fish of his life only to watch as the sharks eat it all the way back to shore."

We enter the open-air establishment where patrons sit around the bar in various states of relaxation. Some are dressed in bikinis, while some wear shorts and tees. It feels like south Florida to me. Easy life at the beach. *This is home.*

"I know it's supposed to be a metaphor, but it's hard to appreciate when it feels so close to reality," I say.

"Not like the movies should be?"

"Right." I take a seat on the high wooden stool, and he cages me in his arms.

"I can protect you from the sharks."

For a moment only our mutual attraction is between us. His eyes level on mine, and my chest tightens.

"What if *you* were the biggest fish I ever dreamed of catching?" My voice is low. "I'm not sure I could watch you slowly taken from me, piece by piece."

"Not happening." He breaks the moment, pushing away and taking the stool beside me. "How can you lose a dream you never had?"

I'm still recovering from our plunge into intimacy, and I don't have a comeback. He's using my words against me. Instead, I look across the bar at the chalkboard listing the day's menu. "I guess we're having cheeseburgers and fries," I say. "And quarter beer."

Our lunch arrives relatively quickly. I think it's delicious, but Cal complains the beer is basically colored water. I only roll my eyes.

It's an honor bar, which means we pay what we

think our meal is worth. Naturally, I leave way more than I would probably pay at a regular burger joint. After a big score, I'm always too generous. Or guilty. I suppose it's why I never seem to get ahead, but I can't help it. It's what Ava says makes me "small time."

A glass case of cigars is near the entrance. Cal studies it as I walk slowly down to the water. The path is worn and the beige sand is packed hard from almost a century of wear. I pass under ancient palm trees with thick trunks like elephant legs. When the foliage opens, I stand for a moment watching the waves breaking softly until Cal joins me, looking out at them. If things were different, I could imagine living here. Starting over and building a new life.

"So you never want to go back?" His voice is quiet. "What about Ava?"

"She's always in my thoughts," I confess, looking over at him. The wind moves his golden-brown hair, and I long to thread my fingers in it. Instead, I think about my little sister. "She's better with Rowan. He loves her. He's the Prince Charming she always dreamed would rescue her."

My phone chooses that particular moment to vibrate and ring. It's the call I've been dreading all day, and I do a little wave before leaving Cal at the shoreline and walking back toward the bar.

"Where are you?" I hate Seth's temper. He's been showing it more and more lately, which makes me suspicious.

"I'm sorry." I can't keep the sarcasm out of my tone. "Were you concerned something might have happened to me after you abandoned me in the street to figure it out?"

Guess what? I get mad, too.

"Maybe," he says, easing off the gas.

"More like you were worried about your money."

"So where the fuck are you?"

"I'm with Cal at Smuggler's Cove." That shuts his big mouth. "I guess you thought he wouldn't find me. Well, think again."

"You told him exactly where we were headed in Miami." He does a little exhale into the speaker. "I don't care about this bullshit. You need to come in and meet me at Blix's."

"Why? What does he have to do with it?" I don't like mixing with Seth's old South Beach crew. I heard rumors they were mostly drug dealers and uniquely cruel. Maybe that's Seth's problem — he's using again.

"He's got ways to move money around undetected. When can you meet me?"

"Not today. I'm with Cal."

"Fuck your prince."

"Fuck you." I'm about to hang up when he stops me.

"What about tomorrow?"

Looking over my shoulder, I see Cal has run out of patience and is headed my way. "Tomorrow's pretty open. I'll text you."

"I'll send you the address."

It's the last words I hear before I end the call. I shove the phone in my pocket, looking up at the sexy man walking to me, wanting to take me out of this life I've built.

"Had enough of paradise?" I tease.

Suspicion is in his eyes. It's in his lowered brow and the way his mouth is a straight line. "No, I was just thinking I'm more a fan of *Blue Lagoon* than *The*

Old Man and the Sea."

Shaking my head, I tease, hoping to move us away from my phone call. "Always with the breasts. I'm not as pretty as Brook Shields."

He catches me by the belt loops, jerking my pelvis against his. "I'm tired of arguing. Let's get naked."

Chapter 6: Suspicions

Cal

I sit on the sand watching Zelda pace as she talks on her phone. She's doing it again. I can't protect her when she hides from me, and I'm losing patience with the secretive phone calls and partial information.

She's talking to Seth. He's pulling her into another web, and from where I'm sitting it can only lead to danger.

Logan has been keeping tabs on Wade and Reggie since they disappeared from Monagasco. They popped up again in Turkey only to be lost in the sea of Syrian refugees headed north. Last week one of our agents spotted my uncle in Morocco. It's the last stop before crossing the Atlantic, and he's had plenty of time to make it here.

Tortola is beautiful, and Zelda is equally gorgeous prancing around in skimpy cutoffs with her long, sexy legs on full display. I want to see her in a bikini on the beach, and I want to take that bikini off her and fuck her in the ocean. Still, every moment we stay, my tension grows. We can come back and enjoy the island when I'm satisfied we've dealt with the current threat.

I walk slowly toward where she's pacing, arguing with that bastard. Her long blonde hair swishes around her shoulders, and she's so beautiful. I wonder what it will take for her to let this shit go.

She sees me getting closer, and her demeanor changes. She ends the call and shoves her phone in her pocket, fueling the irritation rising in my chest.

"We should head back to the villa," she says, only a hint of nervousness in her voice. "I'd love to take a swim, and then we can change and head to Bomba's Shack for dinner? They have a full moon party."

Stopping in front of her, I place a hand on her waist and pull her to me. Her eyes are heavy with guilt, and I reach up to trace my thumb along the side of her jaw. "Is tonight the full moon?"

Her throat moves as she swallows. She does a little nod, and I know my impatience is clear in my expression. I want her to go to Monagasco with me willingly, but I'm one secret away from taking her home by force.

"You have the keys," I say, releasing her.

We're alone at the villa. I'm standing on the balcony in my swim trunks and an unbuttoned short-sleeved shirt while I wait for Zelda to change. Taking out my phone, I shoot Logan a quick text.

Any news?

It doesn't take long for him to respond. *Nothing, but we're watching everything. If either of them arrives on the island, we'll know about it.*

The noise of a splash draws my attention from my phone and I look across the yard to see Zelda already in the large, L-shaped pool below. I watch her swim a moment until I realize... she's not wearing a swimsuit.

I place my phone on the desk just inside the master bedroom before heading down the wide stairs to the first level. I'm crossing the lawn in record time, following the winding stone walkway through palm trees and past metal statues of herons and other fauna to the blue tile-lined swimming pool.

"You didn't wait for me," I say, watching her a moment. The water is clear, and even though she's submerged to the neck, I can see everything below. "Did you forget to pick up a swimsuit?"

"No..." her voice is high, thoughtful. "I just realized we have this enormous place all to ourselves. Who needs swimsuits?"

"It's a valid point." Sliding the shirt off my shoulders, I push my swim trunks down and off before stepping out of them and into the warm water.

She watches me, and I take my time walking out to her, enjoying the way her eyes change as the water line rises to my knees then over my thighs. I'm tempted to pause a moment, but I'm only torturing myself. With a slight push, I glide to where she's waiting and wrap my arms around her body.

As soon as we meet, she exhales a little sigh. My lips are immediately on her neck, just behind her ear. "Were you waiting for this?" I whisper, and a shiver moves across her shoulders.

"Yes." She pulls up and kisses me, pulling my lips between hers and lightly touching our tongues. She tastes like cool water and mint. "Please?"

We're at the side, and I reach out to hold the tiled edge. Her legs are around my waist, and she breathes a moan in my ear. I'm rock-hard and ready.

My tip is just at her entrance when she pulls the side of my ear between her teeth.

Turning my face I capture her mouth, kissing her until her head is in my hands as I plunge deep into her core. It's hotter compared to the pool water, and she moans into my mouth. I'm rocking, working out the frustration I felt earlier, surrendering to the love I'm growing weary of holding back. I can only stay angry with her so long.

She's already told me she loves me. I'm addicted to her like I've never been to any woman. She brings out this possessive, *protective* side of me I never believed possible. I won't let her stubbornness threaten her life.

I feel her hand go between us, moving fast as she massages her clit. Her moans become more frantic, and she whimpers and gasps in my ear. "Faster... oh, Cal! Deeper."

My mouth travels behind ear. "That's right, beautiful. You love my cock."

"Oh, god!" Her body trembles.

"You love to feel me taking you, making you mine."

"Yes," she gasps.

I grip her soft ass and move my mouth into her hair to the place I know gives her pleasure. We spent so much time in Monagasco exploring each other's bodies. As new lovers, we learned every erogenous zone.

Now I bite her, pulling the soft skin at the back of her neck lightly between my teeth. With a jerk, her body erupts into orgasm. Her legs tremble and her insides spasm, sending waves of pleasure snaking up my thighs. She's holding me as I thrust deeper, chasing my own release. It doesn't take long.

The noise of splashing water recedes as the rising tide of orgasm grows tighter and tighter... then breaks. My body is rigid, and I'm holding her flush against me as I pulse, balls deep in her gorgeous body.

Her mouth finds mine, and her kisses are lush and soft, fresh and delicious like water in the desert, bringing me back to Earth. For a moment we only hold each other, her legs around my waist, my arms around her torso. I'm still inside her, and we kiss slowly, languidly, making out in the afterglow of our reunion. After a moment, she leans back, sliding her fingers along my scruffy jawline.

"Are you still angry with me?" Her voice is soft, her eyes so deep.

"Are you still keeping secrets from me?"

Her eyes drop, and I have to hold back a growl. She lowers her legs and swims to the other side of the narrow pool, leaving me cold in the water without her.

"What if I say yes?" Her back is to me as she holds the opposite side of the narrow pool.

I cross it in three strokes. Pulling up beside her, I slide her pale blonde hair away from her shoulder. "I'd want to know why."

She lifts her chin to look at me. "Because it doesn't concern you?" It's a question, not a challenge.

"Does it concern you?"

She turns her gaze back to the blue-tiled wall and nods. I reach out to run the back of my finger down her flushed cheek. "Then it concerns me."

For the space of several breaths, she doesn't answer. Then she swims to the steps leading out of the pool. I watch as she slowly walks up them, water tracing down her creamy skin in rivulets. I'm transfixed as she takes a fluffy white robe off one of the lounge chairs and wraps it around her body.

"We should shower and dress," she says quietly. "I read dinner at Bomba's is buffet style, and if we're late, nothing will be left."

I make my way to where she's standing. Her eyes are on my chest, and all the things I want to say feel redundant to me. I won't repeat myself. Instead, I lean down and kiss her once more, gentle but possessive, communicating in a way words can't capture.

A little noise escapes with her sigh, and her slim fingers lightly touch my stomach. When I pull back, her cheeks are flushed, and I nod. We're on the same page.

"I'll be ready in ten minutes."

Chapter 7: Making Up

Zelda

Twinkle lights are draped over the trees and around the plywood structure of the roof, which is also littered with lacy bras and panties. The walls of the shack are made of driftwood, broken surfboards, scrap tin, and more plywood with names and phrases written all over them.

It's a total beach hangout, and Cal and I both have huge glasses of the "secret family recipe" punch in front of us, which tastes like oranges and bananas and pineapples, and I can tell is strong as shit. I'm already tipsy.

Cal is casual in long shorts and Patch's penis tee. It stretches nicely across his broad shoulders, and I watch every delicious ripple of muscle as he moves. I'm dressed in a pale blue sundress with spaghetti straps. It hangs loose on my body, and I'm not wearing a bra.

Standing beside our chairs, I sway to the lilting reggae music played by a live band. Cal watches me, and his sexy smile is finally back. I wonder how much the punch has to do with it.

"You should toss your panties on the roof," he says, leaning into my ear.

Wrinkling my nose up at him, I laugh. "You want me naked under my dress!" It's possible my voice is a little loud.

"Always," he says, wrapping a strong arm around my waist and pulling me hard against his chest for a kiss.

"I was misinformed," I shout when he lets me up for air. "They don't have food here."

"I'm way ahead of you," he says, still smiling. "Logan's getting food."

It makes me so happy to see him smile. He's done nothing but frown at me since we reunited. Even when we were making love, I could feel the tension in his body, but not tonight. Tonight he watches me with those burning eyes and that slight grin. It makes me want to do naughty things... like toss my panties on the roof.

A motley blend of patrons is on the floor moving in time with the music, and I watch them from where I stand beside the bar. I take another long sip of punch. It's sweet and now has only a little burn in the aftertaste. Cal's eyes rake over me, dark and electric. My skin is humming.

"I love you," I say, wrapping my arms around his neck. That gets me a special appearance by that dimple at the corner of his mouth. I touch it lightly. "That too."

He slides a lock of hair away from my face with his finger. My eyes close, and I lean into his hand.

"Is this a concession?" His voice is low, near my face. "Is it possible life with a playboy prince might not be so bad after all?"

I'm against his chest. Strong arms surround me, and I melt into him. Leaning down, he steals my breath along with a kiss. Our lips part, and he gives my tongue a teasing touch.

"Mm," I sigh, resting my cheek against him.

I listen to his heartbeat mingling with the soft shush of the breakers crashing so close. When he speaks it vibrates my cheek.

"What changed?"

I lean back and look up at him, confused. "What do you mean?" *If anyone changed, it's him.*

"In Monagasco, you said you didn't think of me as a prince. What changed?"

"Oh." His question catches me off-guard. Stepping away, I turn to face the bar. I pick up a small umbrella and twirl it back and forth in my fingers. "I don't know. Nothing, I guess." Lowering it, I blink up at him. "I told you. It's all the things around you."

"Rowan?" He watches me, studying my nonverbal cues.

"No."

"I know it's not the ocean. Or the racing. And you love Occitan — it's just like here."

"Your mother?"

He exhales a laugh. "That's pretty clichéd, Zee."

I shrug and hold my hands out, swaying to the music again. It's a Bob Marley tune I love. "So sue me."

"I can handle my mother," he grins, watching me. "If that's all that's worrying you, don't."

My eyes narrow. "Isn't that what men always say about their mothers?"

"How would you know?"

The bartender refills my glass, and I lift out a maraschino cherry by the long, curling stem. "I wouldn't," I say before sliding it into my mouth.

He's quiet again, and I'm still dancing. "I don't want to wait in vain for your love," I sing softly.

Cal is back on his stool, and he pulls me between his legs. "We've got to get past this."

Closing my eyes, I listen to the music. "Why?"

"Because I told Ava I wouldn't come back without you."

Those words squeeze my chest. I open my eyes and meet his. "How is she? I've been too afraid to call her. I don't know if they're monitoring her phone or —"

"She's much better. She's out of the hospital, and Rowan moved her to the palace. Their engagement is official, and the citizens love her."

"Of course they do. She's the perfect princess." A sad little smile crosses my face. I don't know why I feel like crying. "She must be in heaven."

He moves a lock of hair behind my ear. "She misses you."

I blink up, looking around the ceiling and out at the band. I take a deep breath, trying to calm my emotions. "We've never been apart. Not once in our lives."

He catches my chin. "I love you, Zelda. Come home with me. You're not helping anyone being so far away."

"Maybe not, but I'm also not putting anyone in the line of fire."

The beefy man from the Divi appears carrying a paper sack. "Logan, at last," Cal says, taking it from him.

Logan gives me a little nod.

Cal lifts out two paper boxes and opens them to reveal fried fish and chips. "Looks like cod," he says, holding out a French fry.

I take it and pop it in my mouth.

"Oh!" I grab my drink and take a quick sip. "They're blazing hot!"

"Sorry—I just picked them up." Logan does a little bow then gives me a small smile.

"Thank you," I say as he starts to go. His eyes seem to linger on me, but Cal draws my attention.

"You need to eat something." I watch as he opens a packet of malted vinegar and shakes it over the fish. Then he passes over a plastic fork while I open the small cup of coleslaw.

"Perfect beach food," I say, scooping out a bite of the savory salad. "Isn't this great?"

"I'm sure you'd think anything was great at this point." His eye narrow slightly, and I lean into his chest.

"Are you saying I'm drunk?" That makes me giggle, and I sway to "Could You Be Loved."

His eyes travel over me slowly again, and it's like warm honey in my veins. "Perhaps not drunk, but you're definitely switching to something non-alcoholic. I want you sober tonight when I fuck you."

"Jee-zus," I sigh. This man.

Shaking my head, I fork a large piece of fried cod and slip it in my mouth. Then I let out a little groan. "This is so good." I fork another one as he watches me.

"Traditional British fare," he says.

"For the British Virgin Islands... Aren't you eating?"

He does a little laugh and picks up the entire piece of cod with his hand. It's like a fried brown football, and he bites the pointed end off, giving me a wink.

I laugh and rest my head on my hand. "See? You can do the simple life. What if we just stay here?

It's not such a bad place."

He's wiping the grease away with a paper napkin. "I'd stay anywhere with you."

He means it, and he has no idea what those words do to me — the rush in my stomach, the tingle between my thighs. "Cal."

I watch as he flags down the bartender. "What sort of... non-alcoholic drinks do you have?"

The man turns and digs around in a box of ice. "Coke?"

A red can is placed in front of me, and I give Cal a sheepish grin as I pop the top. "Thanks?"

"Happens to the best of us." He winks and leans closer.

The song changes to "Is This Love," and Cal's eyes light. "I love this song."

My hand is in his, and we're on the dance floor faster than I can say "more cod." One strong arm is around my waist, the other holds my hand near our shoulders. I'm thankful I wore my platform espadrilles so my chin is just at his collarbone. Our bodies touch from shoulder to hip, and citrus, cedar, and Cal fill my senses with every sway.

"So I throw my cards on your table," he croons softly in my ear, and I hum as little chills skirt down my arms.

Tingling warmth swells in my chest, and I close my eyes, floating in his arms to the perfect soundtrack. I'm not sure if my head is spinning because of the punch or his proximity, but it can't get any better. Or it couldn't until his warm lips touch the side of my neck.

"Oh, Cal," I sigh, melting into him.

I'm more sober and completely horny hours later as we're walking, fingers laced, up the sand path to the villa. Strolling in the moonlight after the evening we've just shared, I reconsider my reasons for staying.

"Ava once said I live for the adrenaline rush."

He stops us midway to the house. "Okay?"

It's late, and the moon is shining down. I want to strip out of our clothes and run down to the ocean. Still, I continue. "I wanted her to get her GED, go to community college, and get a real job. I wanted us to leave that life of crime. She said I was small time. She said I live for the adrenaline rush of nearly getting caught."

My eyes drop, and I study the front of that ridiculous tee. I'm still ashamed of what I am—of him knowing, but I think of that little girl who watched me grow up. Ava knows me unlike anyone in my life. She'd also been the one begging me to stay in Monagasco. She said she'd never seen me with anyone the way I am with Cal.

"Are you worried you'll grow tired of me?" The slightest tease is in his voice—still, it's laced with seriousness.

"I'm worried I don't know what I'll do." My throat is tight, and I'm doing my best to be as honest as I can without hurting him. "What will I do if I go back with you? Sit around and knit?"

"I have never seen any woman knitting in Monagasco." His voice is full of authority. "Under the age of eighty."

I snort a laugh and step into his body. His arms go around me, but just as fast he lifts me off my feet. I'm in his arms, and my legs loop around his waist. I'm holding his neck and the floodlights on the corners of the villa light us while casting deep shadows.

"What if I promise never to let you second guess your decision?" His voice is thick. I hold his cheeks, staring down at this beautiful man I love.

"You can't promise something like that."

"I just did."

I sigh and lean forward into our hug. I don't want to think anymore. Turning my head to the side, I speak softly in his ear. "Take me to bed or lose me forever," I tease.

"I can't believe you just quoted *Top Gun*," he laughs.

"Me either, but you'd better do it."

CHAPTER 8: DECISION

Cal

Warm yellow light from the bathroom illuminates the master bedroom. Zelda sits on the edge of the white mattress looking up at me. Her blue eyes are so round. I touch the top of her cheek with my thumb. She's been more honest with me than she's ever been, and my anger has faded away.

She's afraid she'll get bored. It almost makes me laugh, considering my past. But none of that is what she needs to hear. I remember her question on the yacht the night of the Rose Gala. So many things she said to me in those days are so clear now.

"What do you see when you look at me?" I say lightly, repeating her words back to her.

She exhales a laugh and wrinkles her nose in an adorable way. "I didn't really think through that question before I asked it."

My thumb moves to her chin and the off-center line running down it. "I told you all the things I love about you."

"You basically said I look bucktoothed, have a weird voice, and an off-center line in my chin."

"Bullshit!" I shout, pushing her back on the bed.

I trap her under me, and she squeals a laugh as she tries to twist away.

"Stop struggling," I say. "I won't let you go. Now answer my question."

She exhales dramatically and stills. Those blue eyes move around my face, and I can't imagine what she might say.

"I see something I never thought in a million years would happen to me."

That's better. "And what is that?"

"A really good man who loves me. Not a criminal or a low life."

Moving to the side, I rest my head on my hand as I study her face. "Does this mean you're coming back with me?"

"Cal," she sighs, rolling into my chest. "You're a prince. Princes go with ladies, debutantes. Not redneck hicks with bruised knees and bare feet who say *fuck* all the time."

"Mm... my favorite thing." I kiss her shoulder, sliding the thin strap of her dress down her arm.

She shrugs out of it, and I continue down to the swell of her breast. A little shiver makes me smile. Her fingers thread in the sides of my hair, curling, warming up.

"The best part?" she says softly. "The part that makes no sense? I actually like my life. It's easy. Simple."

I take a momentary break from her perfect tits. "Then why did you come after us?"

Her lips quirk, and she hesitates before answering. It's just long enough for me to say it with her. "Ava."

Zelda sighs. "She's never been a redneck hick with bruised knees. She was born a lady."

"I think you idealize her." I kiss the top of her shoulder.

"Oh, she was a pickpocket, mind you," she laughs. "But that was my influence. Ava would have done better. The only thing stopping her was me."

Lifting my head, I hold her eyes. "The only thing stopping you now is you. You might have passed her to Rowan, but you're not alone."

Her eyes divert, and for a moment the only sound is the noise of the ceiling fan and in the distance, the sound of the waves breaking along the shore. When she turns back to me, she places her hands on my cheeks and leans up to kiss me.

I roll her onto her back deepening the kiss. Her mouth opens with a little noise, and our tongues curl together. Lifting my head, I pull that full top lip I love between my teeth lightly before sliding down her body, kissing a line down to her breasts. I smile as I feel her body respond. Her hands slide into my hair as I pull that sundress all the way off her.

She's wearing only a lacy white thong. "You never threw this on the roof," I say, hooking my thumbs under the sides and pulling it down her luscious legs.

"I guess you're too distracting." Her shoulder rises with her sigh, and I smile. She's so beautiful.

"Come here." Moving to my knees at the side of the bed, I hook my arms around her thighs and jerk that bare pussy to my mouth.

She lets out a little squeal as I slide my tongue over the little bud hidden there.

"Oh, god, Cal," she gasps, touching my cheek. "I'm so close."

"Hmm," I kiss the crease of her thigh and her stomach quivers. I slide my palm flat over her, circling my thumb around her navel.

Her knees bend, and she holds her hands to me, "Come up here."

One last pass over her clit, and her back arches. "Cal! Come to me." Her fingers flex, and I laugh, kissing her stomach before diving into her arms.

A little fumbling, a little rotating of our hips, and I rock deep into her. Our mouths fuse together, and her arms are tight around my shoulders. I'm pretty close to the edge myself. I feel when she breaks, and I pull up, driving deeper. Her mouth is on my neck, and when I feel her teeth, I shoot over the edge.

"Fuck," I groan as I finish. My forehead drops to her shoulder, and her legs are tight around my waist. Her lips are right at my ear.

"So good," she whispers, and my arms flex around her.

Moving my palms to the sides of her face, I look into her eyes. They're hazy and tired, and I catch her around the waist, dragging us up to the pillows before I pull her back to my chest, circling her in my arms.

"Sleep, beautiful," I say, and it isn't long before I hear her breathing smooth out as she falls asleep in my arms.

For a little while, I listen to the sound of the waves breaking far below us as I think about what this means and the idea of a perfect life. I've given up trying to understand how my life changed when this woman entered it. Now I'm determined to bring it all the way home.

The sun wakes me, streaming through the open French doors, and I blink a few times at the white wooden ceiling, the dual fans moving ocean breezes around the airy room. The sound of soft laughter brings me completely around. I sit up and see Zelda's on her side watching a movie on the large, flat screen television.

Sliding in behind her, I wrap an arm around her bare waist and kiss that place where her neck and shoulder meet. It gets me a little squeal.

"Tickles!" she says, turning to kiss my lips briefly before returning to whatever is holding her attention.

"What is this?" I say, leaning on my hand.

"I don't want to hear it, MacCallum."

I watch a moment as Matthew Perry grabs a young Salma Hayak and kisses her deeply (as if). "Oh, now you're going to get it. You gave me shit for *You've Got Mail*, and you're watching *Fools Rush In*?"

"This movie is a million times better than *You've Got Mail*," she says in that sassy voice, and I can't resist.

Pulling her shoulder toward me, I pin her against the mattress. "I'd love to hear your justification for that incredible statement."

"For starters, what self-respecting *man*..." (love how she emphasizes the word) "...watches *You've Got Mail*?"

"You might recall I was trying to lure you back into my bed."

"Second, two words: Salma Hayak."

"We have a little girl crush, do we?"

Her eyes roll. "She's fun to watch, now let me up!" She struggles, and I kiss that little hollow at the base of her throat before releasing her.

She giggles, and with her back to me, she scoots her back against my chest, her ass right at the level of my cock. Needless to say, it's a few minutes before we're watching any more of the show, and I'm far more relaxed with my morning wood gone.

"I missed my favorite part!" Zelda pushes to a sitting position, and her blonde hair is standing nearly on end.

I can't help it. I laugh out loud. "Your sex hair is insane."

She blinks and tilts her face to the side. "I worked on it all night just for you!"

Something hits me right in the gut, and I know I can't put this off one more second. Zelda sees my expression change, and her teasing disappears.

"What's wrong?" she asks.

Sitting up beside her, I grab her waist and pull her across my lap in a straddle. Her hands are on my shoulders, and I reach up to hold her cheeks in both my hands.

"Zelda?"

She does a little smile. "MacCallum?"

"I want you to marry me." *Fuck.* Yep, I said it. "I don't have a ring yet, but there are several jewelry stores in Road Town. We have to go back to Monagasco, but I'll talk to Rowan about us living here—in Tortola—once things are resolved, of course..." Her eyes blink faster the more I speak, and I see the glisten of tears in them. "What's the matter, beautiful? Did you think I wouldn't ask?"

"What are you saying?" she whispers.

"I'm saying I want you to be my wife, Zelda Wilder. Shit, we're fucking made for each other, and if you can't see it... well, I won't believe you. You're too smart not to see it."

She pushes off my lap to sit beside me. "But what will you do? I know you're a prince and all, but you must have some job—"

"It's true. Sadly, I can't lie around all day fucking you and drinking champagne, but they have French Virgin Islands."

"They do?" Her brow lines.

"Technically, they're called the West Indies, but Martinique, St. Garth, Guadalupe…"

"But… what does that mean?"

"I don't know exactly, but I'll discuss it with Rowan. I'm sure we can figure out some diplomatic reason for me to be here. We'll work it out." She's quiet, looking at me with her lips slightly parted. I exhale a laugh, and shit. My stomach is tight with nerves. "Just say yes, beautiful."

Her mouth closes, and she blinks down to her lap before she starts fucking shaking her head. "No," she says softly.

My jaw tightens. "Why the devil not?" I don't mean to be sharp, but god dammit.

She looks up fast, blue eyes round. "Not yet."

Okay, that response eases my temper slightly. "Go on…"

"I can't marry you with dirty hands." She slides to the edge of the mattress and stands. "I have to meet with Seth today and settle our accounts. Let me…" she looks around before pulling that silly penis tee over her head. "Let me end things with him, separate. Then…"

Her breath catches, and I'm out of the bed standing in front of her. She's so small without her heels, her head is only at the center of my chest. In a sweep, I lift her, her legs going around my waist, her arms around my neck.

"Then?" I say, looking up at her worried expression.

She exhales a nervous laugh and covers her mouth. "Then… yes?" Her voice is so small, but my insides are exploding with satisfaction.

"YES!" I shout, and she really laughs then.

"You have no idea what you're getting into."

Lowering her to standing, I cup her face in my hands, lifting it to mine. "I'm getting everything I never knew I always wanted."

Her eyes go wide, and she does a little shriek. "You just quoted *Fools Rush In*! You love that movie!"

I laugh and kiss her smart mouth. "I love you."

"I love you," she says, all joking aside. I kiss her again, and she struggles free. "Let me get this over with, and we can meet for lunch."

I sit back on the bed watching as she retrieves a halter-top denim sundress from the armoire. "Where are you meeting him?"

"Road Town," she says, pulling the halter dress over her breasts and tying it around her neck, leaving her lovely lined back exposed. She grabs a brush and begins pulling it through her wild hair. "He's staying with some guy he knows from South Beach. I'll give him his money, and then we can meet for lunch at Bomba's!"

"As much as I love that place, we'll meet at the Sugar Mill Restaurant."

Giving up, she twists her hair into a cute little bun. "That's a very fancy place."

"This is a very important moment."

She leans across the bed to peck my lips. "See you in a few short hours."

"I have a better idea." Throwing the blankets back, I'm across the room and pulling a pair of jeans over my hips. "I'll drive you."

Her full lips twist, and she shakes her head. "Seth is too paranoid."

"I don't like that guy," I say, pulling on a thin navy sweater.

"Don't worry. I can handle Seth." She disappears into the bathroom and I hear running water and the sound of her brushing her teeth.

Reaching up, I rake my fingers through my hair before following her into the luxury space and doing likewise.

"Then I'll drive you into town and pick you up when you're done."

We're finished, and I get a minty kiss. "Deal," she says with a little grin.

I catch her before we leave in a long hug, closing my eyes and memorizing the feel of her small body against mine. My fiancée. My Zee. It's perfect.

CHAPTER 9: BETRAYAL

Zelda

We're in Road Town at the very spot where Seth left me our first night on the island. That night, at two a.m., it had been deserted and empty, with long shadows and ominous, dark alleys. I'd been so angry at Seth for walking off and leaving me here alone.

Now, in the light of day, it's simply a bustling tourist market. The streets are lined with souvenir stores, clothing stores, jewelry stores, and little kiosks with hair wraps and alcoholic slushies. I look ahead two blocks to where my old hotel was situated while Cal peruses the signs.

"Samarkand or Little Switzerland?" he asks.

Our fingers are entwined, palms pressed together, and I evaluate the competing jewelry stores. "Exotic or more conservative?"

"Switzerland has a higher GDP, which means I might get the better deal at Samarkand."

That twinkle is in his eye, and I step into him, lifting my chin for a kiss. "Surprise me."

"Here." Pulling us up short, I watch him take a small gold coin from his pocket and place it in a red gumball machine.

A few twists, and out pops a clear plastic container. Inside is a copper band with an American flag etched on it in red, white, and blue.

"It's so pretty!" I exclaim.

"It's tin," Cal says as he slides it on the third finger of my left hand and presses the adjustable band until it fits. "How does that feel?"

Tilting my hand side to side, I admire the painted enamel. "It's so cute for something in a gumball machine."

"Does it fit?" he asks, and I nod still admiring the trinket. "Take it off."

My chin jerks up. "I want to wear it!"

He laughs, catching my waist. "You can wear it after I use it to size your real ring."

"It's the first piece of jewelry you've ever bought me." I make a little pouty face, and he laughs.

"It won't be the last, and I'm not giving you a tin engagement ring."

"It's like the one they had engraved in *Breakfast at Tiffany's*."

"I think that one was plain tin."

"Get another one." I clutch my hand to my chest. "I want to keep this one."

Digging in his pocket he laughs. "It'll turn your finger green."

I watch as he repeats the process of small coin, turn the dial, out pops another plastic container. This time when he opens it, it's a dull silver ring. He frowns at it.

"See! It's one of a kind! I'll never take it off."

"Must've been in there fifty years." He reaches for my hand and pulls the first ring off, using the second, dull one for sizing before sliding it back.

"Zelda Wilder, will you take this American flag ring, which isn't even the flag of my country, to be my wife?"

"Since I am an American, and it is my flag?" I put my arms around his neck and peck his lips. "I will!"

His hands slide down and cup my butt, and I laugh as a tingle of heat surges in my lower stomach. "Text me when you're done. I'll be here."

"This shouldn't take long." Another brief kiss, and I head off in the direction of Seth's hotel. "Five blocks this way," I say to myself, lifting my hand and examining the cute little ring.

It might be tin, but it has so much significance to me. I kiss it and continue walking, looking up at the palm trees, the blue sky overhead. Optimism is a new mood for me, but I love the feeling. Even thinking about the coming months doesn't scare me. I'll see Ava again. I want to talk to her and see her well and happy—not like the last time I saw her.

The memory of my beautiful little sister pale and weak in a hospital bed dampens my otherwise happy mood, but I hastily shake it away. Cal said she's completely recovered! She's at the palace with Rowan and the country loves her.

"Of course they do," I say softly to myself, reading the signs as I pass.

I notice none of the buildings are taller than the palm trees, and I vaguely recall Seth saying something about that when we were driving down the first time, before we took the unexpected detour into St. Croix.

The black American Express card is in my clutch, and I pick up the pace a bit, wanting to be done with this obligation and running back to Cal in as little time as needed.

I pass a sign for a crafts store and another that says Simply Delicious.

"I suppose that's a restaurant," I say to myself. Wrong, it's a market.

At last I see the sign for Maria's. It's a two-story white structure that faces the shore. I'm approaching it from the opposite side, and it's larger than I expected. I was expecting a private residence or a small, five to six bedroom establishment.

"Leave it to Seth to give himself the better room," I say under my breath.

The hotel lobby is like the entrance to an embassy — or the waiting room of a nice hospital. Square, navy leather chairs are positioned around the space, mixed in with potted palms. A large check-in counter is staffed with locals in white shirts with navy epaulets on the shoulders and little hats. It takes me a moment to recognize the nautical theme.

Pulling out my phone, I text Seth. *I'm in the lobby. Let's get this over with.*

I walk over to one of the low chairs and sit while I wait for his response. It doesn't take long. *Give me just a second. I'll come down and get you.*

I'm growing irritated. I don't understand why he played games the first night, considering we were right on the shoreline. It's like he walked me further into town just to hide where he was staying. *What kind of bullshit are you up to, Seth?* I muse. Why would he feel the need to hide his location?

The optimism I discovered only moments ago dims, and my survival instinct rises in my chest. Something feels wrong here. Standing, I'm about to cut out and reschedule, taking Cal up on his offer to escort me here next time, when the elevator door opens, and I see my partner in crime emerge.

He's dressed in dark jeans and that same long-sleeved navy sweater he had on when we left

Monagasco. His eyes dart around the lobby as he looks for me, and I survey his body language. I've worked with Seth for years, and when he's pulling a stunt, his shoulders hunch and his green eyes dart around the perimeter looking for cops. It's his tell, and he's doing it right now. I'm on my feet stepping around a palm when his eyes hit mine.

His auburn brow lowers and his jaw sets. "Zee." His voice is low, and he makes a beeline for me.

That does it. I'm out of here. I do a quick step to the side, keeping as many chairs, sofas, palm trees, and trash cans between him and me as possible as I head for the door.

"Stop," he hisses, darting to the side, trying to catch me. "What are you doing?"

"You're not at someone's house. What is this?"

I'm out of obstacles between us. I'm going to have to make a break for the door, but he's on me. His iron grip closes around my upper arm so tight, I wince.

"OW!" I exclaim, and he squeezes me harder.

"Shut up," he snaps, continuing to the door and pushing outside.

Now I'm really panicking. "What are you doing?"

It's the only thing I'm able to say before a black SUV pulls up beside us and the doors open. I jerk and try to feint right, but it's too late. Seth shoves me inside, following right behind. The doors are still open when I see a face that shoots ice through my stomach.

Sitting in the passenger's seat, wearing a navy suit, his greasy, black hair slicked back and his thin mustache twisting is Wade Paxton.

"We meet again, Miss Wilder," he says, and I immediately start to scream.

"NO!" I thrust away, charging across Seth's lap for the still-open door.

A tall man, beefy and hairy as a gorilla steps into the empty space. He's wearing a black suit and a scowl, and with a hand the size of my face, he shoves me backwards as if I were a doll, into the truck. The door slams shut.

"Nice work, Mr. Hines," Wade Paxton says.

"Let me out," Seth's voice is urgent. "This is as far as I agreed to go."

"Of course," Paxton says, extending a hand to my ex-partner in crime. "I believe you wanted her card?"

Seth snatches my purse and digs inside, taking the American Express card.

"You fucking liar!" I lunge forward, slapping him as hard as I can.

Seth's green eyes flash, and he grabs me by the throat, slamming me against the opposite door. The handle jams into my back painfully, and my eyes water as he leans into my face.

"Don't fuck with me, Zelda Wilder! You're the liar. There's twenty thousand on this card. You said it was only ten."

"You're a bastard!" I struggle against his chokehold on my neck.

He releases me and starts for the door, but I push off, right behind him. "You'll regret this!"

"Stop her," Wade says calmly, and Gorilla Man has my shoulder in his meaty fist, pulling me back.

My survival instinct kicks in. *Never go with a kidnapper to a second location.*

"I'M BEING KIDNAPPED!" I shout as loud as

88

possible while the door is open. "IN THE BLACK SUV! THEY'RE TAKING ME AGAINST MY —"

BAM! Lights explode behind my eyes as Wade's hand smacks across my face. I fall to the floor of the vehicle, and my mouth fills with the coppery taste of blood.

"SHUT UP!" Wade snarls. "Reginald Winchester is not here to protect you, and I'd advise you to be still and be quiet or I will cut you."

He hit me so hard, it takes me a moment to regain my bearings. I blink several times before I'm able to see the grey-carpeted floor. Blood is in my mouth, and a towel is shoved over my face quickly. Something else... Moving my lips, I work the hard object around until I pull out...

"A tooth," I mumble through swollen, slippery lips.

It's a small tooth. Without a mirror, I can only guess it's from beside my canines.

"Give it to me." Wade snatches it away. More blood in my mouth. He shoves the towel harder at me. "Stop that bleeding."

I take it from him and pull myself onto the back seat again. "Where are you taking me?"

"That is none of your concern."

We're moving at a steady clip down the road. I must be in shock because I don't feel any pain, only adrenaline. Outside the windows I see trees and vegetation on the roadside. My heart beats painfully hard and my cheek pulses in time with my fear. I watch frantically as mile after mile goes by, and I'm taken further from Road Town, further from Cal waiting in the little shopping area.

Cal... it's a plaintiff cry in my mind and tears heat my eyes. *I want Cal...*

Gorilla Man is to my left. Another, black-suited man is driving. Wade is in the passenger's side on his smartphone when the vehicle slows at what looks like a stop sign. Without hesitating, I lunge for the door, gripping the handle and pulling. It could be my only chance.

The door doesn't budge. The rear door locks are disabled.

"NO!" I scream, jerking it over and over. Tears are slick on my face, and I throw all my weight against the door.

"Deal with her," Wade orders.

His words echo in the small space, and I'm fumbling with the power window mechanism. It's also locked.

Movement behind me. I barely have time to glance over my shoulder when Gorilla Man closes the space between us, brow lowered. His bottom jaw juts out, and he looks like a true ape swinging his meaty fist almost faster than I can see it. It slams into my temple, and everything goes black.

CHAPTER 10: REGRETS

Cal

Samarkand is elaborately designed with striking mosaics in an assortment of turquoise, sea, and royal blues. Pointed arches line the walls, and the jewelry cases are low, square boxes arranged in a maze around the room.

I enter, and a few clusters of obvious tourists are ahead of me looking at the array of Rolex watches and glittering cocktail rings. I stroll to the one filled with diamond engagement rings and pause. A beautiful art-deco style ring with a square setting and what look like tiny angel's wings flaring on each corner catches my eye. It's perfect.

A salesman in a white linen coat and pants approaches me smiling. He is clean-shaven and wears a black skullcap.

"May I help you, sir?" He smiles and does a little bow.

"I like this setting." Pointing in the case, I fish in my pocket and pull out the dull tin ring. "I need it in this size."

His brow lowers and he squints, taking the piece of tin from my fingers. "You did not get this in our store."

"No, actually, it came out of a gumball machine," I say with a smile.

Black eyes dart up to mine. "A... *gumball* machine?"

I haven't been addressed with such disgust since my mother saw the photo of me snorting coke off the toned ass of an unidentified supermodel. I can't help wishing Zelda were here, since she was the one who mentioned *Breakfast at Tiffany's*.

"It's just outside the store," I happily turn and point to the door, but the man shakes his head and raises his eyebrows as if I've offended him.

"It matters not," he says.

"Either way, I didn't know the lady's ring size. It was my only idea."

He shrugs and holds out his hands. "It will have to do. Now, which one did you say?"

"This one here, the rose-gold art-deco—"

"Ahh!" he clasps his hands. "An excellent choice, sir!"

I take that to mean I've just picked out the most expensive piece in the entire shop, but I don't give a shit. Only the best for my girl.

"If you could just be sure it matches that size," I say. "How soon will it be ready?"

He looks over my shoulder. "Will you be staying overnight? I can have it sized, polished, and gift wrapped for you by tomorrow morning?"

It's not what I had in mind for our lunch date today, but I like the attention to detail. "What time tomorrow?"

We're settled up, and I have the claim ticket in my pocket as I sit outside in the warm afternoon sun. Pulling out my phone, I notice it's been more than an hour. Tightness moves across my shoulders, and I look up the street in the direction I last saw Zelda headed. She'd been so pretty in her halter dress. Her pale blonde hair was styled away from her face, long down her back, and I smile remembering how excited she'd been about a silly piece of tin.

Opening my messenger, I tap out a text. *Did you get lost looking at ur first piece of jewelry?*

Leaning back, I wait for her reply. A cool breeze sweeps through the courtyard, and I watch a slim woman with skin the color of milk chocolate dance to a classic Billy Joel song. "Zanzibar."

Examining my palm, I try to dismiss the tightness in my chest at the delay in Zelda's reply. It's been longer than she said, but perhaps it took longer to transfer the money than she thought it would?

Looking again up the street in the direction I last saw her walking away from me, I don't like the uneasiness settling in my gut. I push off my knees and start to walk the direction she went. My hands are in my pockets, and I'm taking a leisurely pace. I'll meet her on the way back. I don't want her to think I'm going to be one of those helicopter husbands always checking up on her if she's the slightest bit late.

I'm a block from where I was sitting, about to cross the street, when a black Mercedes cuts me off with a screech. Anger tightens my throat, and I'm about to shout at the driver when the door opens and Logan stands out of the driver's side.

"Sir!" His voice is sharp, and a lead weight is in my stomach.

Pulling the rear door open, I'm in the car before he's had a chance to say another word. "What happened?"

Freddie is in the passenger's seat, and he turns to face me. "We've just received a communiqué from Wade Paxton."

His voice is grave, and the skin on my forehead tightens.

"What does it say?" I ask, my voice flat.

His eyes are full of concern, and he looks down. "It says, 'When you're ready to discuss terms, we'll be waiting.'"

My voice is a notch below a shout. "What the fuck does that mean?"

"I'm sorry, sir." He turns his phone to me, and the image on the face almost makes me lose it.

"Stop the car!" I shout, and Logan immediately pulls onto the shoulder.

I'm out of the vehicle in a flash, pacing the small space between the car and the road. My hands are clutched in my hair, and all I can think is *No, No, NO!!!!*

On the face of Freddie's phone is a grainy photo of my love sitting on a brown tile floor against a dirty beige wall. Her hands are tied behind her back, and a black sleep mask is over her eyes. Her pretty hair is messy, but what guts me is the palm-sized purple mark on the side of her face and the brown stain of blood on her mouth.

"Jesus!" I shout, bending at the waist. *How the fuck could I be such a fucking idiot? How could I let her go alone like that to meet that bastard?* "If anything happens to her, I'll never forgive myself."

"Sir?" Logan approaches me with slow, measured steps. "I've already alerted His Royal Highness of the situation, and we've gained access to the security cameras at the hotel where she went to meet that man. We'll find her, Sir."

I take a few deep breaths before straightening. Logan is in front of me, hands open at his sides, palms up. Freddie is behind him, nearer the car, and both share the same expression of concern mixed with quiet determination.

"We can't let this happen to her." My voice breaks, and my insides are a mixture of rage, fear, and desperation. "Take me to that fucking hotel."

"Sir," Logan starts. "We—"

"NOW, god dammit! I want to see that fucking security footage NOW!"

Freddie is in the car, and Logan nods, turning swiftly to head to the driver's side. I'm in the back seat, and we're speeding down the parkway in the direction of the hotel in less than a minute.

Ice is in my stomach as I watch the black and white image of Zelda crossing the lobby sideways. That fucker Seth tracks her movements, and my chest is tight as I watch her keeping as many obstacles as possible between the two of them. She's trying to run, but he's not letting her go.

"God help me," I exhale. I can't see her eyes, but I know my girl. She's doing everything to reach the door, to survive, and I see the moment she knows she's not going to make it. I can barely take watching this unfold.

"Run, Zelda," I say under my breath, even though I know that isn't what happens.

My fists are so tight my knuckles ache as I watch him grab her arm. Seth Hines will be the first to die when I catch these bastards. We all stand like incompetents as we watch that dick push my love into a black SUV that rushes into the circular drive.

A knot is in my throat and my muscles ache with needing to help her. I see her jerk back, trying to escape, before she's shoved inside.

"No..." Turning fast, I pound my fist against the wall.

Logan is at my side. "I've compiled a list of all Americans living on the island. Unless you need me, I'll start questioning them now."

"Go." I clench my aching fist. My teeth grind. "Tell me the minute you find anything. Tear this island apart. If anything happens to her—"

"Nothing is going to happen to her," he says, his large hand grips my shoulder briefly before he's out the door.

Freddie is at the laptop running plates and crosschecking what we have. "The SUV matches a vehicle currently in long-term parking at the Beef Island Airport."

He looks up at me, and I can read his expression. "FUCK!" I shout, slamming the heel of my fist against the wall again. I look toward the door where Logan just left.

"Let him search," Freddie says. "He might find a clue to where they're headed. In the meantime, I think we should return to Monagasco."

My brow lowers. "You think Paxton will go to the continent?"

"He has the most support in Totrington," Freddie says in a measured voice. "It's been a long time since I've tracked a thug, but I wouldn't put anything past this... *prime minister* when it comes to your fiancée."

This *thug* has my Zelda. I'm unfolding strategy, regarding and discarding ideas in my mind when I register what he just said. "My fiancée... How did you know? We only just agreed—"

"As you know, it's our job to keep eyes on you at all time." A sad smile crosses his solemn face. "We step away when we're sure you're not in danger, but your brother... His Royal Highness, has given us strict orders to protect your person."

I've grown up with guards and security, so it would be ludicrous for me to act modest at this point. "It's always a surprise when someone knows information no one else has been told." I think about my brother's decision to enter the Grand Prix two weeks ago. "We have a mole at Occitan."

"What's this?" Freddie's on his feet, concern lining his face.

"Someone in the house — it has to be someone on staff — is keeping tabs on us. It's got to be how they knew she was here."

Freddie's chin drops, and he speaks slowly. "Seth Hines appears to be how they knew she was here. We have reason to believe he's been working with Paxton since he appeared in Monagasco."

"WHAT?" Acid burns in my stomach. "How long have you known about this?"

"It's only been confirmed in the last twenty-four hours. Your brother's team has been working nonstop to find the man who shot Ava. It's possible Seth Hines was the shooter."

"We have got to find that bastard."

"Of course," Freddie says, giving me a slight nod. "Your car is out front waiting to take you to the villa so you can pack."

I start for the door. "Contact the airport and have a plane standing by. Tell them it's for me, the Prince of Monagasco. No point in being undercover anymore."

"I'm on it." Freddie is holding his phone to his ear. "I'll text Logan to let us know if he uncovers anything."

A brief pause as I consider my stocky guard's interest in my fiancée. "He cares about her," I say.

Freddie's stern expression falters. "We all do. She's a captivating subject."

Nodding, I think about my Zee and her cons, her globetrotting, and her penchant for besting the bad guys. "She's pretty incredible."

"We're going to find her, Sir."

Digging in my pocket, I place my hand on the claim ticket for her ring. "Text me the second you find Hines."

Chapter 11: Lost

Zelda

Consciousness fades in like the raising of a dimmer switch. I open my eyes slowly, but all I see is dark. A black hood is over my head, and I'm lying on a very cold, very hard surface. Placing my palm on it, it feels like metal, and a sudden vibration followed by the echo of what sounds like a drill comes from somewhere far below me.

Inside the hood, my lips are crusted and dry. I taste salt and coppery blood in my mouth, but I'm not actively bleeding. Still, my jaw is painfully sore from my missing tooth, and I'm so thirsty.

Lying here, I feel rocking, an occasional dip. As I listen, I try to place the sensation until at last I realize, I'm either on a boat or I have a concussion. Or both. The last thing I remember is Gorilla Man's fist slamming into my skull.

If I live through this, I'm going to stick a shiv in Seth Hines.

"She'll stay on the island," an accented male voice I don't recognize says.

"It's not on any map." That voice I do recognize. It's Wade Paxton. "They won't even know where to start searching for her."

"How did you find this place?" the other man asks.

"When I was in Turkey, they told me about an island where the Australians sent Islamic refugees.

It's larger, more densely populated, so I continued searching. I found this little island about a thousand miles east of there."

Fear trickles through my veins. I don't move. *Where are they taking me?*

The noise of the door, and another male voice joins Wade and his companion. "We're twenty feet off the shore of Uranu."

"Good work, Blix," Wade says. "You'll stay with them until it's time to dispose of her."

"Yes, sir." More noise of doors, and we're back to just the three of us.

"Who knew she would prove so useful?" From the sound of his voice, Wade is standing above me. It's almost impossible to keep from shivering. "To think I almost wasted her life in Monagasco."

"What do you expect to get for her?"

Wade is back, and I lie still, listening. Perhaps if I know what he wants, I can figure out how to escape.

"Power. Leverage. She's the sister of the crown prince's fiancée. She's the presumptive heir's girlfriend. They'll come to the bargaining table in exchange for her life." My stomach tightens, and I can't help the shiver that passes over my shoulders. "Ahh, and it seems she's awake."

The hood is jerked off my head, and bright light dazzles my eyes. It takes a few moments of blinking and squinting before I'm able to make out Wade's greasy hair, slimy face, and thin moustache.

I'm in a small cabin on a boat that has three twin beds arranged around the walls. In the center is a small table and one long shelf system runs along the perimeter. A veranda is in the very back, and I can see the green brush of an island through the glass door.

The clicking of a photograph makes me jump and look at the other man. He's holding his phone up and taking pictures of me.

"Hold this." He shoves a newspaper at me, and I look down at the cover. It's a *USA Today*, and the date is June 12. "Turn it around."

"May I please have a drink?" My voice is dry and rough as sandpaper.

He grabs a tumbler and fills it with an inch of water from the small sink before handing it to me. I drink the small amount so fast, but it's not enough to ease my thirst.

"Do as you're told." Wade steps forward and roughly shoves the newspaper in my hand again. I place the tumbler on the floor beside me and look up at him. The camera snaps come quickly.

"Where are we?" I ask, not sure how long I've been unconscious, and trying to figure out how I can possibly escape.

We're on a boat, in the ocean, headed to a small island. It's all I know.

"The last place you'll ever live." Wade sneers, and a cruel light is in his eyes. "Make yourself at home, and don't make trouble. Your guard's only instruction is not to kill you. As long as you're useful."

My insides shudder, and I'm afraid I'll be sick. The door opens again, and a tall man with white-blonde hair and dead blue eyes surveys me up and down.

"Zelda Wilder, Blix Ratcliffe." Wade pushes me toward the man.

My head is still dizzy, and I have to grab the corner shelf to keep from falling. The edge digs into my hip, and I exhale a painful noise as tears burn my eyes. I will not cry. The last thing I will do is appear weak before these men.

Blix only turns and walks out into the hallway. I look in the direction he went then back to Wade Paxton.

"We have all we need for now," he says, walking forward and pushing me out the door.

I stumble over the bottom lip, across the narrow hall, and the door slams shut in my face. I'm left standing in only the denim halter dress I put on... this morning? Yesterday? My espadrilles are gone, and cheap rubber thongs are on my feet. My hair is matted, and my arms and legs are bare, except...

Looking down, my throat tightens, and I almost lose my battle with the tears. The tin ring is still on my finger. I lift my hand to look at it, and I see the purplish-green mark it's already leaving on my skin. It's the only reason they didn't bother taking it, but they have no idea how much strength it gives me. With a shuddering breath, I hug my hand against my heart. *Cal...*

Blix is back, and his expression has gone from dead to livid. He grabs my upper arm in an iron grip and shoves me ahead of him in the walkway. "Stay with me," he says, continuing on at a fast pace. I have to trot to keep up.

"No one told me what to do." My voice is so dry, I sound like a forty-year-old smoker.

He stops so fast, I almost bump into him. "Don't make me speak to you again." His voice is very deep and his accent is clipped.

I don't smile. I don't nod or acknowledge his directive. He starts to walk, and I continue after him to the center of the boat and then down flight after flight of stairs until we're at the bottom. I wait as he shows documentation to the men waiting at the exit. They look Indian or possibly Turkish, and I wonder how far we've traveled... or maybe they're simply a foreign crew. It has to be the latter.

Outside, on the long pier, a white Jeep-truck hybrid is waiting. Blix shoves me toward the back, and I climb over the tailgate as he gets in the driver's seat. He turns the ignition, and I barely have time to stumble forward and sit with my back against the cab before we're moving.

The sun beats down on me strongly. It heats my skin, and I know I'll burn quickly on this small island. I don't have anything to pull over my shoulders. I look up and around. We pass a series of short buildings with tin roofs. They look like military housing, and they're painted white with bright pink squares on the sides. I don't know what it means, since I'm relatively sure there are no military personnel on this island.

I look in the opposite direction, back toward the beach, and I see a hollowed out gray structure. It's an enormous, four-story barn of a building with rusted tin walls and a long gable roof. It's completely deserted.

My head hurts from my injury and the sun is making me squint. I don't want to lower my eyes. I need to see where they're taking me, so I can try to run away. Only, I don't see any people who I might convince to help me were I to escape.

Blix takes a sharp left turn and we drive further inland. The canopy of green on each side of the Jeep grows thicker the further we drive, and the despair twisting in my chest grows tighter.

We must still be in the Atlantic, but where? If only I could see a native, I might be able to signal to them or at least examine his or her clothes for signs of what country I'm in.

The truck bounces violently, and my head feels like it's splitting in two. I splay my hands and feet out like a starfish trying to stay seated in an upright position.

Another sharp turn, and we're out of the forest. We're plunged into sunlight, and my breath catches. Blix pulls the Jeep up to park at a line of small, cinderblock buildings. They're all painted white, and they have holes where windows and doors should be. Only, they have no glass or wood. They're empty except for faded white curtains hanging over the space.

I hear the truck door slam, and a dark face appears in the window of one of the small buildings. It's a woman with long, straight dark hair. Her brown eyes are round as she stares at me. I don't move. I sit and stare back at her.

"Halo," Blix says.

A male tenor voice replies. "Bon bini."

"Mi tin un muhé a abo," Blix replies.

"Bon, bon," the man says.

I have no idea what language this is. I don't move. I only sit in the bed of the truck, my eyes locked on the black ones staring back at me from the shack.

The loud slamming of a palm against the side of the truck snaps me from my trance. I look up to see Blix is there, his blue eyes simmering with anger.

"Get out," he orders. "I'm leaving."

Terror grips me at those words. "Where am I?" I say desperately. "You can't leave me here. What is this place?"

He steps forward and grips my arm, dragging me roughly across the bed of the truck. I let out a little squeal, and he jerks me up and over the side of the truck then releases me.

"OH!" I shout, flailing for anything to grab as I fall all the way to the sandy ground. I hit the sand with a hard *Thud!* that rattles my teeth and sends screaming pain through my head.

I lie on my side on the sand unable to move. I don't fight the tears this time as my vision tunnels. Too late, I realize Blix is in the truck and revving the engine.

He hits the accelerator so hard, the tires spin, shooting sand into my face and all over my body. I twist quickly away using my hands to protect my nose and mouth. He's gone before I even open my eyes. I don't want to open my eyes. My limbs are heavy, and I'm so tired. I feel like I might vomit again, but instead, I give up the fight and fade into the blackness.

CHAPTER 12: PIECES

Cal

Ava sprints across the tarmac as I descend the steps of the small jet. Her green eyes are red-rimmed, and I see unshed tears in them. "What's happening, Cal? Where is she? Do you know anything?"

I put my arm around her shoulders and pull her to my chest in a hug. My eyes squeeze shut as I fight my own desperation. I feel every bit of the pain tearing her apart. "I'm sorry I didn't keep my promise to you."

"NO!" she wails, and my insides crumble.

Her body shudders as she cries, and I look up to see Rowan waiting beneath the covered walkway. The moment he sees her break, he's across the space to where we're standing and pulls her into his arms.

"Welcome home," he says, giving me a nod.

I can't answer him. I told Ava I wouldn't come back without her sister, and here I stand, empty-handed.

Rowan and I have been communicating since I left Tortola, and he's up to speed on everything we've been able to uncover over the last four days—which isn't much.

"Wait," Ava turns in my brother's arms, pushing the tears off her cheeks. "You found Seth, right? What did he say?"

My jaw clenches in frustration. "We didn't find Seth. He left the island before I even knew Zelda was gone."

"What do they want?" Her voice is almost a shriek. "I understand trying to hurt me, but not Zee! Zee doesn't have connections to anyone! She doesn't possess state secrets..."

It's a question I've been turning over and over in my mind. No one knows about our engagement. We weren't at Occitan when I proposed, and the villa we rented was completely secure. Even more, this kidnapping was planned. It's the only explanation for how easily they took her and disappeared so fast and so thoroughly.

I've only been able to reach one conclusion.

"It's my fault," I say quietly. "By going after her, I basically confirmed their suspicions about her value. If I had sent someone in my place, someone nobody knew to bring her back —"

"Stop!" Ava grabs my arm with surprising strength. Her green eyes are wide, and she infuses her words with so much emotion. "You couldn't help going after her. You love her, and what she did was... What *we* did was wrong."

Rowan's deep voice cuts her off. "We've already gone over this. Reggie tricked you, and Zee felt compelled to keep you safe."

"Still, Cal needed answers." She slides her hand down to mine. "It's not your fault."

"Thanks," I say, unable to smile. "I'm sorry I don't share your opinion. I was angry, and I wanted to make her confess what she'd done. I wanted to..."

My voice trails off. I can't say the truth out loud, that I'd wanted to hurt her the way she'd hurt me.

The truth of that statement cramps my stomach. *If anything happens to her...*

"I'll do whatever it takes to get her back," I continue. "We'll never stop searching until we've found her."

"Let's go to the palace." Rowan says, leading us to the waiting Towncar with Ava tight against his side.

Once we're on the road, she uses a tissue to wipe her eyes. "Seth disappeared, Zee disappeared, they all just vanished?"

My lips tighten, and I look down at my hands. "From what we pieced together, they were only there for one reason—to take Zelda."

"Do you have any idea what they intend to do with her?" Her voice is just above a whisper, and I hate that I don't know.

"They took her for leverage, which is a good thing," Rowan says. "It means..." I watch as he covers Ava's small hand with his larger one.

"It means they won't kill her." Her voice wavers as she says the words.

Bending my elbows, I rub my hands across my face. I'm tired and I'm anxious, and I haven't slept since this ordeal began. "It would be a lot of pointless effort and planning if they did," I say.

She blinks rapidly and manages to smile. "So she's alive, and they want something. We just have to wait and see what it is."

My brother puts his arm around her again, hugging her close. "That's exactly what it means. In the meantime, you need rest. You're still getting over your own injuries."

Looking up at him, her expression softens. She touches his face and places her thumb on his lips.

The familiar gesture causes me to turn away and look out the window. I don't know how I couldn't see they were sisters before. I was so blind.

"I'll be so much better once I know something," she says.

"Still, when we get back, I'd like you to go up and rest." He says gently. "I'll tell you anything we learn. Okay?"

She smiles and nods as Hajib guides the car through the enormous palace gates and into the circular drive leading to the entrance.

Once we're alone in the war room, I rehash what we know bit by bit. After viewing the security footage... *Jesus, that security footage.* The sight of my Zelda fighting for her life still sends shards of rage ripping through my chest.

We'd gone to Seth's hotel room and found the entire place scrubbed clean. We tore it apart anyway, looking for anything—a scrap of paper, a notepad, a magazine, anything that didn't belong. We found nothing.

We went to Frenchman's, where he'd put up Zelda that first night, but the owner claimed not to know Seth or any of the men in Wade's group. She insisted she took the reservation over the phone from an American for his sister, and the sister left the next day with another man. A man who she thought looked a bit like me.

No fingerprints, fibers, paperwork, or even scraps of trash were found in the abandoned SUV. It was emptied the same as Seth's hotel room and left in long-term parking.

No one matching Zelda, Wade, or the large hirsute man from the video passed through airport security that day or the next. Freddie scoured the security footage and found nothing. The port authority had no unscheduled cruises. They even provided the roster of every charter in or out of Tortola for the past two weeks, and nothing.

"God dammit!" I shout, pushing back against the heavy mahogany table. I'm frustrated again that we have no leads. "It's like they disappeared into thin air."

Rowan's voice is even. "When Zee left, she said they'd been planning this for months. She said they had everything in place before they even locked her in that bathroom. They've been ahead of us from the start."

"Now is the time for the succession referendum," I say, leaning forward in my chair. "The wisdom you showed cleaning out the cabinet after father died couldn't be more obvious than it is now."

We're alone in the ornate cabinet chamber. A heavy mahogany table monopolizes the space, and thick velvet curtains hang over the twelve-foot windows. Our family's coat of arms stands oversized above the head chair.

"I remember a time when this room was filled with men our father trusted," my brother says. "Now they're all trying to seize control."

"Not all, brother," I say, rising from my chair. "Have you made any progress tracking down the leak at Occitan?"

I consider how dangerous our position has become. Everyone is at risk, and until we know more, I don't even want to visit that gorgeous estate on the coast. The first place Zelda and I ever made love...

"No," he says, anger clear in his tone. "It's like we're in the middle of an undeclared war!"

He turns to the window and looks out. His hands are clasped behind his back, and I'm struck by how kingly he appears tonight, trying to solve our problems and protect our country. I wonder if this is Ava's influence in his life.

A sharp knock on the door draws both our attention. "Come in!" Rowan says.

The large door opens slowly, and Logan enters. He's carrying a brown envelope, and his expression is grave. I'm on my feet at once.

"Logan, what do you have?"

"You might want to sit down, sir."

My brow tightens, and I take the envelope from his hands before he can stop me. Pulling the tabs, I hastily open it and reach inside to remove three large photographs. They're black and white, and I do sit when I see the subject.

"Zelda..." I whisper.

She's still in that denim halter dress, but a large bruise covers her face. Dark circles are under her eyes, and her mouth is smeared with dried blood. Her hair is messy like she's had something over her head, and she seems disoriented. My fists clench at the sight of her this way.

"I'm going to kill Wade Paxton with my bare hands," I growl.

"That leaves Seth to me," Logan says with equal intensity.

Sliding the next photograph from the stack, it's her again, but this time, she's holding a newspaper.

A man's hand is in the frame, holding the cover page under her chin. I can't see what it says.

"What is the date?" I ask.

The stocky guard pulls a scope out of his pocket and hands it to me. "The date is what he's showing us."

Dropping the print on the table, I place the round piece over the date field and lean forward. June 12. "Yesterday." I look up at him.

"Where were these taken?" Rowan demands, and Logan is quick to answer.

"We're not sure yet, your majesty. As you can see the walls are bare beige, and the newspaper could have come from anywhere in the Western Hemisphere." He flips through the three photos, and pulls out one, pointing to a glass on the floor beside Zee.

"Use the scope again and look at the reflection on that tumbler," he says.

I do so, and the setting opens before me. They're in a room with a veranda. From the arrangement of the beds and the shelf, it looks like...

"They're on a ship? But we checked all the cruise ships..."

"Yes," Logan says, slowing down as if leading me to the answer. "We checked all the *cruise* ships."

In a flash it hits me. "They sneaked her out on a cargo ship!"

"It's the only option that makes sense," Logan smiles, and I'm out of my seat. It's the smallest break, but we need it so much. "We checked all the cruise ships and charters," he says. "They must have known we would do that. But a cargo ship—"

I'm pacing, thinking. "They could carry her onboard and wouldn't even have to worry about papers."

"Especially if they knew the captain," Logan says in a knowing voice.

My eyes flash to his. "You found a connection?"

He shakes his head, dampening my enthusiasm. "Freddie is searching the list of captains operating cargo ships in and out of the area. He's looking for any who might have a connection to Totringham. It's only a matter of time."

It's the best news we've had so far, and I turn to Rowan. "We need to tell Ava —"

I stop short when I see his face lined with concern. He's holding a sheet of what looks like printer paper. "How much time will Freddie require?"

Logan's face drops as if he knows why my brother is asking. "He's moving as quickly as possible. He knows about the deadline."

"What deadline?" My tone is sharp, and my brother passes me the sheet.

My throat tightens as I read.

Dear Sirs:

We are holding Miss Wilder at a secure facility on an uncharted island. If you ever want to see her alive again, you have six weeks to complete the following tasks:

1-Cancel the contract with the American tech company.

2-Reinstate Monagasco's oil leases in Tunis and reinvest the profits in future leases there.

3-Decline the succession referendum naming Rowan Westringham Tate King of Monagasco.

4-Sign the Open Borders Treaty uniting Totringham and Monagasco as one united, free-trade cooperative overseen by elected members of parliament.

5-Sign the pardon for Wade Paxton for his alleged role in the Grand Prix assassination attempt and reinstate him as Prime Minister of the newly united kingdom.

Confirmation these tasks have been completed is required by August 1 or you will receive a piece of Miss Wilder every day until either it is done or until nothing is left.

Enclosed are photos starting the clock, and your first piece of Miss Wilder as a gesture of sincerity.

We look forward to working with you.

Dropping the sheet, I rip the envelope open looking for what the hell they've done to her. "Where is it?" I shout.

My eyes fly to Logan's, and he slowly reaches into his pocket. "I'm sorry, sir, I wanted to keep it safe."

"Give it to me!" I'm nearly blind with fury and fear and anger when he produces a small, white bundle.

Snatching it from him, I quickly unroll the parcel, searching for what might be inside. It unrolls and unrolls, "Good god," I mutter in exasperation and impatience.

Until with a little tap a tooth drops onto the table. I scoop it up in my fingers, feeling my insides straining.

Grasping my forehead, I can't bear to think how this happened. "Did they use medication. Did she suffer?"

"We have no way of knowing," Logan says quietly. "Although if you look at her photograph again, you can see this large bruised area." He moves his finger over my love's battered face. "It's possibly a byproduct..."

He doesn't finish, and I feel as if I might be sick. Dropping into the chair, my face is in my hands, and I clutch my hair trying to hold it together. Rowan's warm hand covers my shoulder, and he gives me a squeeze.

"Six weeks," he says quietly. "It's more than enough time. We will find these bastards. We will stop them, and when we do, they will pay."

I'm fumbling for control. I take the small tooth and carefully roll it in the damp gauze as if it's a precious artifact. *Pieces of Zee.*

"We have to decide how much to tell Ava," I say quietly. "Until we know how this happened, I'll take responsibility for keeping it from her."

Rowan's expression is grave. "Only for a few days. We will tell her when she's stronger."

"We have to double our efforts," I say, rising from my chair. "Take me to where Freddie is working."

Chapter 13: The Women

Zelda

I'm lying on a stiff cot when I wake. The ache in my mouth has diminished, but my head feels like the top of my skull is breaking open. I'm pretty sure that blow to the temple did more than knock me unconscious. The bright light hurts my eyes, and I try to remember the signs of a concussion.

When I try to sit up, my head spins and my hip throbs from where Blix ripped me over the side of the truck and then dropped me flat on the sand.

"Bon bini," a soft voice is at my side.

Squinting, I see the dark eyes I remember from the open window before I blacked out again. Her skin is the color of mocha and her long, dark hair hangs stick-straight down her back. She looks Hispanic or some kind of Native American. I remember seeing a photo of the Anasazi once. She's like that.

"Where am I?" I say with my sandpaper voice, easing slowly into a sitting position.

Her brow lines, and she stands, crossing the room to a small table where a bucket sits. Using a gourd, she scoops water and returns to me.

"Bebe," she says.

Her voice is soft but direct, and she only meets my eyes briefly before looking down again. I take the cup and hold it to my lips. The water is warm, but it's wet, which is all I care about. I slurp it down with all the decorum of a Labrador retriever.

"Thank you," I say, gasping for air.

She's up and across the room repeating the procedure and giving me another scoop of water. Again, I drink it down in record time.

We repeat this process once more until I've had enough. She looks around the space, and I do the same. We're in a one-room, cinder-block structure. The table is in the center, and an ancient, small stove is in the corner. A box, which I guess is a refrigerator, is a little further down. My cot is against the eastern wall under an open square that serves as a window. Two other cots are on the opposite wall from me. I assume that means another person shares this shelter with us. Is this woman married? Is it for another woman? I have no idea what to expect.

"Baño?" she says, doing a nod and holding her hand toward the door.

I think about the word. I've heard this word in Miami. It means bathroom. Suddenly my bladder feels like it might burst.

"Yes," I say, nodding. "Si," I try, and she lights up at that.

"Si!" she repeats, smiling and nodding.

She stands. I try to do the same, but my knees shake so hard I have to sit down again. Dizziness hits me. I don't know what I'm doing as instinct takes over, and I lean forward moaning, holding my head.

"Dushi!" she says, sitting beside me and rubbing my back. "Sori!"

It's hard to think through this hurricane of pain, but I recognize the last thing she says. I need to make it to the toilet. I'm not sure if I'm about to vomit all over myself or pee in my pants — or both.

"Help… me." I say, barely able to see. "Help," I whisper again. "Baño."

Her arm is around my waist and mine is over her shoulder. Together we rise slowly, and I lean heavily against her as she walks me across the dirt floor to the thin cloth constituting the door. It gets caught up around us, but we keep going until it gradually falls free. Thankfully, the bathroom is only a few paces down from where the line of side-by-side cinder block houses stands.

It's a closet-sized tin room and inside is a chair with no cushion over a hole in the ground. The tin door slams shut, and the smell of urine and fecal matter hits me full force. I immediately vomit all over the ground and flies rise around me. I start to cry again.

"Oh, god…" My shoulders shudder, and my heart feels like it's breaking.

Breathing through my mouth to avoid the stench, I pull my skirt up and my panties down and hover over that bottomless chair as I pee in that hole. When I'm done, I look around. No toilet paper. No surprise.

I wait, doing a little hip-shake, hoping the final drops fall away. When I can take it no longer, I step forward, pushing through the door. The blast of fresh air that hits me has me gasping frantically.

"Oh, god!" I gasp, leaning against the wall of the outhouse.

My new friend looks at me and nods. "No bon." She motions to the trees around us. "Baño."

Blinking at her a few moments, I try to understand. Is she telling me to pee in the woods? It would certainly make more sense than enduring that torture test every time I need to relieve myself.

I nod as if I understand. The vomit followed by peeing cleared my head a bit. I'm able to walk back toward the cinder-block houses by myself, but I need to lie down again. I stagger through the cloth hanging over the door and make it to my bed.

For a minute I sit watching the makeshift door, but my new friend never joins me. After what feels like an eternity, but is probably only a few minutes, I give up and lie on my side to sleep.

Voices rouse me, and when I open my eyes again, I see my friend is back and with her is a little girl. I say "little," but she's probably twelve or thirteen. She's skinny and tall, and her dark hair is wavy, unlike the woman's.

I watch a few moments as they move around the kitchen talking in their strange language. The girl is animated and fun, as if somehow she's managed to rise above the squalor surrounding us. She's also dressed in a plaid skirt and a white, button-up shirt. It looks like a school uniform.

Whatever my friend is cooking smells delicious. Or maybe it's because I haven't eaten in two days. Sitting up, I rub my eyes and wonder if I can figure out a way to communicate with them.

"Wak! Wak!" The woman motions to me, and the girl turns.

She looks at me, and I'm struck by her clear green eyes. Clear green eyes, wavy dark hair, tall and skinny... She's so much like —

"Hello!" the girl says, skipping to my cot. "I'm Selena. What's your name?"

I'm taken aback. "You speak English," I say through an exhale.

"I go to school," she says with a cute, superior look.

Her friendliness and happy manner are so out of place. My throat tightens, and I miss Ava. "That's good," I say, blinking fast, swallowing my tears. "I'm sure you're a very good student."

"I'm at the top of my class!"

The woman says something, and she replies in their language before turning back to me. "Mama says do you feel like eating?"

"Yes," I answer quickly. "Si!"

Her mother smiles and returns to stirring the pot on the stove. I smell tomatoes and peppers, and I wonder what type of meal she's cooking.

That makes my little companion smile. "So what is your name?"

"Zelda," I say. "But you can call me Zee."

"Selda," she says, substituting the Z sound with an S.

"I like the way you say it."

"I've never heard that name before." She walks to the table. "Where do you come from, Selda?"

"Miami." I'm starting to feel better, and I push the blankets aside to try and stand. I've got to move around. I've got to get my strength back.

"It's in America," Selena says. She looks down as if I said I came from heaven. It gives me an idea.

"Where are we, Selena? What is this place?"

She blinks around the tiny room. "This is our house."

"Yes, but where are we? What is this island?"

"The island is Uranu."

It's the same name Wade said on the boat. The tiniest spark of hope lights in my chest. "And where is Uranu?"

Her slim brows pull together. "I don't know what you mean."

Taking a careful step forward, I do my best to remain friendly and not intimidating. "I just mean... Where is Uranu? Is it part of Mexico? Puerto Rico?"

Again, she looks confused, and her mother interrupts our conversation. "Tempu na kome."

My eyes flicker to the woman's then back to the girl. Selena smiles, "It's time to eat now."

Three plastic chairs surround the metal table. We each have a small bowl containing corn meal mash mixed with tomatoes, jalapenos, and okra. I take a bite, and exhale a groan. It's delicious. The slimy okra cuts the spice of the jalapeno, and the tomatoes give it a savory goodness. I'm so hungry, Selena and her mother have barely started eating, when I empty my bowl.

They don't notice or comment, and I sit at the table, feeling the comfort of a full stomach. That small flicker of hope grows stronger, and I start to think I might be able to get out of here. I just need to know *where* is here.

I'm on the verge of trying to find out again when a man bursts through the curtain door.

"Tendé!" he shouts.

He's not very tall, but his presence sends Selena running behind her mother's chair. My friend rises quickly and holds her daughter behind her as she backs toward the wall where their cots are placed.

"Bo a na hasi un trabow!" He crosses the room to my friend, and she starts to scream.

"NO! NO! NO!" She's wailing, and Selena is screaming with her, holding her arm and crying.

The man shouts back, and the cacophony of noises, violent, shrill, and piercing, cuts through my head, reviving the intense, nauseating pain. My hope and optimism disintegrate as I stagger, practically crawling to my cot.

Tears are in my eyes as I squeeze them shut. Lying down, I pull the skimpy blanket around my head, trying to cover my ears. I hear a struggle in the room, but I'm helpless to intervene. The pain in my head paralyzes me.

Selena is crying. That man is taking her mother away, but I can't do anything to help them. I can't even stand. With every beat of my heart, pain flares through my limbs.

I don't understand what's happening. I don't know what's wrong with me. I'm hurt, and I miss my sister. I want to go home. I want Cal. I close my eyes and without even trying, the darkness comes.

When I open my eyes again, it's morning. Selena is gone, and my friend is on her cot with her back to me. Sunlight fills the space, and from the angle of the light, I think it must be noon. For a moment, I blink around the room. The table is clean, and only the bucket sits there with the gourd beside it. All signs of struggle are gone, and it's the same as it was when I opened my eyes the first time.

I'm starting to question reality when my bladder tells me I have to pee. Slowly I climb out of the bed and stand straight. The first thing I notice is my head is better. I don't feel like I'm pitching over the edge of a cliff or I'm about to vomit all over my shoes. I do feel like I'd better get to the baño quick.

Slowly, I go to the door, encouraged that I don't have to hold the wall to stay upright. I'm getting better... For whatever that's worth. I have two things going for me: Selena speaks English, and I can actually walk on my own to pee.

I bypass the outhouse of horror and opt for peeing in the bushes behind a tree. As I make my way back to the cinderblock house, I'm able to look around at my location better. Another woman watches me from the window of an identical house as the one we're in. Her eyes are just like my friend's — dark and curious.

Pausing for a moment, I give her a little wave. Then I smile. Her expression doesn't change, but she walks away from the window. Only an empty black hole stares back at me.

A wave of loneliness passes through my stomach, but I dismiss it. Why should any of these women trust me? I don't know why I'm here, and I'm sure they don't. If Wade is as cruel to them as he is to me, they're right to be wary.

Thinking back to last night, I wonder who that angry little man was. I want to know why he came in here and why he upset my friends so much. Entering the room, I pause for a moment, surveying Selena's mom. She's still lying on her side facing the wall, but she isn't covered with a blanket.

It's not particularly cool or warm, but I decide to return some of the kindness she showed me. Crossing the room, I go to where I assume she's sleeping and take the thin blanket from the foot of her bed. I'm just about to spread it over her shoulders, when she gasps and turns to face me.

"Kí bo ke!" she shrieks, and I jump back.

"I'm sorry! Sorry!" I say holding my palms out.

I drop the blanket. She's shivering, and I see now that her face is battered. Her lip is split and dried blood is in the corner of her mouth. My insides twist, and I understand they needed me last night. The man who came here was a bad man, but instead of helping, I was too weak. I hid under the covers when they needed me.

"I'm sorry," I whisper again, picking up her blanket and putting it on the foot of the bed.

I go to the bucket on the table. Taking the gourd, I fill the bowl and make my way slowly back to where my friend has returned to facing the wall.

"Are you thirsty?" I say, knowing she can't understand me.

She doesn't move for a few moments. I wait, looking at the clear water in the bowl and wondering if there might be a way to make it cooler. I know I would've preferred cool water when my own face was so beaten.

I'm about to walk away when she moves. She turns onto her back and looks up at me with red-rimmed eyes. "Danki," she whispers, cupping the gourd with her hands and drinking slowly.

I know that word. I heard it on that old *Heidi* movie I watched as a kid. Heidi was a little orphan girl from Germany... or Switzerland. Why would they speak German here? I don't know if any of the islands are owned by Germany. I didn't even know France owned some until Cal told me. Once again, for the millionth time, I wish I'd stayed in school.

"You're going to be okay," I say, trying to encourage her.

She only turns to face the wall again. I have no idea what happened last night, and I don't even know where I am. Returning to the small table, I put the gourd beside the bucket and force myself to rally.

I've been injured. I don't know where I am, but I'm still Zelda Wilder. If Ava were here, I'd grab her hand and figure it out. Ava's not here, but I haven't changed, and I'm not giving up.

Selena will be back this afternoon, and Selena speaks English. I'm going to find out what's going on here, and I'm going to figure a way out of this. It's what I do. I might not be Cinderella, but I am a survivor.

Chapter 14: Double Agent

Cal

Another day gone, and still no answers. Freddie has scoured every cargo captain, and not a one has connections to Totrington. Most cargo ships are based in the islands or in the U.S. and they carry produce or oil.

"What about this guy?" Freddie says, pointing to an online manifest. "Adem Tanipar?"

"That sounds Turkish," I say, walking to the large computer screen and leaning forward.

I'm holding the papers on a Russian captain Logan ran background checks on yesterday. No connections to any southern European countries. Still, it's the closest we've come — until now.

"Your uncle fled to Turkey after the shooting at the race." He looks up at me, and my eyebrows rise.

"Where is Reggie now?" I drop the Russian captain's papers on the table as adrenaline spikes in my veins.

"We haven't been able to locate him." Freddie moves the mouse, and I hear the printer start to work. "He didn't accompany Wade to Tortola. It seems they've split up."

"Where could he have gone..." I say it as much to myself as to Freddie.

We're in the large library on the first floor of the palace, and an oil painting of my mother reading a book is situated over a burgundy leather chair with shiny brass buttons. My eyes fix on her, and an idea flashes through my mind.

"Have Logan run a full background check on Adem Tanipar. I'm going to speak to the Queen."

My mother is sitting at the blonde wood writing desk in her bright, yellow study with a stack of linen thank you cards beside her. The tall windows are covered in thin, lace curtains, and it all feels very cheerful and summery. I'm working hard to keep my temper under control.

It's not my manner to be angry with Olivia, but the realization I just had makes me want to shout at her.

"I need to speak to you, Mother," I say, striding into the room.

"MacCallum," she says without looking up. She's holding a cloisonné fountain pen, and she doesn't pause in writing on the pale linen notecard in front of her. "I haven't seen you since you returned from your trip. Are you well?"

"As well as can be expected," I say, pacing the room. My hands are clasped tightly behind my back. It's going to be difficult to keep this up for long.

"You seem agitated." She's still focused on her letter. "Would you please fetch a bottle of the Canard-Duchêne?"

My eyes flicker to the clock. It's four-thirty in the afternoon. A bit on the early side, but not shockingly so, and the Canard-Duchêne is her favorite champagne as well as mine.

I go to the small wine refrigerator and open the door. Taking a black bottle from the rack, I set it on the counter and proceed to remove the foil, loosen the basket, and carefully slide the cork from its place.

Two flutes are on the portable wet bar at the window behind her desk, and I pour us each a glass before returning to where she sits.

Finally, she places her pen carefully on the blotter and folds the linen paper. "Now, what in heaven's name is troubling you, MacCallum?"

I let a moment pass, watching as she calmly seals the envelope with a stamp and places it to the side.

"You, Mother," I answer, and her blue eyes flicker up to mine. "You've been keeping up with Reggie. You never stopped communicating with him when Rowan turned him out of the kingdom. You know everything he does and you can get in touch with him whenever you wish."

Leaning back in her chair, she lifts the champagne flute and takes a small sip. "I don't know if every word of that is true. I don't know everything he does, and I can hardly reach him whenever I want."

I'm at my limit. Stepping forward, I place my palms flat on her desk. "Where is Reggie, Mother?"

"I'm not sure where he is at the moment, MacCallum." Her eyebrow arches, and she looks up at me. "Despite what you think, my brother does not send me his daily itinerary."

My jaw clenches, and as much as I respect my mother, murderous thoughts flicker across my mind. "When is the last time you spoke to him?"

Standing, she walks to the empty fireplace and sets her champagne flute on the mantle. "You and Rowan are determined to make Reggie into a villain.

129

If you would take a step back from the situation, I can explain how you are wrong."

The tightness in my chest makes it difficult to be patient. "I'm all ears."

"When your father died, Rowan was thrust into a position of leadership whilst at the same time attempting to deal with a tragic loss." Her blue eyes are fixed on the blackened grate in front of her.

For a moment I study her short grey hair, cut in a flattering pixie style. Today she's dressed in a new, severe pantsuit. It's cream with navy pinstripes, and her pearls are, as always, perfectly arranged at her neck. Total control.

"I think Ro did a fine job stepping into leadership," I say. "He's never been one to be overcome by personal matters. Even now. He inherited your nerves of steel."

I add that point in case she might try to implicate Ava somehow for distracting him from his "duty," although the whole idea he should find a wife originated with her.

"He did a fine job," my mother says with a slow exhale. "You're right. Rowan is a true Westringham. He has the sophistication and the innate elegance to lead. The fire he inherited from the Tate side." She looks at me and allows a little grin. "You, my dear, seem to have received a straight injection of Tate fire with only a touch of Westringham to temper it."

"Enough of this talk." My patience is gone, and whether it's the Tate in me or simply my love for Zelda, I don't have time to sort it. "My uncle has been working with Wade Paxton, and I want to know how much you know about his plans."

Her face grows serious, and she returns to her desk.

"It's true. Reggie has been working with Wade since your father died."

"You've known about their connection since Father died?" I take a step forward, and my hand brushes over a brass statue of a pointer dog positioned on an end table. I'm angry enough to smash it through a window.

"Control yourself, MacCallum!" My mother's voice rises, and her eyes flash. "Your uncle has been working with Wade Paxton on my orders. I'm still the Queen of Monagasco!"

Her voice echoes slightly in the room. My lips part, and for a moment, I'm not sure how to proceed. She is still the leader of our country. Rowan has not succeeded her yet. The succession referendum has not even been drafted, so for all intents and purposes, our mother is still in charge of this country. She is eager to retire and has been increasingly ceding responsibility to my brother, but she has the power.

"Mother," I say, dropping to the seat. Her confession changes everything, from the ransom demands to the reason I entered this room in the first place.

Only one word crystallizes in my mind: "Why?"

"Your father had a heart condition, MacCallum. He had a short temper and he was significantly overweight." She looks down at the table and murmurs a brief prayer. "I'm not speaking ill of the dead, but the fact is, you cannot blame your uncle for Phillip's death."

"I might not, but Rowan certainly does." It's not an attack. I'm simply stating the facts.

"Your brother was very hurt and angry by what happened to his father, and it was a most

131

appropriate way to respond. However, our country has been in jeopardy since before the two of you were born. Reggie and I made a vow to save Monagasco at all costs."

"At all costs? What does that mean, Mother?" My tone is edged with ice. "What do you consider a cost?"

"Hubert joined forces with Wade, and Reggie was determined to stop them. He is as committed to keeping Monagasco independent as your father ever was. His goal was to infiltrate their plans, report them back to me, and help us destroy them from the inside."

Silence. The ticking of the brass clock on her desk.

"You say that was his plan." I'm thinking about what I know. "How did it change?"

"When Rowan kicked the entire cabinet out, Reggie went with them." She returns to her desk and lifts the cloisonné pen. "He had to choose whether to continue tracking your father's betrayers or come clean and lose all access he had to them and their plans."

"He chose to stay in league with Twatrington." I say, finishing her sentence.

"To protect his country. Reggie is one of us."

For a moment, I think about what I know of my uncle's involvement in the plans to overthrow our government, in the plans to sabotage Rowan's car at the grand prix, in the attempt to kill Ava, in the kidnapping of Zelda... I know very little, actually.

"When he returned with Zelda and Ava, did you have a role in that as well?"

She does a little shrug. "I only know your uncle needed to get back into the country somehow."

"So this bit about him finding an heiress for Rowan to woo—all of it was simply a coincidence, considering you had just proposed the exact same solution and planned a ball to facilitate it?"

Her blue eyes snap up to mine. "Your uncle has always been very resourceful."

"You told him what you were planning." It's all clicking into place. "He simply had to find a woman—or in this case two—to be his ticket back inside Monagasco."

"Wade Paxton was already here. He secured a pardon from Hampton de Clare and had begun drafting the treaty to unite our countries. Hampton was already in the process of strong-arming members of both parliaments behind the scenes, creating stories of Rowan's risk-taking and inexperience—"

"So Rowan was right. The King of Totrington is supporting Wade's efforts," I clarify.

"Once Hampton let him back in, I needed your uncle to return from exile."

My brow lines, and I walk around the space trying to piece everything she's saying together. It's going to be hard to think of Reggie as an ally in this.

"Why not simply tell Rowan everything?" I ask.

She lets out a long sigh. "Remember the part about his Tate fire? Rowan has a tendency to overreact when he feels threatened."

"He can't throw *you* out of the kingdom, Mother."

"Either way, Reggie is in a precarious position. If we embrace him now, if Rowan pardons him and brings him back into the fold, we risk losing everything we've worked so hard to accomplish." She levels serious eyes on mine. "Wade Paxton is a thug. If he finds out your uncle is a spy, he will kill him. Most likely in some sinister way."

Now I'm at a loss. I'm trying to figure out what to do next or how to move forward. Rowan needs to know about this. He needs to know everything, and we need to make a new plan.

"Do you know about the ransom note? Their demands?"

I watch as she takes a sip of champagne. "I heard something about it. They want Rowan to forego his right to succession in favor of uniting the countries."

"Among other things."

"They seem to think the succession referendum has already been drafted, that I'm already planning my retirement celebration."

"They've given us a pretty tight deadline."

She pushes out of her chair and starts for the door. "I think we should take a holiday at Occitan. I think we should go there and discuss my displeasure with Rowan's choice in fiancée. We should have several very loud and clear debates on my decision to continue on as the titular leader until he comes to his senses. I'll be sure to use simple language even a rat can understand."

I'm on my feet and following her to the exit. "You know about the security breach at Occitan?"

Pausing at the door, her voice is thoughtful. "I think we should feed our rat some poisoned cheese and see where the carcass leads us."

It's an idea that can definitely buy us time. "You'd better tell Rowan everything before you start attacking Ava, even fictitiously. He can handle it."

"My thoughts exactly," she says, giving me a sly smile.

"The three of you go ahead, and I'll join you in a day or so." I kiss her cheek, heading back for where I left Freddie. "Please let my uncle know I'll be here waiting to speak to him."

Chapter 15: Mako

Zelda

I find a mirror in a drawer under the kitchen cabinet. Beside it are a tiny canister of talc and the smallest bottle of cologne I've ever seen. I open the bottle, and it smells like baby powder.

"This must be Selena's," I say, deciding against borrowing her brush.

Lifting the mirror, I'm startled when I see my face. The bruise on my lower cheek is purple, and my mouth is swollen. Dried blood is stuck in the corners of my lips. I smile, and the hole where my tooth used to be is exposed.

"At least it was in the back," I say pulling my lip down. I don't look as terrible as I could, but my hair is insane. "I need to get cleaned up."

I glance over at my sleeping friend. She hasn't moved since I tried to put the blanket over her, and I don't want to bother her over something I can probably find myself. One last look in the mirror, this time I study my eyes. My pupils are not dilated, which gives me a bit of relief. I'm still not okay, but maybe it's not a concussion.

Shoving the mirror back in the drawer, I take off out of the house determined to learn about my surroundings. A different woman is watching me from the third cottage, and I try again doing a small wave, giving a little smile. She doesn't run away, but she doesn't return my greeting. I decide to wait for

Selena before attempting to make contact. They can't understand me anyway.

Going to the back of the house, I find a little garden. It's four rows wide, and I see tomato plants, okra, what looks like cabbage growing in it. Green sprouts over what must be carrots are beside the longer tops of onions. I'm impressed and a little discouraged. She's growing her own food?

Between the outhouse, the lack of electricity, no glass for windows or even wood for doors, I'm concerned we really are cut off from everything. My only hope is Selena goes to school somewhere, which means she has a teacher, and a teacher will have contact with the outside world.

Walking through the brush, I look down at my hand, and I see Cal's ring. My chest squeezes as I remember the twinkle in his eyes as I begged to keep it. He was right. A purplish-green line is on my finger just beneath the tin band. I hold it against my chest and wonder what he's doing. Is he worried? Is he searching for me?

I try to imagine what he thought when I never returned to meet him. Wade took my picture holding that newspaper as some sort of "proof of life" image, but what kind of demands is he making?

No one knows about our engagement—I'm not even sure it's official. Even if it were, Cal isn't Rowan. I remember Reggie said if something happened to the crown prince, Cal would take his place. Does that make me valuable? I don't know enough about the politics of their countries to answer this question. Although, if I'm not valuable...

The thought churns my stomach. It's only a matter of time before they get rid of me. Looking around, I know I've got to find a way off this island.

138

The dirt path continues to the edge of the forest. A strange succulent that looks like a giant aloe vera plant is at the tree line. It's as tall as I am, and makes me think of something out of the dinosaur era.

I'm away from the little camp, but I'm not any closer to signs of a town or civilization. The trees are thinner, and I keep going, a few more steps, and they part. I've found a deserted beach, but it isn't sandy. It's covered in stones the size of my palms.

Picking one of them up, I study the smooth surface. It's large and gray, but others are red. Some are blue. Some are yellow and green. It's actually a vivid assortment of colors. Massive rocks are up ahead, and I climb over one to find several smooth, gray boulders surround a clear pool of turquoise water. It's like a hidden bath. This place is so beautiful—pristine and undisturbed. How is it possible no one's found it?

It's completely deserted as far as I can see in all directions, so I carefully untie the halter-top of my dress and slide the zipper down my side. I ditched my panties after the first night, so I'm totally nude when I lower my aching body into the cool water. One enormous boulder is in the center, and a little ring of soft white sand surrounds it. I sit on its flat surface and reach down for the sand to rub over my skin.

I don't have soap, but the salt water is cleansing, and the sand scrubs away the feeling of dirt. Lifting handfuls of water, I clean the blood off my mouth and cheeks, and I lean back to clean my hair. For several long moments, I float on my back with my eyes closed. I feel like a castaway lost on a deserted island, and except for the small band of women back at the camp, it's possible I am.

When I finally decide it's time to head back, I sit on the rock a while, letting the sea breeze dry my skin. I feel refreshed and encouraged, and I wonder if Selena will be home when I get back. I'm finally dry, and I climb over the rocks and put on my dress.

It takes me a few minutes to find the path I followed to get here, but I'm headed back, noticing familiar landmarks as I make my way. The dinosaur plant is at the edge of the path. As I walk, I notice another large palm with brilliant pink flowers up ahead. I didn't notice it before, and I consider picking some of the blooms for my friend back at the house.

I'm about to step into the forest to do it when the man from last night charges out of the brush screaming.

"ABO! ABO!" He grabs my forearm in a vise grip, and the bruises and blood on my friend's face send me into a panic. I'm not sure I can take another beating just yet.

"ABO NO TA SALI ESAKI KAS!" He yells, black eyes flashing with rage.

Still holding my arm, he drags me behind him a few paces in the direction of the houses. He's not very tall, but he's strong, and he's talking so fast... Well, I wouldn't be able to understand him anyway. Still, the way he's shouting in a foreign language makes my heart race.

"I don't understand!" I scream, and he gives my arm a violent, forward jerk that sends me scrambling to the path in front of him.

"ABO NO TA SALI ESAKI KAS!" He yells, storming toward me, black eyes blazing.

"Saying it louder doesn't help me understand!" I scream back.

I'm on the ground, and my relaxing bath is ruined. I'm panicked and dirty, and I don't know what he's saying. Reaching down, he catches me under the arms and hauls me to my feet. Then he pushes me forward in the direction of the houses.

I stumble catching my balance, relieved when I see the small garden I explored on my way out. Once I know where I am, I pick up the pace and start to run to where I hope Selena is waiting.

Rounding the corner of the house, I charge through the curtain that serves as a door, and relief hits me so hard. My little friend is sitting at the table with a book in front of her. When she sees me, her green eyes go round.

"You're alive!" she whispers, and my stomach drops.

The door behind me opens in a swirl, and the small dictator is in the house again, causing my friend and her daughter to fly screaming to the back corner, crouching on the floor between their cots.

"ABO NO TA SALI ESAKI KAS!" He says, looking at them but pointing at me. "Bisa su! BISA!"

Their panic caused me to panic, and now I'm standing with the small table between him and me. I look from him to my friends and back again quickly.

"INGLES!" he says, and finally Selena speaks.

"He says you're not to leave the house." Her voice is so small, I want to run and stand in front of her and her poor battered mother.

Instead, I nod quickly. "Si, SI!" I shout at him.

The man's eyes flash and he storms toward me. I circle the table, keeping the small furniture between us.

"Abo hasi problema pa mi," he hisses, "Ami hasi problema pa abo!"

My eyes are straining as I look to Selena. Her voice is barely audible. "He says if you make trouble for him, he'll make trouble for you."

Holding my hands up, palms facing him, I nod as quickly as my aching head will allow. "SI, SI!"

He stands in the house several moments longer surveying me with that evil light flashing in his black eyes. Finally, he seems satisfied and starts for the door. I move around the table, still keeping it between us in case he changes his mind before he leaves. He doesn't, and when he's finally gone, the room feels very quiet and empty.

The soft noise of Selena's mom crying is the only sound apart from my panicked breathing. I look over to see Selena hugging her mother and stroking her hair. The woman clings to her daughter, and I feel my heart breaking.

"I'm sorry," I whisper, going to them.

The woman continues crying, and I sit on the cot reaching out to touch her back gently.

"I'm so sorry, Selena," I repeat, trying to keep from crying myself. "I wanted to bathe. I was dirty."

"We have a shower in the trees behind the toilet," she says, her voice still trembling. "I can show it to you."

"Who is that man? What did he do to your mother?"

She blinks down as if ashamed. "His name is Mako. He owns us."

"Owns you?" My head involuntarily jerks back. "What does that mean? Is he your father?"

"NO!" she shouts, causing her mother to jump and whimper.

Selena speaks to her in their language, and I stand off the cot. "Let's help her lie down."

The girl speaks to her again, and they rise slowly off the floor. Her mother moves onto the bed and resumes her position facing the wall.

"What... happened to her?" I'm almost afraid to ask.

Selena's voice turns cold. "A boat came."

My heart leaps at those words. "A boat? That means —"

"The men come, and they take my mother. They take the other women." Today there is no fear. Today she is quiet rage. "One day they will come for me."

Now I'm the one gripping her arms. "No!"

I'm in no position to promise anything, but it's like having Ava again. I won't let Selena be hurt.

The little girl walks to the kitchen, and I watch as she reaches into the cabinets, taking out a bag of cornmeal. A bowl holding carrots and onions is beside that, and today she goes to the box I guessed correctly was a small refrigerator. In it is what looks like a very small piece of meat.

Looking back at the woman on the bed, my voice is quiet. "What is her name?"

My young friend looks up. "Ximena."

I take a step forward and touch her shoulder lightly. "I'm going to get us out of here, Ximena. I don't know how, but I won't leave you behind."

CHAPTER 16: UNEXPECTED ALLY

Cal

Reginald Winchester stands in the green drawing room of the palace facing me. My instinct is still to be furious with him, but after what my mother told me, I'm trying to curb it.

"What do you want from me, MacCallum?" he says in the reproving tone he always uses with me.

"I want you to help me find Wade Paxton."

Exhaling dramatically, he steps to the small wet bar and lifts a decanter of scotch. "I have distanced myself from Paxton. He's a thug, and he can't be reasoned with anymore."

"It's not a request, uncle. You will help me find Wade Paxton, and you will do it now."

Drink poured, he replaces the crystal stopper with a soft clink. "I don't take orders from you, nephew. I'm in your mother, the queen's command."

Anger tightens my jaw. "Then I will have my mother command you to help me find Paxton."

"Don't you mean Zelda?" He watches me with those steel blue eyes as he takes a sip. "She's who you're really interested in finding, correct?"

"Yes." I return his gaze with matching intensity. "Do you know where she is?"

The idea that he might know her location almost provokes me to cross the room and grab him by the lapels, but I won't let him see my level of desperation. The last thing I need is for him to think I'm not in control.

"No." His answer is clipped, and my shoulders drop.

"Fuck," I hiss, dropping to the sofa.

"However, I know what they were planning. It's possible we can compare notes and see if it leads us to the prize."

My head snaps up. "Tell me what they were planning!" I'm off the sofa and closing the distance between us.

He takes another deep breath. "When you lit out of here on her trail with two of Rowan's best guards, Wade abandoned his plan to kidnap Ava in favor of her sister."

"He was going to kidnap Ava?"

"She's engaged to your brother. She was his first-choice bargaining chip."

I nod as I listen, thinking of her words. "It makes sense to take Ava."

"However, at the palace, with the assassination attempt and everyone on red alert, he knew he wouldn't be able to get within fifty feet of her."

"Or more," I mutter.

"Zelda, on the other hand, took off running with the very man he'd hired to be his ears inside the palace."

Nodding, I look at my palm. "We knew he used Seth to get to Zee and Ava, but we didn't know why."

"Wade Paxton is a thug, but he's smart. He never trusted me. He doesn't trust anyone as far as I know."

Touching my uncle's arm, I motion to the door. "Come with me to the war room. Freddie is there with Logan. They have all the information we've gathered so far."

As we pass through the corridor heading for the grand staircase, I think about what Logan uncovered. "How did you leave it with Paxton?"

"We parted ways in Turkey, when he set out for Tortola. I intended to stay undercover in Antalya until the time we rendezvous in Totrington."

We're at the large office, and I tap on the heavy wooden door as I push it open. "He's here," I say, and my two guards do a brief nod. "Your grace."

Reggie steps around to what I assume is his usual chair and pulls it out to sit. I take the seat opposite him.

"We don't have time to waste. Paxton has connections all over the Mediterranean, the Caribbean… He mentioned several small islands off the coast of Venezuela that are uncharted."

My eyes widen, and I confess, my heart beats faster. "Do you remember any of the names?"

"He never said names. It's possible they don't have names." My uncle reaches for the file in front of Logan. "Is this the roster of ship captains?"

"We isolated a Russian and a Turk."

"It's the Turk," Reggie says, flipping the pages quickly. "Antilles or Agnan?"

"Adem?" Freddie says.

"Yes — Adem Tanipar captains cargo ships from Brazil to Turkey." He drops the file and slides it back to Logan. "He'll know where they are."

I'm out of my chair, pacing the room. "How fast can we find this Tanipar?"

"We're searching for him now…" Logan's tone is solemn. It makes my stomach twist.

"What's the problem?"

"We've been unable to locate him since his ship left Paulista." He's standing, and his large arms cross over his broad chest. "We have everyone looking, but nothing."

"Did he take a different ship? A different route?" I confess, I'm out of my element when it comes to cargo ship lines.

"He took his usual ship. He simply disappeared once he entered international waters. A local captain said he seemed to be changing course."

"Heading for Tortola," I say, clenching my fists. "We have to find that ship."

"Have the crown prince request a satellite search," Reggie says. "He has contacts in the tech industry."

"Will that work?" I look from Logan to Freddie.

"It's worth a try," Freddie says.

The last thing I hear as I'm pushing through the door headed for Occitan is Logan addressing my uncle. "Can you help us locate Seth Hines?"

Chapter 17: A Pass

Zelda

Mako likes to play blackjack. It's an unexpected stroke of luck I can't believe dropped right into my lap.

The night he left, after I'd wandered away from the camp, Selena was quiet. Ximena never left her bed, but the girl managed to get her mother to eat a piece of the flat bread she'd prepared with our meal. I felt mild nausea again, which I'd assumed was because Mako had thrown me down on the path and irritated my existing injury.

My little friend had taken out a worn pack of playing cards, and I watched as she played a round of solitaire. When I felt better, we'd played a game of Twenty-One. Now card games are our favorite way to pass the time.

Another week has passed, and no one has come to the island. I don't know if I've been forgotten or if I should be looking over my shoulder every morning, noon, and night. The problem with indefinite imprisonment is the tendency to grow complacent.

"Mako loves to bet," Selena says holding a handful of cards. Today we're playing Go Fish. "Give me all your aces."

I pull a pair of aces from my hand and pass them to her. I'm sitting across from her in a light cotton dress scattered with tiny pink flowers. It's loose and flowy and keeps me cool in the rising heat.

The denim dress I wore to this place is soiled and tight around my middle, which I know is the result of doing nothing but sitting on my ass in this house all day. I'm going to be so fat by the time this is over Cal won't even want me anymore.

"Give me all your kings," I say as I study the hand I've been dealt. My hair is piled on top of my head in a bun. "What happens when he wins?"

"He takes away a pass. Go fish."

A tiny bead of sweat is lingering around my hairline, and I reach up to flick it away before pulling a card from the pool. "What's a pass?"

"When the boats come, if we have a pass, we don't have to go."

My brow lowers, and I look across the table at her. "How many passes does Ximena have?"

"None. Give me all your twos."

I hand her the deuce I just took from the pool. "How do you earn passes?"

"One week with no violations is a pass."

"A week?" I think about the time that's passed. "But I've been here at least a week. Ximena never does anything wrong. She should have a pass!"

"She had many passes."

"What happened to them?"

Selena is quiet, and I lower my hand slowly.

"How did she lose her passes?" My eyes are fixed on the girl.

She only shrugs. "It's your turn."

Reaching across the table, I grasp her forearm. "How did she lose them? That first night he took her? What happened?"

150

Selena shakes her head so that her dark waves bounce around her cheeks. "It's not your fault. She chose to do it."

"Do what?" I can't move. I feel as if all my muscles are frozen while I wait for what she's about to say.

"The day you came, everyone left, and you were lying on the sand in the yard unconscious and bleeding." Her green eyes are fixed on her cards. "Ximena wouldn't leave you that way even when Mako told her not to touch you."

Folding my hand, I put the cards on the table and stand. We're in the small room, and her mother is outside. I go through the curtain door and around the cinder block structure to where she's in the little garden on her hands and knees digging.

"Ximena?" I say, going to where she's working. I stop and lower to my hands and knees beside her.

Stopping, she pushes a lock of straight dark hair behind her ear and studies me with those black eyes. A knot twists my throat when I see the faded yellow bruise still on her cheek. My stomach twists when I realize she got that beating, and god knows what else, because of me. She was abused and probably raped because she took pity on me. She carried me into her house and gave me water. She gave me her food. She carried me to the bathroom.

The night they took her, her screams and Selena's cries, fill my mind. I remember how I crawled onto that cot, clutching the blanket over my ears. I remember how I couldn't help them, my splitting head, and I'm so ashamed.

Reaching for her hand, I blink fast to clear the heat from my eyes. "Danke."

151

Her thin black brows pull together, and I know she doesn't understand why I'm thanking her. Still, I scoot forward and hug her.

"Danke," I whisper again.

That's how it started.

Mako doesn't come to the camp very often — at least he never did before. Selena told me he makes weekly checks to be sure all the women are in their houses. Unlucky for me, I happened to have wandered off to the shore on the day of his weekly check-in.

Today when he appears, I make a point of having Selena play blackjack with me.

"It's the same as Twenty-One," I tell her. She's afraid, but she trusts me. She's so much like Ava, I know I'll never be able to leave here without her.

On the table in front of me showing is a king. Selena has an ace.

"Hit me," I say, and she puts a six on my king.

She stands, and when we turn up the remaining cards, I have a ten. She has a king. Mako explodes with a loud laugh, causing us both to jump in our seats. Selena looks so afraid, I'm worried she peed.

"Abo bust!" he shouts, and bends at the waist laughing because I lost.

It's exactly what I hoped would happen.

I nod to Selena. "Go again."

Her small hands tremble as she collects the cards and shuffles them in her clumsy manner. I told her not to let me shuffle. Nothing gives a card shark away faster than an expert shuffle.

I wait as she deals each of us a card facing down and then a six to her, a three to me. "Hit me," I say fast.

I watch as she deals me a king, and I know what's coming. It's all playing out perfectly. She deals herself a five, and it's time to flip our remaining cards.

Selena has a ten, and I get a nine—and even louder laughter from Mako.

"Un mucha bati abo!" he laughs, pointing at me. "Un mucha!"

His laughter and taunting makes me think of bullies on the playground. I remember when Ava and me were little, and I would kick their asses. I got in so many fights in foster care.

I allow the anger to show on my face as I glare at the little man who holds so much power over us. He sees me glowering and laughs more.

"Abo rabiá!" then he changes his voice, so he sounds like John Wayne. "Abo *pissed*."

"I'll play you!" I say loudly to him.

He only looks at me, not understanding. I nudge Selena. "Tell him what I said."

Her eyes are wide as she looks at me. "No, Selda, we don't play with Mako."

"I'll play you!" I say, infusing my voice with as much fury as possible.

He speaks quickly to my young friend in their language, and she answers equally fast. I sit at the table watching, warm satisfaction filtering through my insides. *Get ready to get hustled*, I think, still holding my expression steady.

Black eyes are on me, and I can see him gloating.

"He wants to know what you're playing for," Selena says, nervously.

"If I win, Ximena gets a pass," I say and Selena translates.

Mako sits back, looking from me to her. I don't know what he will ask for if he wins. I don't know if he's been instructed not to touch me. If I'm a bargaining chip in Wade Paxton's plot to win Monagasco, I might be off-limits.

He looks at my young friend a moment, and a sick gleam sparks in his eye. It's so fucking familiar. I've seen that lecherous look before, and I know what it means. His words come fast, and Selena's face goes white. Her head jerks to me.

She jumps up from the table and runs out of the house. Mako explodes with laughter, but I only pause a moment to give him an angry glare before I'm fast on her heels.

I find her in the back garden kneeling in front of the tomato lattice. She's sniffing and holding her legs, and I see her little body tremble.

I drop beside her in the dirt and put an arm around her shoulders. "What did he say?" My voice is soft.

She doesn't answer me right away, she only shivers, and I'm right back in that fucking culvert in Florida holding my little sister as she shivers and cries. Only this time, I'm ten years older and about a hundred casino cons smarter.

"He said if he wins, he gets me." Her voice is so soft, and I know she's terrified.

I want to tell her not to be afraid. I want to tell her while it sounds scary and she might think it's a huge risk, it's not. I know I'll win. I know it as sure as I'm standing here looking at her. I'll get that pass and Selena will never be in danger.

"I'll beat him," I say. It's not a wish. It's not even me being reckless or bragging. I've been winning at blackjack against tougher competitors than a jacked-up pimp since I was old enough to sneak into bars. "Come with me and tell him it's a deal."

Her green eyes are huge when they flash to me. "You can't even beat me! How will you beat Mako? I won't do it!"

She crosses her arms over her stomach and turns away. I hate putting her in this position, but I don't have a choice. I can't tell her about a hustle. I can't tell her anything she might accidentally slip up and repeat.

I touch her gently, turning her back to me. Our eyes meet, and I smile my most reassuring smile. "Trust me. We're going to get Ximena her pass. We're going to get her twenty passes."

Selena doesn't move. She sits in that garden watching me, turning over my words. "How?"

"Trust me!" I say. "I know what I'm doing."

"And if he wins?"

I catch her arms and hold her tight. My eyes level with hers, and I make a promise I mean with all my heart. "I will *never* let him touch you."

She still hesitates, but I take her hand and pull her up with me. "Tell you what," I say. "If anything goes wrong, I'll take your place."

Her face jerks, "Don't even say that!"

Giving her a little hug, I laugh. "I wouldn't say it if wasn't sure I'd win."

That seems to reassure her.

Mako is waiting when we round the corner of the house, and I feel Selena's body tense. I give her another reassuring squeeze, and she tells him in their language it's a deal. The three of us return to the table, and I'm determined to win those passes for

155

Ximena. I didn't say it out loud, but that's another thing I won't let happen again. No one suffers for me.

With trembling hands, Selena places two cards face down in front of us, followed by two cards face-up.

Silence falls over us as we examine our hands.

I have a three; Mako, a Jack.

My breath stills. I do my very best to channel all the casino-cool that's been pounded into me through the years.

"Stay," he says, leaning back and grinning.

"Hit me," I say, and Selena turns a ten up next to my three. Mako begins to laugh, and Selena's eyes flood with tears.

I want to reach over and squeeze her hand, but I can't. It's the moment of truth, and I can't appear to know what's coming.

Selena takes a shaking breath as she reaches to flip the final two cards, but Mako is eager. His hand shoots forward and he flips up a two for him...

An eight for me.

We're quiet a moment as the truth sinks in. Selena does some fast math, and then her breath explodes from her mouth with a laugh.

I glance up through my lashes to see Mako's face turn bright red. "NO!" he points to the table and shakes his head.

"A deal's a deal!" I say, scooting back in the chair. "A pass for Ximena."

His eyes cut to me, and for a moment he considers reneging. I can see it in his shifty eyes. He's a double-crosser. He makes deals and then changes them when they don't go his way.

Standing, I go to the door and pretend to call into the yard. "I should tell the other women what happened here. How we won fair and square, and you're taking it back."

His eyes move from me to the table, to Selena then to Ximena. He doesn't know what I'm saying, as far as I know, but he gets up and walks fast to where I'm standing at the door. Selena is still at the table, frozen in place as if she's unsure what might happen next.

Mako leans into me, says something in his language, and then pushes through the door, storming out into the yard and away.

I explode a breath. "Shew!" I say, leaning forward.

I want to laugh, but instead my head spins. My breathing is labored, and while I'm so happy I won, I have to close my eyes against the rising nausea.

"Are you okay?" Selena asks, walking to me and touching my arm.

"Yeah," I say, trying to nod, but I'm afraid to make any fast movements. "It might not be twenty passes, but it's a start," I manage.

"Do you want to do it again?" she asks.

I want to say yes, but my stomach is churning. I don't know if it's my head injury. I don't know what's the matter, but I dash out the door and around the corner of the house just in time... to lose my lunch all over the ground.

I hold the side of the house, gasping, my eyes damp with tears. I don't know how much more of this I can take. I'm not getting better. In fact, I'm afraid I'm getting worse. What if I have internal bleeding? What if my brain is swelling?

Ximena appears at my side, and she touches my arm. She reaches around my shoulder and helps me move back, away from my vomit, back to the front of the house facing the yard.

"Na estado?" she asks, dark eyes large, face lined with worry. "Beibi?"

My eyes hold hers a moment. I don't know their language, but some words sound the same in any language.

"What did you..." I can't finish my sentence as I race through the math, as I race through all of it.

From the time I arrived in Monagasco and met Cal, we'd pretty much had a long, sex-filled holiday until I ran away. Then when he found me, we'd spent the proceeding days making up for lost time.

How long has it been? I don't remember having a period since... before we left for Monagasco. So many weeks ago... A month ago? Two months? Oh, god, I don't even know!

How could I be so careless? I've *never* been careless about such things... It's yet another way MacCallum Lockwood Tate came in and turned my carefully controlled life upside down.

Sliding my hands over my cheeks, I know none of that matters now. What's worse is it only makes me long for him more. Tears flood my eyes. *Cal... I need Cal.* I can't be here in this... prison camp away from him, possibly facing death, and pregnant with his child.

Pushing away from Ximena, I shake my head. "No!" I gasp. "Not like this."

I have to get back. I don't know how, but I have to get out of this place. I have to save our baby.

Holding the wall, I trail my fingers along the blocks as I make my way to the house. Selena is inside humming a tune while she cleans up the dishes.

"Hey," I go around to where she's standing and hold her hands. My desperate mind is scrambling for any possibility. "Tell me about your school."

She smiles so big when she sees me and jumps forward to hug me. "You saved my mama. You are a good person."

"It was nothing," I say fast. "Tell me about your school. Do you have a teacher?"

This makes her laugh. "Of course, I have a teacher! Miss Jimenez. She's my best friend Elana's mother."

"Elana? Does she live here on the island?"

Selena nods. "Her mama is one of Enrique's women. They stay on the other side of the island.

My insides plunge. "What do you mean? She's not a real teacher?"

"She has a book, Will-iam Shakespeare," Selena only stumbles slightly over his name. "She taught us to speak English and write our names in English."

Closing my eyes, I shake my head as my hope begins to die. "But she never leaves the island? She doesn't know how to get away from here?"

Selena's brow wrinkles, and she looks at me as if I just suggested the most outrageous thing. "No one leaves the island."

"But the boats... How do you think I got here?"

"Yes," that makes her nod. "You were brought on a boat. But the boats don't take us away."

Pacing the small space, I chew on my nail. "How old are you?" I ask, pausing.

"Thirteen," she says, "but Mama says I'm twelve. Mako leaves us alone if we're twelve."

My throat tightens, and I start to panic. "Selena, I need a doctor. I need to leave the island."

She drops the plate she's holding into the sink and takes my hands. "What's wrong? Are you sick? Is it your head?"

"Beibi," Ximena says.

We look up and she's standing in the doorway watching us. Her face is calm. She's entirely focused on her daughter and me. In the meantime, I'm terrified. I have to have a doctor, vitamins, Cal...

Selena smiles and walks to the door. We're all standing in the space when noise breaks out behind us. Mako is back and the women in the other house are howling and crying. It sounds like they're struggling. Ximena holds her arms out, guiding us all to the back wall of our tiny shelter, then steps to the window to peek out.

Mako is speaking rapidly, and one of the other women is arguing with him. We all hold our breath. I've never heard the other women speak much less argue with Mako. Selena is beside me, and I can feel her body rigid with fear.

"Another boat has come," she whispers. "He's telling them they must go, and they're angry. They say it's not their turn."

The three of us hold our breath, and all I can think is how I have no leverage. I have no money, none of us has anything, and we're counting on some pimp to keep a deal he made over a game of cards?

"What kind of boat is it?" I ask, but Selena doesn't know. "Ask your mother. Is it a cruise ship? A cargo ship? Some kind of kinky yacht club?"

She speaks to her mother in their language, and Ximena gives a short answer.

"She said they are workers. It's a big ship, and they all work."

Chewing my lip, I think about this. "It's a cargo ship," I say, still thinking.

They must dock here, and the men pay to be with these women. A shudder moves through me as I realize no one probably even knows about these unscheduled stops on unknown islands. It's inhumane, and no one knows.

Only now I know, and I have to stop it. *How* is the question with no clear answer. Instinctively, I opt for what could be the stupidest thing I've done so far.

Pushing through the curtain, I go out to Mako. "Hey!" I say, pulling his arm.

He's angry when he turns to face me. "Kí?"

I motion to him and me, and then I hold my hands like I'm holding cards. I point around at the women, and I point to my hand. He frowns and he shakes his head no, placing a hand on my face and shoving me backwards.

Stumbling, I manage to regain my footing before I fall on my ass, only now I'm furious. "No!" I say, shaking my head. "Pass!" I say, pointing to my hand again.

His jaw sets, and he reaches out to push me by my face again, but I dodge. He only manages to push my shoulder. I'm right behind him as he grabs the woman I've watched a few times from the other house. She begins to wail, and I reach for his other arm, holding him back.

"NO!" I shout. "It's wrong! It isn't right!"

The woman he's taking is crying, and I'm hanging on his arm. I'm not sure this will work, and he starts to shake me off. Finally, he releases the woman, but he isn't stopping. He steps right into my face and yells in that foreign tongue words I can't understand. His hand is around my neck, and he walks me backwards to Ximena's house. I can't breathe. I grip his hand, stumbling the entire way until he pushes me up against the wall, banging my head against the concrete blocks.

Selena and her mother rush out and take my arms, pulling me away from him and inside the one-room structure. The curtain door swings shut and the shouting and yelling outside resumes. Ximena is speaking rapidly under her breath and Selena is answering her in short, one-word responses.

I'm on my side on the cot, injured again. Pain, debilitating nausea grip me. I'm pregnant, and I can't risk being seriously injured. Still, the women's cries tear at my heart. I can't let them be hurt. Oh, god! I close my eyes as I cover my ears with trembling hands. What can I do?

Chapter 18: Going Back

Cal

Rowan is on the phone with the American tech company, and I'm sitting across from him with my fingers steepled in front of my lips. Another week is gone. We're running out of time, and I've passed from worried to frantic. We've got to find Zelda. We're a week away from our deadline, and even with Reggie's help we haven't been able to locate either the Turkish captain or the mysterious island.

"Is it possible to engage a satellite to search for the island?" He waits, and I'm on pins and needles waiting with him. "How long does something like that take?"

Another long pause. Another eternity.

"We don't have that much time. Is there a way to move ahead in the line? We're dealing with a life or death situation. Matters of extreme urgency."

He listens, and I strain against the minutes. "Thank you, Gil. I'll be waiting for your call."

Disconnecting, he turns to me. "We can get the images," he says, and I'm out of my chair.

"It sounded like you were going to say it was impossible!"

"Using his personal connections would take a month," my brother says, "But he's on the board of DigitalGlobe, and they're going to scan the area where we think she's being held and send us what they get."

"How long will that take?" I'm pacing the White Drawing Room, my heart beating fast in my chest.

"They have to turn the satellite. It could be a day or two."

Exhaling a loud breath, I go to the windows and look out over the gardens. I can't bear another minute of this intense worry. I can't bear being without her, without knowing she's okay. My body aches for hers. I want to hold her in my arms and feel her warmth against my skin. The idea that she might be taken from me forever has me on the brink of desperation.

"Any word after our conversation at Occitan?"

"Still waiting," he says, walking to stand beside me. Bracing my shoulder, he looks in my eye. "You've got to stay strong. We're so close now. We're going to find her."

"With every day that goes by I'm sure I can't take another one."

All the stress of these last several weeks is enough to break me. I lean forward, placing my head against the cool glass. "I can't sleep. I close my eyes, and I see her fighting to get free. The image of her battered face is in my mind, and all I can think is it's my fault. I should never have let her go alone."

"We asked for proof of life. If we're lucky, we might catch a boat headed to one of those uncharted islands on satellite."

For a moment, I think about this incredible possibility. My mother had the bright idea of using the rat at Occitan to manipulate Wade Paxton into showing his cards.

She went with Rowan and Ava to our family beach estate, and the three of them spent several days arguing over succession and discussing how she plans to fight the referendum. It was all an act, of course. My mother has wanted to retire since before this nightmare began.

Our hope is that her pretend disapproval and resistance to succession will gain us more time with these kidnappers. If Rowan is not the titular leader of our country, he can only fulfill the first ransom demand and possibly the second.

The first was to break his deal with the American tech company, and he made a big show of putting that contract on hold until he's named King of Monagasco. The second demand was to re-energize our oil holdings with Fayed in Tunis. Rowan is dragging his feet on that one, but still making a show of fulfilling the request.

Turning down the throne, signing the treaty with Totrington, and pardoning Wade Paxton—the final three demands—are all items he can only fulfill as king, and he can't be king so long as our mother refuses to step down.

We have no idea how these problems are impacting our timetable. Personally, I couldn't take the silence anymore and went to Occitan yesterday to tell Rowan we needed proof of life. I need to know she's okay. I need to see her.

It was an impassioned plea. Now we simply have to wait and see if it makes a difference—if we get another photo and if we can tell anything about where it was taken.

Standing in the plush drawing room, I make a decision. "I'm going back to Tortola. They won't expect me to be back there, and perhaps we've been gone long enough that some of these guys might have come out of hiding."

Rowan presses his lips together. "You're going alone?"

"I might take Logan with me. We need to stay off the grid, under the radar." Truth is, I can't stand waiting around here anymore. I'm ready to charter a boat and drive it all over the Caribbean searching for her.

Rowan doesn't try to stop me, he only nods. "I can't imagine the level of stress you must be feeling. If it were Ava..."

"Just keep her safe. Zelda will be worried about her, and I want to be able to tell her Ava is safe when I find her."

"Who are you telling I'm safe?" Ava enters the room quickly. She's dressed in a sheer black dress that swirls around her body, and my brother's eyes track her as she moves.

"Cal is going to Tortola."

She turns quickly, sapphire eyes on me. "I want to go with you."

"I-I can't." My eyes move to Rowan. I can't tell her no. I know she's as worried about her sister as I am. We're all coming apart with the helplessness of this situation.

"You have to take me with you." Tears fill her eyes. "I can't stand sitting here waiting anymore, Cal!"

Rowan steps up behind her, sliding a large hand around her waist and pulling her back to his chest. "He needs to go alone." His deep voice seems to calm her. "He's less likely to be caught, and he can move quicker, perhaps uncover something we missed the first time."

He manages to talk her down, but I see the worry full in her eyes. "I promise," I say, squeezing her hand, "If I learn anything — anything — you'll be the first to know."

Looking down, she nods. "Not like that tooth situation?"

With a wince, I shake my head. We finally told her about the piece of Zelda, and she handled it far better than I expected. She took it better than me.

"I won't hold information back from you again," I promise.

A little smile, and I'm out the door. I don't even pack. Touching the face of my smart watch, I alert Logan to meet me at the airport. The faster we move, the more likely we'll catch someone off-guard.

CHAPTER 19: PROOF OF LIFE

Zelda

It's a typical, nameless day when everything about my situation changes. I've lost track of time, but I've been trying to rest more. Ximena took a chance and sent a note to school with Selena saying we needed extra milk. We haven't said a word to any of the other women or to Mako about my pregnancy. I don't know if it will put me at more risk or less if they know I'm expecting a royal baby.

Now when Selena comes home from school, she has a little box of milk in her bag along with her pencil and notebook. We've been doing this for five days when that Tuesday comes.

I'm sitting on the floor and Ximena is behind me on the cot braiding my hair. It's growing hotter by the day, and we're in this landlocked location. My mind drifts to the beautiful baths I found down the dirt path away from this camp.

I wish we could go there, but if we're caught, it would be a very bad thing for Ximena. It wouldn't be good for me, but at least I'm protected from the true horrors of this island — for now.

We haven't heard another word about passes, and I'm pretty sure she doesn't have one, judging by how angry Mako was at me winning that round of blackjack. I haven't been able to get him to play me again. Every time he comes to the area, he doesn't look at me. He acts like I'm not even here.

Today ends that arrangement. The curtain over the door flies open, and I jerk back against the cot. Ximena pulls her legs up and gasps. Mako glares at her then glares at me.

"Bini ku mi," he says, reaching down and grasping my arm.

I'm on my feet and being dragged out the door with Ximena right behind us speaking quickly in their language. I think she's asking him what he's doing. I'm slowly picking up bits of their language.

We're out in the yard when my heart slams to the pit of my stomach. Fear races through my veins like electricity, and I fall behind Mako, even though I know he'd throw me in front of a train as soon as help me.

"What the fuck?" Blix is standing in the yard beside that Jeep-truck hybrid vehicle. He charges across the space to where Mako is holding me and pulls me out of his grip.

Turning me to the side, he smooths his hand over my stomach, then he turns to Mako. "Did you fuck her?" he shouts, and the man only holds up his hands and shakes his head.

"Can't you see she's clearly pregnant?"

I'm stunned he knows right away. We don't have full-length mirrors here. I've only been able to see my face in Selena's little hand mirror since I came here. Considering I just put the pieces together, I wonder what I look like to someone who hasn't seen me in four weeks. I wonder what I'll look like to Cal.

Blix speaks to me, which is a surprise, in view of his "never make me speak to you again" policy. "Are you pregnant?"

My heart is beating hard in my chest. I don't know the correct answer to this question. I could lie

170

and say I've merely been eating heavily and not moving, but I don't know the consequences of lying to this man. I have to think about my baby now. I can't be as reckless as I was when I was just Zelda Wilder.

"ANSWER ME!" he shouts getting right in my face.

Dropping my head, I look down at the sack dress I've been wearing. It's tight around my stomach but hangs on my arms and shoulders. I suppose my condition is obvious.

"Yes," I say quietly.

He exhales loudly and pulls a phone from his pocket. I watch as he dials, pacing back and forth in front of me. At once he begins speaking rapidly in what sounds like German into the phone. His dead blue eyes are trained on me, and I look up at him. He has a cruel face. He makes me think of people who like to torture their victims. He makes me think of little boys who catch birds so they can kill them. He makes me think of every evil person I've ever known.

"Is it the Prince's baby?" he asks with no smile, no emotion.

My insides are racing. Will they hurt me if it's Cal's baby? Will they use this for something even worse than whatever made them kidnap me initially? I don't answer right away. I've learned in my gambling jobs sometimes it's better to wait and see if the person asking a question will answer it for himself.

Blix is not one of those people. When I don't answer his eyes flash and he crosses the space to grab my arm. "Are you deaf as well as stupid?"

He's holding me so hard, I let out a little cry of pain. "No," I say, struggling for breath.

My brain is screaming. This is the same guy who threw me on the ground. I have to protect my baby from this guy.

"Then answer me, bitch," he hisses in my face. "Is this the prince's baby?"

Oh, god, I mentally pray before nodding slowly. His grip tightens and the scariest, most evil smile spreads across his face. Tears spring to my eyes, I'm so afraid. He returns to speaking on the phone, but his terrifying eyes are still on me.

Disconnecting, he takes my arm again and drags me to the side of our cinderblock house. It's the white wall with nothing on it. Reaching in his back pocket he pulls out a newspaper.

"Hold this up," he orders.

I look at the cover. The date is July 5, and for a moment I think of home, America, grilling and fireworks on the fourth of July. I didn't even know what day it was. A large hand reaches to the nape of my neck and jerks my hair.

"I said hold it up!" Blix is glaring at me, and I turn the *USA Today* around and hold it just under my chin.

His phone clicks several times and then he snatches it back. I don't even get to look at the headlines. My mind is thinking one word: *Cal.* I need to see him. I want to tell him about the baby. I don't want him to find out this way.

Blix goes to his truck and digs around in the cab before returning with a small Coke bottle. "Pee in this," he says, shoving it at me.

I hold the dirty bottle out and look at it. "Should I wash it first?"

172

"No," he says. "Piss in that bottle so I can get the hell out of here."

Despair fills my chest. As much as I hate Blix, his awful presence is at least evidence the outside world still exists. People are out there asking about me. Cal is still searching for me. The thought floods tears in my eyes. If only there were some way to send him a message. I miss him so much. Every night I dream about his arms, and every day I long for his touch. When I'm feeling very low, I fear I'll never see him again.

Taking the dirty bottle, I go around the corner and pull up the cloth dress. It's difficult but I manage to get an inch of urine in that small bottle. When I give it to Blix, he uses a napkin to hold it as if it's covered in germs.

Without a word, he goes to his truck and leaves. I'm standing in the courtyard watching him go with only Ximena by my side holding my hand.

CHAPTER 20: A MESSAGE

Cal

The G650 is waiting when I arrive at the airport. Logan has texted he's onboard and in the cockpit chatting with our pilot. Hajib lets me out at the tarmac, and just before I go, he touches my shoulder.

"Good luck, sir."

I cover his thick hand with mine and give it a firm squeeze. "Thanks, Hajib."

"No Odd Job?" he says with a smile.

"Reggie suggested we might be offending you with our old nickname." I say, feeling the need to send good Karma ahead of me.

"It always made me laugh, sir. No offense taken."

Pressing my lips into a smile, I nod. "I'm glad to hear it. We never meant any harm."

"I'll be glad to see Miss Wilder again."

My stomach tightens. Anxiety has become my constant companion. "Me, too."

With a fortifying breath, I jog across the space separating the town car from the gleaming silver private jet and up the short flight of stairs. Our flight attendant is waiting when I arrive.

"We're all onboard, your majesty," she says. "As soon as you choose a seat we'll prepare to leave."

"Thanks," I say, ducking inside the aircraft and planning to sit in the first open spot.

I stop in place when I see my uncle already at a window seat with a glass of champagne in front of him.

"Reggie!" I hesitate before going forward. "What are you doing here?"

"Your brother told me where you were going. I'm coming with you."

My brow lines and I walk quickly down the row and take the chair directly across from him. "Rowan told you where I'm going?"

"He said you're flying to Tortola. I hope you don't mind I changed your flight plans. We need to stop in Miami first."

Gripping the arm of my seat, I lean forward. "What happened? What do you know?"

"It seems the criminal is returning to the scene of the crime."

He pauses for a sip of wine, and I barely manage a calm, "Please continue."

"Ronald Delahousse in Miami heard about a man with an exaggerated southern accent working roulette wheels on the cruise circuit. I'm willing to bet it's Mr. Hines."

My throat tightens. It's such an incredible break in the case if we've found him. "But... would he be so careless to return to Miami?"

"I don't expect Mr. Hines is aware we're working together, and as such, I'm sure he expects your focus has shifted."

The flight attendant steps into the small cabin. "We're cleared for takeoff, your grace. May I get you something to drink?"

"Scotch neat, thanks," I say, sitting back and considering this new development. "If he's working cruise ships, are we sure we'll catch him in port?"

Reggie nods, and glances at the magazine on the table in front of him. "The ship he's currently on returns to Ft. Lauderdale tomorrow. He's been sticking close to the dock, renting rooms under an alias and leaving again within days. We'll have to act quickly, but we'll catch him this time."

Pulling out our flight plan, I survey our schedule. We stop once to refuel in three hours, then the remaining eight are spent over the Atlantic. We'll arrive in Florida tomorrow morning. Sliding my palms down my legs, I try to relax, something I haven't been able to do since this ordeal began.

My uncle looks up from his magazine. "There's a bed in the back. You should try to sleep. We'll want to be alert when we get there."

I glance up at him. "I'm afraid the chances of me sleeping are slim to none."

The flight attendant returns with my tumbler of scotch, and I nod my thanks. She takes her own seat as the plane picks up speed for takeoff. It's a smooth ride for a small jet, and it isn't long before we've reached our cruising altitude.

Reggie looks out the window, his voice thoughtful. "The night I met Zelda Wilder, I was impressed by her brains. She sees every angle."

I still haven't decided how I feel about my uncle's involvement in this affair, but I agree with his statement.

"You're right." Leaning forward, I rub my hand over my mouth as I think. "She'll keep her eyes open."

He nods, looking back at me. "She'll survive."

It's the one thing I've been holding onto as we've scoured manifest after manifest, as we've gone from hotel room to hotel room. I've held onto that fact through every day that has gone by with no word.

"She *will* survive," I repeat. "And we'll deal with the men who've hurt her."

Reggie makes a noise of assent then he leans back and stretches his legs. "I wasn't thinking of you when I hired her to do this job. Despite everything that's happened, Zelda is controlled. She takes responsibility very seriously."

That makes me almost laugh. "And I don't?" My eyes cut to his, and he does a little frown.

"Up until now, you've had the well-deserved reputation for irresponsibility. Even when you were on active duty."

I trace my finger around the lip of my glass. "You're right again," I say, and all of my indiscretions filter through my mind. "I was a royal fuck-up. I didn't have a reason to care. Rowan has always been on track to lead the country. My position has always been redundant, superfluous."

"The threat of something happening to him, of an assassination attempt or an accident, has always been there. You are far from an extraneous member of the monarchy. If Miss Wilder has helped you to find balance, I'm glad I brought her into this mess."

Inhaling deeply, I try to remember the day I changed. It didn't happen all at once. It crept up behind me when I was holding her, kissing her, laughing with her, and making love to her.

"When I met Zelda, I wasn't thinking about balance. I was thinking about excess." *Excessively indulging in her arms.* "She is responsible — you're right — but she's also sassy and passionate, and quite fun. The more time we spent together, every time she spoke of leaving, I couldn't imagine going back to the way I was before." I slip my hand in my pocket closing my fingers around the engagement ring I'm carrying with me. "I can't imagine my life without her."

Reggie studies his own empty wine glass. "I'm sorry she's been caught up in this crisis. I want to help get her out of it."

Logan emerges from the cockpit, and his expression is determined. He's dressed in his usual dark suit, and his phone is in his hand.

"Sir," he takes the seat across from me, in front of my uncle. "We just heard from your brother the crown prince. Satellite imagery has identified five small islands off the northern coast of Venezuela. We've engaged a local service to scout them and report back any findings."

My chest tightens. "How long before we know something?"

"They have to travel by boat, considering the islands are very small and largely unpopulated. Still, they're starting immediately."

I'm impatient with his answer. "A day? Two?"

"Some of them are fifty or so miles apart."

Reggie reaches across the aisle and holds my arm. "Seth will know where they have her. We'll have her location in the next twenty-four hours."

Now it's my turn to look out the window and say a silent prayer. It's what we're counting on making this unexpected stop.

The Ramada across from Port Everglades is as fast and dirty as they come. "It's like *déjà vu* all over again," I murmur, walking toward the two-story beige building.

The only difference is instead of raining the sun is beating down on us, and the air is so heavy with humidity, it feels like a warm washcloth against my skin. We're so close to the port, I can hear the drill of the ships anchors being raised and lowered, and the smell is wet pavement mixed with gasoline and rotting garbage in the side-by-side dumpsters.

Logan and I split off from my uncle, him taking the left and me right. Reggie will do the honors of pretending to need a room, then he'll let us in the back door. Unlike this time, we don't have a room number for Seth.

Walking through the narrow, two-lane parking lot, I pass a man loading a small bag into a faded white Jeep with a bed like a truck. Our eyes meet briefly, and I nod, not wanting to appear suspicious.

He doesn't return my greeting, and I make a quick note of his appearance — tall, pale blonde hair and flat blue eyes. His grey tee is stained with sweat and has *Fish Aruba* on the front over a cartoon wave. It draws my eye to a spatter of what looks like oil or mud on the hem. All of this is seen in a moment, but I don't stop. The noise of a truck door slamming and an engine turning over tells me he isn't stopping either. In fact, he seems in a hurry to leave.

My watch thumps, and I look down at my wrist. It's a text from Logan saying, *Room 220 — STAT!*

Breaking into a sprint, I jerk the back door open without even stopping to think it should be locked. I take the stairs two at a time and burst through the metal doors, making my way fast down the hall toward the open door. Reggie is in the hall looking down, phone in hand.

"What happened?" I'm breathing fast when I reach him.

My uncle's face is grave, and he nods toward the room. "See for yourself."

Using my elbow to avoid fingerprints, I push inside and stop in my tracks. "Oh, shit!" The smell of blood and vomit hits me in the face, and my stomach roils.

Looking around, blood is spattered on the walls. A large portrait is on the floor, smashed into three pieces. Glass is everywhere. Logan is in the bathroom, and his phone camera flashes twice.

The desk chair is in the center of the room. Stepping closer, I see fibers from what appears to have been a yellow, nylon rope caught in the cracks where the arms meet the metal base. The smell of vomit is strong, and looking down, my eye catches something on the floor. I almost lose the small breakfast I had this morning when I recognize it's a fingernail. The base is bloody and it appears to have been ripped out at the roots.

Straightening, I step back and hear a soft crunch under my boot. Looking down, I see another fingernail. Then another...

"Jesus," I hiss, moving away from the macabre scene.

Logan steps out of the bathroom, and his face is pale. He walks straight to the door and leaves without a word. I hear the heavy thud of his boots, and I realize he's jogging down the hall in the direction of the exit.

My stomach is tight as I walk carefully toward the bathroom. Whatever is in here made a definite impression on my retired military partner.

"I'm not sure you need to go in there," Reggie says, peering his head into the room. "In fact, I think we should leave this place at once. They obviously

181

knew we were coming for him. Police could be headed this way now, and we can't afford the delay or exposure."

"They knew we were coming, or they were looking for something," I argue, continuing toward the small facility.

The closer I get, the stronger the stench of urine and vomit grows. I take a cloth handkerchief from my pocket and hold it over my nose and mouth. The door is cracked, and Logan left the light on. In one quick sweep, I see enough to shoot our threat level to fire-engine red.

Seth is in the tub, and his face is blue-purple and bloated. The whites of his eyes are crimson, and what appears to be clear nylon fishing line is wrapped repeatedly around his neck. The tips of his fingers are bloody stumps, and rust-colored lines streak the skin.

It appears he fought to free himself until he died. His clothes are soiled with urine and feces, and foam is at the corner of his mouth.

I stumble out of the bathroom, still clutching the handkerchief over my face. Looking up, I lock eyes with Reggie.

I push off the wall and head for the door. "We've got to find Zelda. NOW!"

My uncle is right behind me, and we waste no time getting out the back door. Ronald Delahousse, our local contact, has the black SUV waiting in the parking lot, engine running. Logan is in the passenger seat, so Reggie and I take the back. As we're slamming the doors, he begins to speak.

"The jet is fueled, and the pilot is filing our flight plans. We should be ready to leave within minutes of arriving at the airport."

We set off at a fast clip to cover the short distance to Miami. My mind is racing, and I keep going back to the man I saw in the parking lot. It could be a coincidence. The hotel is located in a sketchy part of town. Still, fishing twine, "Fish Aruba"...

"It doesn't make any sense," Reggie says slowly. "Why torture him? Murder, yes, but torture? It's like they were trying to get him to confess. Looking for answers. But to what?"

"Maybe they were trying to send a message," Logan says in a grave voice.

"Can we get the satellite images of the islands?" My mind is still on fishing and Aruba.

"I have them on my laptop on the jet," Logan answers. "Why?"

"I want to start with the ones closest to Aruba."

He turns in his seat to face me. "Any particular reason?"

Passing my hand over my mouth, I see the dead blue eyes of the man in the parking lot. *Fish Aruba.*

"It's a hunch," is all I can give.

It's all it is, but I have a strong feeling he's connected. Fishing twine, polypropylene rope, skinning pliers...

We make our way quickly to the waiting airplane, and I'm settling in my seat when Logan strides down the aisle, laptop in hand.

"I have the images here," he places the device on the shiny wood table and takes the seat directly across from me. "You can see how the islands are positioned in relation to Aruba, Venezuela, Curacao..."

His words trail off as a message alert from my brother flashes on the screen.

Must speak to Cal immediately, it says.

My phone is out of my pocket and I'm touching my brother's name as Logan clicks on the envelope to open the message. The message opens, and my chest grows tight. Inside is a photograph, and I'm on the edge of my seat, leaning forward to see her. It's difficult to breathe.

The bruises are gone, and her cheeks are flushed. She's looking up and another damn newspaper is right below her chin. I can't see her beautiful neck or shoulders, and I have to trust they're not battered and bruised.

Longing aches in my chest, and for several long moments, I simply look at her beautiful eyes. I study her full lips. I need to touch her. I have to find her.

"Cal!" Rowan's voice is in my ear. "I'm glad you called. We've received important news."

"The photo—I have it here," I say. "She looks... healthy?"

"She's well..." his voice is haunted, and ice filters in my veins.

"What happened. Tell me!" I shout.

"Open the second photo," he says.

I slide the cursor over it, although by the thumbnail, it looks like a thermometer. A double-click, and I'm looking at a plastic stick. It's two-toned pink and white and it has pink lines on it.

"What is this?" My brows pull together.

"Do you have the email message?" My brother asks. "Read it."

My eyes scan quickly. The subject is Proof of Life. It's very short, only a few sentences.

Dear Sirs:

The proof of life photo you requested is enclosed. Or perhaps we should say proof of lives. *It seems Miss Wilder is pregnant. Perhaps the possibility of a royal baby will motivate action on our demands.*

Your time is running out.

My eyes flash to the photograph of the stick and then again to Zelda. They flash to the two words, and I read them over and over.

Royal baby… royal baby.

I fight back the image of Seth's tortured body from my mind. I fight to keep my insides from spilling out from where I've been figuratively gutted. They win. I can't take another day of this.

"Give them what they want." My voice is a whisper. "I won't sleep until I find her."

CHAPTER 21: JUDGMENT

Zelda

Selena will be home soon, and I'm sitting with Ximena on the ground in the shade of the house with several items of clothing I accidentally scrubbed holes in when I "helped" with the wash.

"I never was any good at laundry," I say, doing my best not to stab myself with the dull needle as I repair a seam I busted open on the scrub board.

Ximena has been working on the same secret project for the last week, and she glances at me with a shy smile. "Laundry?"

"Um…" I look around trying to think of an easy word. "Wash?"

I move my hands in a scrubbing motion and she nods. "Ah. Not good."

"No," I shake my head and return to mending the seams I ripped out. "Ava would sort it all then take it all to the laundromat. I just got the money to pay for it."

She glances up at me and smiles, and I have no idea how much of what I just said she understands. We're both getting better at communicating. I'm picking up a few of their words, like I know *Abo* means *you. Bini* means *come. Kome* means *eat*, and I already knew *baño* (*bathroom*) and *beibi* (*baby*).

"Ta ki bo esposo gusta?" Ximena says, and while I'm not sure about the first part, I know *husband* and *good*.

My cheeks flush when I consider the things Cal is very good at, and Ximena starts to laugh.

"He's masha bon!" she says.

Masha bon. I think about the words. *Very good.*

"Yes," I nod. "Masha, masha bon."

My eyes heat, and I miss him so much. I want him to know about our baby. I want him to hold me. I want to leave this place and be his wife and live wherever he wants to live. I want to tell him I'll never run again or steal or do anything to make his people ashamed of me. I'll go with him to Monagasco and take up knitting, and I'll never be a liability to him again.

"No!" Ximena says, scooting forward and holding my arms. "No ta yora!"

I've heard her say this to Selena. *Don't cry.*

I blink quickly, doing my best to banish the tears. "I miss him."

She nods and pauses, looking at the bundle in her lap she's been working on. I turn back to finish whip stitching the seam of Selena's uniform skirt. I'm right at the end, and I do the back and forth, then tie the ends of the thread in a knot so it doesn't unravel on her.

"There," I say, folding the piece and setting it on the short stack of clothes I ruined. "All done."

Reaching into my lap, I start to wrap the remaining thread around the almost-empty spool. I need to figure out a way to buy them more thread since I keep destroying all our clothes.

"Here," Ximena says, standing. "For you."

My hair is tied up in a little bun on the top of my head, and the loose, flour-sack dress I've worn every day for weeks is damp with sweat.

"What is it?" I say, squinting up at her from where I'm sitting on the ground.

She whips from her lap my old denim dress, only it's completely transformed. She's added a seam under the breast line to create an empire waist and cut long, skinny slits in intervals through the bodice leading down to the hem. In each of the slits, she's added a strip of thin, floral cotton material to expand the width and make room for my growing midsection.

"Ximena!" I gasp, covering my face with my hands. "It's bunita!" *It's beautiful!*

I put my elbows on my bent knees to cover my face. No one has ever done anything like this for me. I never even look for people to do nice things for me. If anyone does a favor, it's always because they want something in return. In my world everything is tit for tat.

Only, here, this woman who has nothing, who carried me off the dirt road into her home at the cost of a beating and god knows what else, has made this dress for me. Tears stream down my face, and I can't take my hands away. I'm too overwhelmed. I'm too... grateful.

"Aki, aki," she says. *Here, here.*

Grasping my arms, she pulls me up gently.

"Off!" she says, motioning for me to remove my dirty dress.

"Let me go inside," I say. "I'll put it on inside."

I motion to the hut, and she smiles, handing me the new dress. For a moment, I only look at it, running my fingers over the perfectly small, neat stitches she made around the new, floral panels.

It's unique and interesting, and I can't help thinking of when Reggie took Ava and me to the

189

designer boutiques at Bal Harbor. Ximena is so creative, and she's an amazing seamstress. She could design clothes...

I'm inside the small house slipping out of my old dress and using it to dry the sweat off my body. She cleaned my denim dress before altering it, and I consider running to the little shower in the bushes to rinse off before I put on my beautiful new dress.

Taking my time, I step into it, pulling it over my tiny pooch. I have to laugh at my silly little stomach. It's not even a bump. I've simply gotten thick in the middle and back, and I look like a sausage. What would Cal say if he saw me now? Would he laugh? Would he touch my stomach in wonder at what we've done, like I do? How would his beautiful eyes change if they saw me? Would they darken with desire?

A lump is in my throat as I pull the dress up and tie the halter part around my neck. I can only see the bottom, but I do a little spin. From what I can tell, it looks beautiful! I'm just about to run outside and thank my friend when I hear the sound of a truck pulling into the yard.

I look toward the cloth door, expecting Ximena to run inside like she always does when anyone comes into our little camp. I wait several moments, and she still doesn't appear. The noise of voices speaking their language is loud in the courtyard, and I hear a shout. I'm stunned, and I run to the curtain. It's Ximena shouting.

Slinging it aside, I see Mako is in the yard. He's with two other men I've never seen before. They're driving a truck and in the back three women are crouched together, their chins tucked into their knees as if for protection.

190

My eyes move fast from them to Mako, and I see he's grasping Ximena's arm. She is pulling back, struggling against his hold, and I run to where they're standing. He speaks sharply. I make out *Selena*, and she instantly stops struggling. Their eyes lock for the beat of a heart and she relents. Her fight is gone, and she starts to go with him.

"NO!" I scream, grasping her arm and pulling hard.

My motions seem to enrage him. Mako shoves my chest, and I stumble backwards.

"Cards!" I scream, holding out my hands. "Cards for Ximena!"

His eyes narrow on me. Stepping forward, he puffs out his chest, and I know he's trying to intimidate me. "You cheat!" he says.

"NO!" I shout. "Cards for Ximena!"

I've got to save her. It's all I can do, even if he's right and I am cheating. One of the first tricks Seth taught me was to count cards. Still, I'm cheating a pimp—that makes it okay, right? I don't care. In my world the answer is *yes*.

Mako looks over his shoulder at his friend and speaks fast in his language. I make out the words *bitch* and *teach her*. Whatever it takes.

Following me back into the house, I go to the drawer where Selena keeps her worn deck. We don't have much time, and I know I only get one round. I need to let him deal so he doesn't renege. I shuffle sloppily and pass the cards to him to deal.

Four cards. In front of Mako is a ten of hearts. In front of me is a three of clubs. We have two cards facing down, and I know exactly what to do.

"Keda," he says. *Stay*.

"Hit me." He puts a card in front of me. It's an ace, and he starts to laugh.

"Djesun!" he shouts pointing at it. *Eleven.*

He won't let me count it as a one because he wants me to bust. I bust and he wins. I nod in agreement. I know what's coming. He flips his facedown card, and it's another ten.

"HAHA!" It's a shout rather than a laugh, and it's right in my face.

"Warda," I say softly. *Wait.*

Turning my last card over, it's a seven of hearts.

Black eyes go wide. He stares at the table several minutes then looks at my hands and back to the card.

His fist flies up, and I brace for him to hit me. It's going to hurt like hell, and I've got to be sure I fall in a way that protects my stomach and my head. I'm not sure I can handle another concussive blow.

Seconds pass. He's trembling, fist raised, and I'm squinting, ducking with my whole body tense. When another moment passes, I sneak a look at him, and I can see something bigger than me is holding him back. He's weighing the consequences of hurting me, and ultimately, he backs down. Wade Paxton is one mean motherfucker, and even this peasant pimp knows it.

His eyes are blazing anger, and he throws the metal chair aside. I watch as he storms out of the cubicle into the yard. I hear the shrieks of a woman from another house, and my stomach sinks. I would save them all if I could, but I can't. I can only save Ximena.

My shoulders droop, and I'm suddenly so tired. I'm still sitting at the table looking at my twenty-one hand when Ximena quietly returns. She doesn't speak as she goes to the small kitchen area and starts to prepare the vegetables for our meager dinner.

I slowly walk to my cot and lie down. I'm so exhausted from the adrenaline, and lately I've simply been tired all the time. I don't know if I'm getting proper nutrition. I don't know if the way I feel is normal. I don't know anything, and I don't have anyone to ask. I only know I saved my friend.

I look up and I watch as she moves around the little space. I don't know how long Mako will abide by the rules of our game, but she's safe for now. Selena is coming home, and the three of us will sit at that little table and eat dinner together. We will be like a little family.

Gathering my strength, I get off the cot and go to the door to wait for Selena. Whenever I see her at the edge of the trees in the afternoon, we always smile and wave to each other until she's at the house. It has become our ritual, and it gives me comfort to see her safely return.

My stomach knots when I see Mako and the men are still in the courtyard with their truck bed of sacrificial lambs. I don't want Selena around them. I know she knows what happens to these women — she knows more than I do about everything — but I don't like Mako near her. It reminds me of our foster father and Ava, and I don't have a lamp to smash over his head.

I see her at the tree line, and I make the decision to go to her this time when the noise of another truck sounds in the distance. It's coming fast, the noise growing louder, until it breaks through the trees. It's the strange Jeep-truck hybrid. It's Blix. His eyes flash at me, and I know at once no amount of card playing is going to save me.

He's out of the truck and circling to the back. His jaw is set, and he doesn't even glance at me. Something is different this time, and I get the distinct feeling he's not here to take pictures.

Selena runs out of the trees toward me, but I stop her. "Go to the house!"

She's confused, and she hesitates too long. Mako is watching us, and that fucker is smart. He's always known I'm special, and now he's trying to see if he can get in on whatever the promise of me entails.

Blix is digging in the back of his truck. He has what looks like a large tackle box, and he rifles through yellow rope, a spool of clear nylon fishing line, pliers. Finally he takes out something that looks like a huge garlic press. He turns to face me, and I don't know why I'm not more afraid. Maybe I think because I'm carrying Cal's baby they'll go easier on me? Looking back, I know I was a fool.

Curiosity drives the men from the truck. They know Blix is one of Wade's men — possibly the worst of Wade's men — and they want to see what's about to happen. They're all speaking fast in Mako's tongue, quietly under their breath.

Blix's dead eyes are fixed on me, and he doesn't say a word. His mouth is set in a straight line, and he doesn't stop until he's standing directly in front of me. I think about our first day — I think about every day since I've met this man. I'm not a human to him. I'm not even sure I'm an animal. I'm a commodity in a deal he's helping play out against the man I love.

Blix grabs my forearm and jerks it up. Instinctively, I jerk it back, out of his grip. His dead eyes flash, and he rears back so quickly, I don't have time to duck.

Light explodes behind my eyes with the force of his fist, and next thing I know, I'm on my hands and knees on the ground. The screams of Ximena and Selena from behind the curtain fill my ears, and I cringe back from the pain in my head.

"Oh, God!" I whisper a real prayer. I'm on my hands and knees, clutching my arms over my head. "Help us."

Tears are in my eyes, and Blix's boots appear before them. He's standing in front of me, and he jerks my hand off my head. I'm handicapped by my injury. I can't fight him. I can barely register what's going on.

I close my eyes and again, I pray. *Please help me. Please don't let them suffer for me again.* The words are in my mind as I slowly lift my head. My eyes open and then go wide with horror.

Blix has the garlic press in his hand, and I just register the touch of metal against my skin when SNAP! He clamps the metal pinchers shut and the end of my ring finger falls to the ground.

Silence fills my ears half a second before pain shoots through my hand.

I scream. I can't stop screaming.

I look at the dead little digit. It's like something out of a haunted house lying on the ground. Blood is pouring down my arm, and I can't stop screaming. I'm staring at it from somewhere far away, somewhere filled with blood and pain, and I can't stop screaming.

The men run back in the direction of the truck, and Blix jerks my hand up, wrapping it tightly in some kind of white material and applying pressure. It hurts a million times worse, and I scream until my throat burns fire and my voice gives out. Pain resonates in my hand and arm, and I'm trembling and whimpering when he finally pushes me back, satisfied I won't bleed to death.

He never speaks. He bends down and plucks the end of my finger off the ground and drops it in a plastic bag, then he returns to his vehicle and drives away. I'm on my knees, one arm tight around my waist, still whimpering, holding my hand at my stomach but afraid to touch it. It's covered in blood and a purple line is below the bandage now stained red with blood. I can't look directly at it. The only thing I see is the ring. The tin ring Cal gave me. *I want Cal...*

Ximena runs out to me. The dizziness is back, and I think I'm going to faint. Hazy shapes cloud my vision, but I feel her taking my arms. I focus with all my strength on getting to my feet, allowing her to take me into the house. Selena is at my other side, holding my waist. She's crying. I see the slick coating of tears on her cheeks, but I can't speak. My voice is gone. My fight is gone. They're too strong, and I can't win this time.

It's the culmination of everything I've done. I've been a thief and a liar all my life, and my time in this place is the prison sentence I ran to Monagasco to escape. My motives don't matter. Protecting Ava doesn't matter. Only my crimes exist here, and I see this moment as the reckoning for everything I've done.

We're at the sink, and Ximena speaks to her daughter. Selena runs to their bed, and I hear the sound of material ripping.

I can't stop shaking. My body is hot and cold. I can still feel the cold metal pliers against my hand. I can still hear the notch sound, and I see half my finger fall like a bit of play dough to the ground. I see Blix's dead eyes, and I wonder if I'm nothing more than another fish to be skinned in his mind.

"You're in shock." Ximena says.

I'm on the cot wrapped in a blanket. She holds a cup of broth to my lips, and I try to drink it. I try to think, but the throbbing in my head makes logic difficult. It's interesting to note the disabling fire of a concussion can take a backseat to the blazing agony of a severed finger. Two pains are warring in my body, and based on my bizarre train of thought, I think my friend is right. I think I'm in shock.

Ximena speaks in a whisper. She's wrapping and wrapping. Selena is pale, but she comes to me.

"It's going to be okay. Mama says it's going to be okay."

She's wrapping my finger as if she has experience with such things. Perhaps this isn't the worst thing she's seen. I can't imagine what that means. I can't imagine anything anymore. I don't know what day it is. Every day bleeds into the next like the blood pouring from my hand. I don't know how long I've been here, and I don't know what I'm looking forward to anymore.

My stomach hurts, and I need to pee. "Baño," I whisper.

Selena takes my arm. I'm still in the beautiful dress Ximena made for me, only now it's stained with blood. It's a sign of our friendship. It's a sign we've protected each other. She's rescued me twice. I've rescued her twice. Now it's covered in my blood.

Selena walks me to the bushes. "Will you be okay alone?"

I nod and step a few paces into the brush to crouch. It doesn't take long for me to pee, and I wait, shaking my hips so the urine can get off me. I look around for a friendly leaf or something I can use to help. A banana plant is nearby, and I reach for a large leaf to pat myself dry. It's slippery, and when I pull it away, I see a dark red stain on the leaf. My stomach cramps, and I know something more is wrong.

"Selena?" I whisper, trying to call her.

Do I dare attempt another prayer? *God, please, no. Please don't take my baby.*

Leaning heavily on Selena, we stagger to the house. I go to my cot and lie on my side. Ximena crosses the room to me, but my head is overwhelming me. All of it is overwhelming me. I can't tell her what's wrong. I can only give in to the pain.

The next several days come in and out in hazy visions. I hear voices. I know Ximena is beside me. I feel her hand on my head.

I drink from the familiar gourd and then pass back into oblivion. I can't do anything. I can't help anybody.

The day I lost my finger, the day I saved Ximena... Was that yesterday? The day before? A week ago? My baby... Is my baby okay?

My eyes are fused shut it seems. Heat rises all around us in waves, and I'm still on the cot. Darkness comes, and I've been asleep. Voices are around me, but I don't recognize them. I hear Cal's rich voice, and I smile. My eyes are closed, and he's with me in the ocean. We're back at our beautiful beach in Tortola, and we've run down to the shore like I'd always wanted to do.

We don't need clothes. It's our private beach, and no one is around. Twilight paints the scene in black and white, and my arms are around his neck. His large hands span my lower back, sliding down over my ass as my breasts press flat against his firm chest.

The water laps around us as our lips meet. He kisses me like he always does, firmly, passionately, demanding, taking. Our tongues slide together as the waves rise and fall, moving us slowly in a rocking motion. I feel the dark waters just at the line of my lower back. I taste the salt on Cal's tongue as his warm, strong hands touch me, hold me, lift me against him.

"Cal," I whisper, tightening my hold on his shoulders.

His skin is against my face. I can smell his delicious scent of citrus and cedar and him. *My Cal...* His strong arms are around me, and it's the most wonderfully secure I've felt in my entire embattled existence.

I want to kiss him again, but he speaks. "Yes, my love. I've got you."

My stomach flashes at the sound. My eyes fly open, and it's not a dream. I'm in his arms. Cal is holding me against his chest. One arm is around my back and one is beneath my legs. It's dark, and he's carrying me into the trees.

We're moving fast, and I'm crying. I'm holding his neck, and my body shudders with joy and relief and sobbing. I didn't know it was possible to feel this way, as if my insides are spilling out from my eyes. I can't speak. I can't stop crying. I can only hold him and weep as he carries me out of this place, away from the nightmare.

"Don't cry, my love," he soothes, but I hear the break in his voice. "I have you. You're safe now."

We're on the path I took that day so long ago when I found the beach and the baths. Someone is with us, and when we reach the beach, Cal lowers my legs to stand while catches his breath. One strong arm holds me firmly against his torso.

"Is she okay?" I recognize Logan's voice.

Cal has me in his arms. My face is pressed against his neck, and I can't let him go. I haven't let him go since I woke up to find him here. I'm almost afraid to look around or speak in case this is all a dream and it fades. I'm not sure I could take that.

"She's going to be okay," Cal says, and joy vibrates in my bones. *It's not a dream!* "Let's get her to the boat."

CHAPTER 22: COVERT OPS

Cal

We've been in Tortola two days, and I haven't been able to get the image of Zee and the pregnancy test out of my mind. Logan convinced me to stay here, let the men we've hired search the islands for her, but everything I touch here reminds me of Zee.

I was such a shit to her. I was so angry. Sitting on the bed, I clutch my head in my hands as regret racks my insides. "When I find you, Zelda Wilder, I'm never letting you go."

My phone rings, and I snatch it up. Rowan is calling.

"What's up, Ro?" I'm desperate for word, especially now with August first looming.

Our men have been searching. We're playing with fire, and I'm ready to say screw the detectives, forget the plans. I'll find her myself.

"Ava thinks she has the coordinates for Zee."

I'm off the bed and throwing open drawers at once. "How? Where did she find them?"

"Ever since the pregnancy test and Seth's murder, she's dedicated herself to finding the leak at Occitan. She hasn't left the estate. She's followed the staff, sneaked into their rooms…"

I hear the pride in his voice, and I can only imagine my beautiful, future sister-in-law invading our seaside estate.

"What happened?"

"It was Juliana."

I almost drop the phone. "Nesbitt's niece?" I think of the mousey girl who dropped out of school and moved in with our housekeeper last spring.

"Ava noticed she was obsessed with Seth's disappearance. She sneaked into her room and found several texts from Hines on the girl's phone."

"Skip ahead," I demand. "Where is Zelda?"

"The coordinates are fifteen point seven thousand north, sixty-three point six three-three west. Hines must have known they were coming for him He told Juliana to give you those coordinates if anything happened to him."

My chest explodes with an insane mixture of relief and frustration. "What the fuck was she waiting for?" I shout in the phone.

"She didn't know he was dead. Ava says the news hit her pretty hard."

"Never mind—I'm hanging up. I'll text you when we get there."

"Be careful, brother," Rowan's voice is grave.

"I've got Logan and Reggie with me." I'm jogging down the stairs, grabbing my keys off the counter. "Tell Ava good work. She found the answer we've been needing."

"I've already requested satellite images. I'll forward them to you as soon as they're in."

The small island is three hundred miles south of Tortola, which requires us to charter yet another jet and fly to Venezuela. I'm frustrated as more time slips through our fingers. We're past our deadline, and while Rowan is working on his end to buy us more time, I don't trust Wade Paxton not to hurt her. I can't shake the images in that hotel room.

It takes another day, but we're on a boat, speeding toward the small island not far from Aruba. Using the satellite images, Freddie found an abandoned pier hidden in the curve of the island where a series of mineral baths are located. I'm at the bow, staring down the wind and wishing I could push the boat faster through sheer willpower, when I feel a text come through on my phone. It's from Rowan.

Proceed with extreme caution. A scout visually confirmed Zelda is in the camp. Sending exact location.

An image appears on my phone, and I make my way carefully to the back of the boat, where Logan is driving, I show him the text. His jaw is set and he nods, taking us around to the location of the hidden pier.

I'm keeping my eyes out for other boats or small planes. Reggie tries texting Wade Paxton. He's determined to facilitate a meeting between the three of us. Personally, I think he relishes the idea of turning our oversized bodyguard loose on that slime.

I make a signal, and I'm heading back for my seat when another text appears — this time from Rowan.

Pax is making good on his threats.

My stomach plunges. His threat was to hurt her. His threat was to send us a piece of her. With trembling fingers, I text a reply. *What did he do?*

Rowan's reply doesn't answer my question. *Whatever force is needed I authorize you to use.*

He's telling me I have his permission to kill, to assassinate the prime minister of Totrington. I can't take it anymore. *What happened?* I text. I'm two seconds from calling when he replies with an image.

I drop to my knees when I see it. My head is in my hands, and I'm barely holding it together. The sound of the boat engine dies, and my head snaps up. "NO! Get us there NOW!" I'm practically shouting.

Logan's face is lined. "Sir! What happened?"

"We have to get to her now, Logan. We can't lose another hour."

Reggie stays on the boat as we make our way through the dark jungle in the direction of the camp. Two camps are on opposite ends of the small island. The one holding Zelda is closest to our hidden dock. A long pier is in the center of the island, and we've learned cargo ships make occasional, overnight stops here leaving or returning to Venezuela. As far as we know, tonight we're alone.

"Perfect place to hide a criminal enterprise," Logan says as we make our way up the dirt road in the direction of the first camp.

We're armed to the teeth and dressed in black. Our plan is to retrieve Zelda, but my additional plan, once she's secure on the boat, is to return to this Blix Ratcliffe's shelter and cut his fingers off one by one then shove them all in his mouth and tape it shut then tie him to a chair and set him on fire. Envisioning his intricately painful execution is the only thing keeping me together as we make our way quickly and quietly to where my love is being held prisoner.

The clearing opens, and in the moonlight, I see a line of small, cinder-block huts. None of them have windows or doors, and in the dim night, they could be hiding anyone. We stand out against the white walls like rocks on the white sand, and I look around for security cameras.

"No time," Logan whispers. "Move fast."

I do as he says, not stopping for stealth. I charge up to the first shack, where our scout said he'd seen her taken. Pushing the curtain aside, I see a tiny room with a table in the center and three cots. In the far corner a woman and a girl sleep together, but to my right...

Emotion hits me so hard. She's wearing that same denim halter dress from the last day I saw her, only it's slightly different, fuller. She's lying on her side in the fetal position, but the light from the window touches her blonde hair and cheeks. Her hair is tied back in a braid, and her face is drawn and stressed. Even sleeping, she looks so tired.

Going to her, I gently smooth her hair away. Her bandaged hand is near her face, and I lift it carefully, moving it against her chest. She exhales a noise, and I have to pause as it cuts into my heart. I want to hear her say my name, but I don't want to scare her. As carefully as possible, I lift her into my arms. Her chest is against mine, her arm over my shoulders, and I slowly lift her.

She presses her forehead against my neck, and I sit on the bed to hold her, hugging her tight, allowing the emotions to pulse through me and into her before we set out into the darkness, heading back to the boat.

"Cal," she whimpers, breaking my heart. I kiss her full lips gently, and her arms tighten around my neck.

"I've got you, my love," I say as I stand. "You're safe now."

My eyes land on a pair of green ones watching me from across the room. The girl is awake, and she sees me. I'm frozen in place unsure if she'll scream or wake her mother; if she'll try to fight us, or if she'll call Ratcliffe.

The girl does none of those things. She simply nods and smiles. I don't hesitate. We have no time to waste, and I'm out the door and back to where I left Logan in record time.

Onboard the ship, I'm holding Zelda in my arms as we decide our next steps.

"I wasn't able to deal with Hines," Logan says, his voice a low rumble. "You stay with her. I'll finish Ratcliffe."

The anger in my chest surges to life. "His ass is mine." Every time I see the finger Zee keeps trying to hide, red floods my vision. "He dared to touch her. I will make him suffer."

"I'll make him suffer." He nods to my fiancée. "She needs your strength now."

It's the only thing keeping me here. Zelda is hugged close to my side, and she seems smaller somehow, broken. My arms tighten around her, and with a deep exhale, I give him the go-ahead. He's off the boat, disappearing into the night.

Reggie is at the stern, holding the wheel and waiting for our next steps. "Wade is in the area," he says, slipping his phone into the coat pocket above his chest. "I'll arrange a meeting with him, and the two of you can plan however you'd like to deal with him."

"That's good," I say, standing and lifting Zee in my arms again. "We'll be below." I take her down the steps of the cabin cruiser to where a small living area fills the space below deck. Bench seating surrounds a table, and through a sliding door in the back is a tiny bedroom.

"I can't believe you're here," she finally says, and I pull her close to me again.

She cried almost the entire way from the camp to the boat, and my heart broke over and over with her sobs. She's been so quiet since we got onboard. I felt her recoil from Reggie, but when she heard us talking she relaxed. Her good hand is fisted in my shirt, and as much as she doesn't want to let me go, I'm not in any hurry to let her out of my arms.

"Would you like to sleep?" I ask gently.

Her eyes close, and she melts into my chest. "I've missed the sound of your voice."

Both my arms tighten around her, and I carry her to the queen-sized bed with me. I'm sitting, propped up with pillows, and she's curled with her head on my chest. We stay that way several long moments as her breathing slows and the hole her kidnapping exploded in my chest gradually heals.

"My beautiful Zee," I whisper, and her arms tighten on me. I stroke her forehead, then I kiss her brow. "I'll kill them for hurting you. I'll kill them all."

She doesn't speak. She only hugs me again, and a little tremble moves through her. It's almost more than I can stand. Rolling her onto her back, I raise up on my elbows so I can see her blue eyes. They're red-rimmed and watery. I'm feeling every emotion I see reflected at me there.

"They said you're pregnant?" It's a question that's been tormenting me for days. "You're having my baby?"

"Oh, Cal," she rolls forward, hiding her face in my chest. "I think I am."

A flash of something I don't expect aches in my chest. I almost can't say the words, but I have to. "You think it might be someone else's?"

Her head snaps up, and she's shaking it fast. "God, no!" Her hand is over her mouth a moment, and she hiccups a breath. "I was... I was bleeding." A little tremor before she's able to speak again. "I'm so afraid."

Pulling her against my chest again, I look up at the ceiling and breathe slowly. Heat is in my own eyes this time, and I can't believe how quickly I've become attached to the idea of Zelda and me as a family.

"We'll take you to a doctor as soon as we get back. We're leaving this place tonight. I'll message Logan and tell him to return."

Her body jerks, and she clutches my shirt in her fist. "Cal! We can't leave them behind. You have to get them!"

My brow lines. "Get who, darling?"

"Ximena and Selena. The woman and her daughter who took care of me. We can't leave them behind, Cal. They're in danger here. If he comes and finds me gone, he'll hurt them!"

She's talking so fast and pulling on my shirt. I run my hands over her hair and try to calm her. "I'll tell Logan to get them. Will they go with him? They might be afraid."

"Selena speaks English. Have him tell her I said for them to come. Tell them my husband is here, and we need them to come with us."

That makes me smile. I cup her beautiful face in my hands and kiss her wet cheeks. She makes a little noise, and turns her face to find my mouth. Our lips part and her tongue curls with mine. She tastes like salt and tears, and with every beat of my heart emotion rolls through my veins. I pull her to me again, holding her so close.

"My Zelda," I whisper. "I'm going to make up for everything that happened to you here, I promise. No one will ever hurt you again."

CHAPTER 23: PRINCESS

Zelda

Cal is above deck talking to Reggie, and I strip out of my transformed denim dress into the most amazing shower of my life. It's a tiny, cramped boat shower, but I have soap and shampoo and hot water. I stand and luxuriate under the spray with my eyes closed until I hear Cal back in the room.

"I don't want to be a tyrant, but we have a limited supply of water onboard." A smile is in his voice, and fresh tears flood my eyes.

Reaching forward, I shut off the water and rest my forehead against the white wall a moment as I let the realization I've been rescued wash over me. Taking a deep breath, I open the frosted-glass door, and he's waiting there looking like the most amazing dream come true, holding a fluffy, white towel for me.

"A towel," I sigh, as he wraps it around me and pulls me to his chest.

Warm lips are on my temple. My arms are pinned against my chest, and he's holding me in those strong arms so safe and warm. My stomach is tight, my insides vibrating with pure joy.

Lifting my chin, I catch his gaze. "Was Logan able to get them?"

"They're right outside at the table," he says softly. "I gave them food, and they seem a bit overwhelmed."

"We're probably all going to need time to adjust to being free."

"Take as much time as you need. I'm eternally grateful to them for taking care of you."

"You have no idea how much they did for me."

Our eyes meet again, and he cups my cheeks. His are so warm, I feel like I'll be lost gazing into them. It's like a dream.

"More good news," he says, and my brows quirk in a question. "Ximena said the bleeding stopped. She said you were asleep for a long time after... your finger," his lips tighten, "but she thinks the baby is okay."

I'm relieved but still worried. "I'll be glad when I'm able to see a doctor. I've been so afraid ever since we found out."

Another simmering kiss, and his strong arms return to hold me. "I'm so relieved we found you. I feel certain you're going to be okay."

"Only..." my chin drops, and I look down at my bandaged hand.

Cal follows my eyes, and I see the muscle in his jaw move. I remember not so long ago when it was directed at me. "I'm going to find that animal. Wade Paxton is next."

Terror hits me like a medicine ball. "You know where he is?"

"Reggie is trying to lure him out of hiding. He has reason to believe he's in the area."

"He's a monster, Cal. Don't go near him."

Fury flashes in his eyes. "I'm going near him. I intend to be very near him, and when I'm done, he'll regret the day he was born."

Turning away, I use the towel to finish drying my body. I can't think about Cal confronting Wade Paxton right now. My head is aching again, and I need to speak to Ximena and Selena. I need to explain what's happening to them. Pausing at the door, I hesitate a moment. Cal's body is warm at my back, and his face moves to my bare shoulder and soft lips close over the skin of my neck.

"Oh," I gasp.

Electric tingles snake through my limbs and I reach back to hold his head, the back of his neck as he devours the skin of my shoulder, moving up into my hairline.

"I've wanted to taste your skin, smell your hair, feel you in my arms for so long. I thought I would go mad from wanting you."

"Cal," I whisper, unable to move.

My back is to his chest, and he holds me. His face is against my ear, and my hand clutches his neck. "When you're strong enough," his voice is low. "I want to make love to you again."

"I want that, too," I say, holding the wall for support. "How long before we're in Tortola?"

"We'll be there by morning."

Cal gives Ximena and Selena their own private room on the first floor of the villa, and we're in the second-floor suite we shared before my nightmare began. We're relieved and cautious after visiting the recommended doctor as soon as we arrived in Tortola.

Several blood tests, examinations, and one ultrasound later, we'd been told our baby girl is

213

healthy and thriving. I'm twelve weeks along, which means, as Cal noted, I've been pregnant since Monagasco.

"I can probably say which night it happened," he says with a grin, holding me against his chest on the enormous, incredibly soft bed.

"The first night you decided condoms took too long?" I tease, watching the two ceiling fans spin in time.

He scoots down and pushes the light cotton blouse I'm wearing open. "I don't regret a thing," he murmurs against my stomach, holding my sides and kissing my navel.

Threading my fingers in his hair, I think about the other news we were given. The doctor said my concussion symptoms could last a year. I have to eat a special, vitamin-enriched diet for the next few weeks while I'm recovering, and holding up my hand, I can't decide if I want to have reconstructive surgery on my finger.

"I think I'd like one of those wooden fingers," I say, considering my damaged digit.

Cal props his head on his hand and studies my expression. "Are you sure? We can have the finest doctors work on it. Remember that prince thing I'm always reminding you about?"

I place my palm against his scruffy cheek. "I think it makes me look like a pirate. Or maybe a Tenenbaum?"

That gets me a sexy MacCallam grin. "I had a feeling there would be a movie tie-in somehow."

"Do you hate the idea?"

He returns to pressing burning kisses against my slightly rounded stomach. "I love everything about the idea."

Strong hands slide under my skirt, moving up the back of my thighs. My insides clench as he gets closer to... "Yes," he hisses, flipping my short skirt over my hips. "I love it when you go commando."

"Cal!" I gasp, but he's distracted, dipping his luscious tongue inside and teasing my clit with slow, gentle circles.

My hips jump with every pass, and he kisses away, moving his mouth to my inner thigh. "Not so fast, beautiful. I want to make this last."

"Oh, god." My voice is a strangled groan. Now that I'm better, I realize how much I've missed him — and how much a healthy pregnancy makes me horny. "I'm going to combust if you go slow."

He only grins and traces his tongue along the line of my hip. Everywhere he touches me sends fire simmering beneath my skin. He traces a path slowly to the center, settling in and covering my lower lips with his. His arms are wrapped around my thighs, and his tongue sweeps faster, circling, making my eyes flutter shut as my hips move in time with his mouth.

Heat spirals up my thighs and down, fluttering like waves in the arches of my feet. My toes curl as my orgasm builds so fast, and when I feel his thumb slide into me, I can't help crying out.

My insides tighten in an irresistible fist of pleasure and with one more teasing pass of his tongue, I break, bucking my hips and begging for his cock.

"With pleasure, beautiful," he grins, kissing my stomach once more, pausing over my breasts to tease my nipples with his teeth.

Currents of pleasure fizz in my veins and every kiss shoots another spark into my clenching insides. "Please... I need you."

He's over me at once, leaning against his forearms and plunging deep into my throbbing core. His hard shaft massages and soothes my aching need, and I'm holding him, loving the feel of his hard body against my soft one. I slip out my tongue and taste the salt on his skin just before his mouth covers mine.

Warm lips and the scruff of his beard mark me. My fingers are in his hair, and I follow his every movement, every kiss as his hips begin to move faster. He's diving deeper into me, and I love the feel of his rising orgasm. He moans against my shoulder, and my insides break into a new wave of clenching pleasure. It's all he needs to fall over the edge. He holds my hips flush against his body, and I feel him pulsing inside me, filling me, holding our bodies as one.

"God, I've missed you," he groans against my shoulder. I wrap my arms around him and smile.

"Not as much as I missed you." I hold him as we breathe together, as his heartbeat slows, and we make our way back to calm.

Another breath. I feel his lips pressing kisses against the top of my shoulder, and I trace my fingers down the lines of his back.

Lifting his head, our eyes meet and his smile is so warm. "I'm sorry."

I can't help a frown. "For what?"

"I wasn't going to do that until you were completely better. I didn't want to force you to do anything —"

"MacCallam Lockwood Tate, are you trying to say you think that was forced?"

A naughty gleam is in his eyes. "There's my dirty girl. I want to fuck you five more times tonight, yes?"

Laughter bursts through my lips, and I cover my face with my hands. "I don't know if I can go five more rounds," I confess.

"Fucking concussion. Yet another reason I plan to kill Wade Paxton with my bare hands." Cal scoots up in the bed and cradles me in his arms. "I'll take it easy on you, but just know I'm fucking you five more times in my mind."

I can't resist teasing him. "I can probably handle once more in a bit."

He leans back and places the pad of his thumb against my top lip. "That's my little trooper." He grins, and I laugh, and he leans down to kiss me, pulling my lip gently between his teeth.

"Oh! Hang on." He's out of the bed and crossing the room in a flash, and I slowly push myself to a sitting position.

My blouse is beside me, so I put my arms in the sleeves and let it hang open over my breasts. Cal is digging in his discarded jeans, and I'm admiring the flex of his fine ass when he stands and faces me. His eyes darken, and he grins.

"You are so fucking beautiful." He walks slowly back to the bed carrying a small parcel. "Look at you with that just-fucked hair and your shirt all open. God, Zelda, you're killing me."

"Stop it," I pretend-scold. "You're making me blush."

"Liar. You are never shy with me, and don't you ever start. I'll spank that out of you."

His words give me a little thrill, and I press my lips together.

"What do you have?" I nod toward his hand.

Climbing onto the bed beside me, he gently lifts my injured hand and studies it a moment. We were able to remove the tin ring he'd given me without cutting it, but my finger is still swollen and now has a metal brace on it as well as gauze and tape.

"More reasons to kill Paxton," he says through an exhale.

Placing my hand on his muscled thigh, I watch as he opens a small silk bag and takes out a tissue-wrapped item. My breath disappears when I see what's inside.

"Cal!" I gasp. It's the most beautiful thing I've ever seen.

"It's rose gold and diamonds," he says quietly. "See the details on the side here? They look like angel's wings. I thought of you, since you're my angel."

Tears blur my vision, and I can't take my eyes off the beautiful piece of jewelry. "I've carried it with me everywhere while they had you. I said I would put it on you the moment we found you. I never expected..."

His eyes drift to my injury, and I reach up to touch his face. "I love it so much."

"Will you still be my wife, Zelda Scott Wilder? After all you've been through?"

"There's nothing I would love more than to be your wife, MaCallam Lockwood Tate."

His eyes light with a tease. "Glad to hear it, and no more carrying on about not being royal enough or whatever. You've got my little princess in your body now."

"You get a player for a princess," I say, doing a little pretend frown.

"I'm the luckiest guy I know."

CHAPTER 24: TROUBLE

Cal

Zelda is recovering so well at our home in Tortola. I bought the villa for us to live in, and I've already spoken to Rowan about a diplomatic position in the West Indies. He's working on it, and I'm focused on tracking down that fucking prime minister of Twatrington.

I'm not joking when I say I want him dead, but I've stopped mentioning his name in front of my fiancée, as it seems to set her back in her recovery. I'm much happier watching her nesting in our new home with the help of her friends Ximena and Selena.

Ximena is understandably having the biggest adjustment period. For now she's most comforted staying inside, close to her daughter. She likes doing familiar, household tasks, and we let her do whatever pleases her as she gradually gains more confidence.

Her daughter is just the opposite. Every new thing, every new experience is another step forward for Selena. She's a smart and very sweet girl, and I've engaged a tutor to work with her. I owe them both more than I can ever repay for taking care of my Zee.

Logan is in my study when I get downstairs, and by the expression on his face, I can tell he's got news about our mission. "He's openly returned to Totrington." Anger radiates off my large friend as he speaks. "Hampton is giving him asylum, and they've refused extradition to Monagasco, despite his indisputable connection to the assassination attempt, Ava's shooting, and Zelda's kidnapping."

"It's as much as a declaration of war," I agree, walking to my desk and waking my computer.

"Your brother is furious," he continues. "Freddie was able to connect Blix and the ransom note to Paxton in less than twenty-four hours."

"What does Reggie say about all of this?" My brother and I are slowly coming around to the idea of accepting my uncle's advice.

Our mother had a hand in our acceptance, pointing out that next to her, Reginald does have the most political experience of us all.

"Your uncle thinks we should wait." Logan's frown deepens. "It's his most infuriating idea to date."

I nod, looking at the latest email from Ro. "I agree with you. I want Paxton's head on a platter today — yesterday, if possible. Why does Reggie think we should wait?"

"He says the prime minister will show his hand. He said if we wait, Paxton will grow impatient and make another power grab, and we can move then and avoid the appearance of aggression."

"After this last ordeal, I'm not comfortable with him walking around free."

"I couldn't agree with you more, sir."

He walks to the French doors and looks toward the pool. I step up behind him and see Zelda placing a fluffy striped towel on a lounge chair. Her hair is twisted on top of her head in one of those cute buns, and her stomach is just starting to round with our baby. She's adorable.

"We don't need Freddie to connect Wade to his crimes." My stomach tightens as I watch her. "She knows everything he's done. She's seen it first-hand."

"He will not threaten her." Logan's voice is thick, and if I weren't so sure of my lady, his overt interest would concern me. As it is...

"I will kill Wade Paxton with my bare hands." Taking my phone off the desk, I slip it in my pocket before exiting through the French doors. "Zelda has survived enough."

Leaving him in the office, I make my way down the stone steps to where my girl is lying back on a chair, a magazine in her hand.

"Hello, beautiful," I say, pausing to kiss her soft lips. She's wearing huge sunglasses, which she pulls down her nose to give me a look. "If you keep looking at me that way, I'll have to carry you inside and fuck you."

"Hmm..." Her cheeks flush a pretty pink. "Is that supposed to make me stop?"

Pulling up the lounger beside her, I can't miss the name of the magazine she's holding. *Casino Player?*" I say with a laugh.

She pulls the cover closed and glances at it. "I know! I've never seen this before. I couldn't resist."

"Already growing bored with your life of leisure?"

"I've only been here two days!" Her eyebrows rise. "Still... it's good to have options."

"You have zero options. You're never leaving me again." Moving to sit beside her, I drape an arm around her shoulders. "How does that sound?"

Her eyes drop, and she studies her nails. "I miss Ava."

I turn so I can face her. Reaching out, I touch her chin. "Let's go to Monagasco."

"It's just..." Worried blue eyes meet mine. "It's so close."

Clenching my teeth, I hate seeing her afraid. "Wade Paxton would be a fool if he dared step foot in my country to hurt you. I hesitate to say it, but I think Logan might be as intent on breaking his neck as I am."

"Logan?" Her pretty brow lines, and she looks over her shoulder. "Why—"

"Don't look now, but I think you've charmed the pants off my best guard. He's no use to me now. I'll have to send him back to the regiment and find a replacement."

"Oh, stop it!" She rolls her eyes and leans back in the chair, flipping the pages of that silly magazine. "You're being ridiculous."

I can't resist teasing her. I exhale a long sigh. "When you go missing again, I won't be searching uncharted islands."

"I will *not* go missing again." She cuts those eyes at me, and I do a little wink in response.

"That's what I wanted to hear."

"You tricked me into saying that."

I lean forward to kiss her firmly. It makes her melt against my chest, and I'm not lying when I say I want to carry her inside and help her out of the bikini she's wearing.

"I'll book the plane and tell Logan and Reggie we're going back. Would you like to take your new friends?"

Her hand is on my chest, and she slides a finger around the button of my shirt. "I'll talk to them.

Staying here will be far less of a shock and there's no reason for them to go with us."

"Give them the run of the house. We can be ready to go this evening."

"I'll go inside and pack."

Rowan stands at the head of the table in the war room, and Reggie, Logan, Freddie, and I are with him, looking at what we know and what we're able to do.

"Hampton has pulled back entirely. You wouldn't even know we were once allies."

"You didn't cave on any of their demands," I say. "We got Zelda back, and you emerged from this ordeal stronger and more ready to lead than ever."

"Your mother is drafting the succession referendum as we speak," Reginald says. "She would like the coronation ceremony to occur around the same time as the wedding, if not before."

I don't say it out loud, but I'm pleased my mother has come around to accepting Ava as her future daughter-in-law. She was downright shitty before Zelda's kidnapping and the assassination attempt on Rowan. Spending time with Ava started her evolution in thought, but once Ava exposed the rat at Occitan, our mother couldn't deny her bravery any longer.

"She's a lovely girl," is how our mother references Rowan's fiancée these days. I haven't presented her with Zelda's and my good news just yet. We'll let her process one royal-commoner mix at a time.

"What is the timeline on the wedding?" Logan asks, holding a small agenda book and scrolling through his phone.

"It takes months if not a year to plan a royal wedding," Rowan says. "Or so I've been told. Ava would like us to be married in the fall."

We all look at him a bit surprised. "By fall, is she meaning September? October?"

"I think she's hoping sooner rather than later," he says, and he can't hide the hint of a smile curling his lips.

"So you're planning to do it in two months?" Reggie straightens in his chair. "It's unorthodox and might shock the people." A minor pause, and he quickly adds, "Or you might catch them at the height of optimism and joy over a new king, a victory over Totrington, and a beautiful new queen consort. It could be exactly right."

"I'm going with exactly right," my older brother says in his usual confident tone. Oh yeah, he's grinning. Then he abruptly turns to me. "And how is my new little niece faring? Have you decided when to broach this joyous news?"

"I confess, it is nice to have control of the flow of information again, isn't it?" I glance up at him, remembering well how trying the last several months have been.

"I'm trying to decide the best punishment for the girl. Apparently she was hired by Lara to keep tabs on my dating habits."

"And she fell for that Hines fellow," Freddie says. "Seems punishment enough."

"Facing the wrath of Nesbit is more like punishment enough," Logan says with a laugh. "She won't sit easy for the next month, from what I understand."

"You're joking," I say, catching his eye.

"I'm not." He gives me a wry smile. "Auntie Edna spanks."

"Well, this is all fine for conversation at high tea," Rowan says, bringing us back around. "What are we doing about this Paxton situation?"

"As much as I hate it, I think Reggie is right," I say. "I think if we go after him now, it will be seen as an act of aggression."

My brother's steel blue eyes flash, and the line of his jaw moves. He's out of his chair and facing the windows before my uncle has a chance to speak. "It's incredible to think he gets away with everything and we have to sit back and wait."

"We're not in a position to wage war with Totrington," Reggie says. "It's what they're counting on—our anger leading us into a rash decision."

"It's far from rash," Rowan argues. "They tried to kill me."

"A justified, albeit hasty attack on our part; an easy win on theirs. Check, mate," our uncle continues. "But I know Paxton. He's a thug and an animal. He'll be miffed when we don't respond as he anticipates. Then he'll seethe when he remembers our prosperity, our access to the sea. He'll grow tired of having to ask Hampton's permission to act... He will make a move."

Rowan pivots slightly and looks over his shoulder at our uncle. "And when he does, we'll crush his head like the serpent he is."

My uncle stands and runs his hands down the front of his coat. "Be patient. It's something your father never could grasp. The reason our country is

227

nearly nine hundred years old is because we're in a position of power. We don't have to go after trouble. Trouble comes to us."

I'm not comforted by this statement, but I agree. He's right.

CHAPTER 25: REUNION

Zelda

The moment Ava and I see each other, we start to cry. We're across the tarmac, hugging and laughing and crying, and I don't even try to hold it back.

"Oh, Zee! I've never been so afraid in my life," she says, wiping her eyes, still just as beautiful as ever when she cries. "I couldn't eat, I couldn't sleep," she says. "I walked around this place thinking I would go crazy, and you were so far away... and I was so weak. And this..."

She gently touches my hand, but I shake my head. "Don't." I pull it back. "It wasn't your fault."

More tears flood her eyes. "I wasn't there for you."

"You couldn't have been. You'd been shot." My brow lines and I inspect her torso. "Speaking of, how are you feeling? You look amazing." I touch her soft dark waves, I touch her face. "You look happier than ever."

"I am—now that you're here, I'm happier than I've ever been in my life. Two weeks ago, I thought I was going crazy worrying about you."

"I heard you had a role in finding me." I'm holding her hand when Rowan steps up beside us.

"It's good to have you back, Zee." He gives me a formal kiss on the cheek, and I squeeze his forearm as I smile.

"Thank you," I say with sincerity. "For saving me."

He shakes his head. "Cal would have saved you no matter what. I only did my best to help him find you faster. I'm sorry it wasn't fast enough."

We're at the car, and the familiar driver holds the door for us. I don't miss him smiling at me, and I do a little curious smile back.

Once inside, driving to the palace, the brothers are embroiled in their own conversation, but Ava's and my arms are around each other's waists. We're together again. It feels right. I feel the stress start to melt from my body.

"When we heard about what happened to Seth..." her voice trails off, and she shivers.

I think about the night after our casino heist in St. Croix, him leaving me alone in the market, then I think about his gruesome demise.

"He betrayed me." He gave me to Wade Paxton for money and then he was tortured to death. We don't even know why.

"You were right never to trust him," she says. "I'm sick every time I think how I encouraged you to date him. I'll never question your judgment again."

"It was the worst time of my life. I thought I was in hell." My voice is barely a whisper. "I can't believe Seth would do that to me."

"Oh, god," she starts to cry. "They would have killed you."

"Hey, Ava-bug," I exhale a laugh. "I'm okay now. Let's focus on that."

She lifts my hand and holds it. My thick gauze bandage and metal brace have been replaced with a flesh-colored nylon pressure glove, and I'm able to wear my engagement ring over it.

"I love your ring," she says quietly. "I love how Cal treats you."

"He's pretty great," I say, unable to stop the grin splitting my cheeks. "Who knew Zelda Wilder would ever settle down?"

"Marrying Cal hardly counts as settling down, buuut...." She singsongs, reaching out to rub my midsection. "Being a mama might slow you down a little bit."

Placing a hand over my eyes, I can't help shaking my head. "Don't even say it. I can't believe I'm going to have a little princess."

"I'm being replaced!" She fake-pouts right before starting to laugh. The tears glistening in her eyes now are happy ones. "I'm so excited. I can't wait to dress her up in all the little clothes and bows and shoes and tiaras..."

"You'll have to visit us in Tortola."

"Oh," she looks over her shoulder at Rowan. I follow her gaze and see his calm blue eyes observing our reunion. Her cheeks pink. "I don't think Rowan will let me be gone that long."

That makes me laugh. "What is he, your father?"

"No." Her voice goes quiet, and a naughty look passes over her face. "He likes me to be here for him."

My eyebrows rise, and I glance from the future king back to my little sister. "Okay," I say before changing the subject. "About this wedding..."

"Oh!" She scoots forward in the seat, holding my hands. "Everyone keeps saying how we have to plan it for a year because there are so many balls and events and things leading up to a royal wedding."

"So we're looking at a year of parties before you can marry him?"

"That's just it," she leans closer. "Rowan thinks we can skip all of that. He hates all the balls and parties anyway. So we're going to do one enormous gala and then poof!" She moves her slim fingers in a starburst motion. "We get married."

My eyebrows rise. "I like it! How can I help?"

"Just be here for me." She turns in her seat as the car slows to a stop.

We're at the palace, and I peek out the window. I still feel like a fish out of water with all these people, but I guess if Ava is happy here, I can help her with her wedding. I don't even go into the fact my own fiancé, the father of my baby, is one of these pampered insiders.

I've just never thought of Cal that way. It's not how we relate to each other.

"So I was thinking a masquerade ball would be the most amazing thing. I saw pictures of the spring masque in Venice, and it is unbelievable..." Ava is off in planning mode, and I'm following along after her.

A quick glance behind us, and I see Rowan talking to Hajib, but my guy, my Cal, is standing beside the car watching us go. I lift my hand and do a little wave. He laughs and gives me a wink in reply. I really do love that guy.

We're in Ava's plush bedroom. I'm lying on an enormous four-poster topped with a pillow-soft white duvet. Material swatches and magazines are spread all around us, and she's showing me sketches from hopeful designers wanting her to pick their dresses.

"It's so weird," she says quietly, as if someone might be listening in. "They all want me to use their designs. It could make their careers if I wear their dress!"

"You're going to be a queen, Ava-bug. You've got to get used to what that means."

Nodding, she pushes a long piece of dark hair behind her ear. "I don't know if I'll ever get used to it."

That makes me frown. "Are you unhappy being engaged to Rowan?"

"NO!" Her eyes are big. "I love Rowan. He's amazing. He's sexy and strong and kind and perfect. I just... I'm not used to this kind of attention."

"I understand that." Picking up a piece of tulle, I turn it over in my hands. "You're pretty valuable now. Cal said the people are in love with you."

Her cheeks flame red, and I love my little sister. "They say I'm like a Cinderella. I guess they don't know I grew up stealing watches and cufflinks off security guards."

Wrinkling my nose, I laugh. "I think it gives you depth. You're not just some bubble-headed bimbo."

Pressing her lips into a frown, she gives me exasperated eyes. "Thanks, Zee. Love the vote of confidence over here."

"Ava Lavinia Wilder! You know I'm your biggest supporter. Hell, I've finally managed to get you into the life I wanted for you since I dragged you out of foster care!"

She shakes her pretty head. "You're still small time, Zelda Wilder. You tried to get me to go to

233

community college, get a business degree, and a nine to five."

"Hell, you're right!" I laugh. "I am small time. You said fuck that, I'll marry a king."

We fall back on her fancy bed, our heads together as we look up at the vaulted ceiling. "It is a fairy tale," she says quietly. "And as much as I tease you about it, I confess, I'm always looking over my shoulder. I'm always waiting for the other shoe to drop. I guess I'm small time, too."

Turning toward her, I grip her arm and look her straight in the eyes. "It's not going to drop, Aves. You deserve this. You were born a lady. I'm small time but you're not. Rowan loves you, and you're going to have a beautiful life."

She blinks up at me, and I know she's hearing me. Ava has always trusted whatever I tell her, and as always, it's something I take very seriously. I won't let my small-time fears, my penchant for looking over my shoulder, trickle into her happiness. My sister is going to marry the king of Monagasco, and anyone who tries to rain on that parade can deal with me. After what I've survived, I'm feeling pretty badass.

A soft rap on the door makes us look up. I'm the new kid at the palace. When we were here before, all our adventures were at the beach estate in Occitan or at the Paris Hotel. Now we're in this place, and it's all very official and palatial.

"Come in," Ava calls, and the door opens slowly. I'm not sure who I expect to see, but it is definitely not Cal's mother, the queen looking curiously into my sister's room.

"I hope I'm not disturbing you?" Her Royal Highness actually seems to be asking if it's okay to join us.

"Not at all! Please come in." Ava is as beautiful and inclusive as ever, and I can tell she's worked her magic on this old lady.

I remember very well her skeptical attitude toward my sister on the yacht before the grand prix.

"I'm sorry to intrude," the old woman says. "I know how sisters love to have their special time together."

"You're not intruding at all," Ava says kindly.

"It's actually you I would like to see." She turns her attention to me, and I feel my cheeks heating.

"How do you do, ma'am," I say, sliding off the bed and doing a little curtsey.

"I believe we've met before."

I don't point out I've met her three times now, because that would be rude. "Yes, ma'am, I met you with Sir Winchester at the rose gala."

"Heavens, with all those other young ladies."

"It was a pretty packed field." I nod and glance at my sister.

Ava's not even following our conversation. She's too preoccupied with having to choose a designer for her dress—or more accurately, with having to reject five other designers when she picks the one she likes. My sister might be too kind for this role.

"MacCallum is my favorite son." Her voice is wobbly, and I'm not sure how to answer that. Is it okay to admit you like one child more than another? "Rowan is my noble leader, but MacCallum is my heart."

"He's quite a charmer." It's all I've got.

"I heard through the royal grapevine he asked you to marry him."

"Oh... well..." Did Cal want to tell her this together? I can't remember.

"I further heard you're expecting his child. A baby girl."

"Wow!" I tease "And I thought we caught that rat at Occitan."

Ava's eyes blink up, and she heard that last part. "It was a girl named Juliana. I caught her, you know?"

"You have always been so clever," I say, not even caring if I sound like a doting mother. I've been looking out for Ava a long time.

"Is it true?" The queen's voice has adopted that air of authority. Because she's a queen.

My chin drops, and I wonder where my man has gone. "Y-yes ma'am. I'm pregnant with Cal's baby."

Sneaking a glance, I see her blue eyes studying me, sizing me up, and as much as I'll defend Ava until the cows come home, I can't bluff about myself. I'm no lady.

"You're going to marry my son?" Her voice is sharp, and I'm sure it's because she knows I'm a con artist and petty thief.

Everybody knows this, right? It's essentially what led to me being in a prison camp for the last six weeks. Poor life choices. I want to tell her my picture is beside *poor life choices* in the encyclopedia. I'm the visual aide.

The queen is not a terrible person. She's a mom who wants the best for her admittedly favorite son. I get that. If I thought I was good for Cal, I never would have run away in the first place. I believed he deserves someone better, with more class than me.

"I love Cal very much," I say quietly. "I love him like I've never loved anyone in my life. Except for Ava."

"Then you should be here with us in Monagasco. Taking him and moving to such a remote location sends a message."

"That we like living in paradise?"

Her cool blue eyes narrow at me. "That there is disapproval at home."

I've never been very good at keeping my mouth shut. "Isn't that sort of the truth?"

She stands. "Of course not. I approve of anything Cal chooses." Going to the door, she stops and looks down. "Except when he was photographed in bed with two models snorting coke off their bodies. I did *not* approve of that."

My mouth has fallen open, but I quickly shut it. I'm not surprised Cal would get busted doing something like that, but I'm floored his super-proper and ultimately controlled mother, The Queen, would acknowledge it out loud and in front of us.

"You should get your rest," she says before closing the door.

When Ava turns to me it's like looking in a mirror — both our eyes are round as saucers. Then we start laughing.

"Oh my god," I wail softly. "Is she the worst or what?"

"I haven't decided," Ava's voice is thoughtful, and her eyes return to the closed door. "She wants what's best for them, and you're always saying we gotta do better."

"I can honestly say we've done better than I ever dreamed when I said those words."

She looks down at the large prints in front of her then up at me again. "So what do you think? I think I'm going with the Nikki Rodriguez."

I join her on the bed to look at the simple, full-length design. A delicate network of silk covers the bodice, and thin spaghetti straps are over the shoulders. The skirt is long, flowing silk, and in the hair is a jeweled tiara.

"I think it's gorgeous," I sigh. "It's perfectly you, and it's perfect for this beautiful place."

She nods studying the print a moment longer. "I'll let him know. Then I want to go to Occitan. The palace is too stuffy, and we can spend every day at the beach and go barefoot and live in bikinis..."

"No arguments here!" I say, giving her a squeeze. "Let's go!"

CHAPTER 26: WATCHING

Cal

Waves break in a gentle swish, and my head is in Zelda's lap. She's wearing a black and white string bikini and her skin is golden. Her hair is pulled back in a ponytail and little pieces fly around her face as she reads the tablet in her hand. I can't see her blue eyes for the aviator sunglasses she's wearing.

"Mrs. Kensington, you are so beautiful," I tease her.

"Yes," her pink lips curl with a smile. "*Austin Powers* is hilarious."

Her hand moves to my hair, and she threads her fingers in the side absently, still reading. My eyes move down to her breasts behind those small triangles of her bikini top, and I wish Ava wasn't in the water behind us.

"You are so beautiful," I say with complete sincerity this time. "I love being here with you. It feels like our place."

That makes her lower the device. "It is the first place you seduced me and totally ruined my assignment."

"You would never have been happy with Rowan." Turning my face, I kiss her barely rounded tummy. "Hear that, princess? Daddy knows best."

She starts to laugh, and I sit up to catch her cheeks and kiss her gently. She exhales a little sigh, and I want to carry her inside. "I was pretty much done for after that night. It only took our next few nights of fucking to know for sure."

"I was pretty completely freaked out." She smiles, tracing a finger along my jaw. "I was supposed to be seducing your brother, and you kept seducing me!"

"You're the one who never wore panties." I lean forward to kiss the line of her neck. Definitely need to carry her inside now.

She sighs a little laugh. "I miss your texts."

"I like checking the status of your underwear."

"It's simply a matter of efficiency. If you're going to be around, it saves time to skip the panties."

"That's my girl. Now I have to carry you in the house and fuck you."

"Cal," she laughs more. "I'm reading."

"You can read." Her hands are on my face, and I hear the noise of feet squeaking on the sand.

"Don't mind me!" Ava calls out as she passes us. "I'm just going inside for lunch."

I break away and look up. "Oh, hello, Ava. Didn't see you there." She laughs and waves over her head as she continues up the boardwalk. I glance behind us toward the ocean. All clear. Perfect.

Wrapping my arm around her waist, I do a quick roll, replacing her position on the beach chair, and holding her in a straddle on my lap. She smiles down and I spread my hands over her waist, sliding my thumbs across her bare stomach.

"I thought I was going to read?" She's teasing, and I'm hard as a rock.

"Read aloud," I say, running my eyes over her breasts still hidden behind that bikini top.

"It's a pregnancy manual."

"Hmm..." I trace my fingers along the line of her top. "Maybe we'll learn something."

Her eyes narrow, and she looks at the small tablet she's holding. "Good prenatal care is one of the most important ingredients in making a healthy baby..."

Hooking my finger in the center of one triangle, I slide it to the side allowing her breast to spill out. "And here I thought it was just semen," I say before covering a taut nipple with my mouth.

Her voice wavers as I slide my tongue around the hardened tip. "Don't delay..." she sighs, and I trace my finger along the edge of her bottoms starting at the top of her hip and moving quickly down.

"As soon as you have a positive... Oh, Cal..." Her voice breaks when I reach the center and slip a finger into her slippery core.

"Mm..." I say, kissing across her chest to the other beaded nipple. "A positive what was that?"

My finger curls inside her, and the device hits the sand. She cups my cheeks and our mouths collide, tongues searching frantically, hands everywhere, quickly pushing what little clothes we're wearing aside.

With a brief lift, we both groan as I sink deep into her clenching insides. "Cal," she sighs, pushing against the chair. It's the greatest feeling in the world.

I'm leaning back, watching her ride my cock. My hands are on her sides, and I slide them higher to circle her beautiful nipples with my thumbs. The bikini top is pushed away to the sides and her breasts are full and spilling out, bouncing with each thrust.

"You are so beautiful," I murmur, sitting forward to cover them with my mouth. She whimpers and rides faster.

My arm moves around her waist, and I pull her soft body flush against my hard one. Leaning up, I kiss her mouth, and our tongues caress. Her warm lips move against mine.

I'm thrusting up now, chasing my building orgasm. My pelvis floods with tingling heat that grows tighter as her inner muscles massage and pull me. Sliding my hand down her ass, I move my fingers along the line between her cheeks, clutching her soft bottom and scrubbing her clit against me. We're moving in one fluid motion when all at once she breaks.

"Oh, god!" she whimpers as her body buckles toward me in a shuddering wave of orgasm.

Her insides clench around me, and I let go, allowing my own release to pulse through us, blanking my thoughts and bonding us together.

Her movements slow, and my hands slide over her heated skin, moving around her waist. I hold her flush against my bare chest, and I can't help smiling as her warm lips touch the side of my neck.

"I'd say that was very positive," I tease, rolling us so her body is beside mine in the chair.

She props her head on her hand and pretends to scold. "I'm trying to learn about all this pregnancy stuff. I'm completely ignorant."

"It's pretty amazing how women had babies all the time before those books were written."

"Yes, but they also had mothers to tell them what was coming."

I kiss her nose. "Not always." My kiss moves to the top of her cheek, and when I pull back, I can tell something's troubling her.

"What's wrong?" I lean further back.

Her lips press together a moment before she says it. "You should be here." Her expression is almost guilty. "Your mother says Rowan needs you here."

"Are you saying you want to move back?"

She blinks down and then out to the water. "No."

"Good, because I really like our villa. I also think we should add another pair of panties to the roof at Bomba's."

That makes her laugh. "Relationship goals?"

"Definitely." I kiss the side of her jaw.

"I'm worried about being so far from Ava. I'm not sure she's safe here."

"Rowan will not let anything happen to your sister. Trust me."

She exhales a sigh. "I wouldn't have let anything happen to her, but it still did."

Catching her chin, I bring her eyes to mine. "We've gone over this. You were alone when that happened. Now you have us, and we know what we're up against. She won't be hurt again."

Her eyes move over my shoulder, and I see her thinking. "It's true."

"Stop worrying." I hug her to me. "We'll stay for the wedding, then we're going back to our place."

"Our place," she repeats softly, and a smile hints at the corner of her mouth.

I give her another kiss. "With our little princess."

Logan has the satellite images spread across the thick mahogany table of the war room.

"Entry points are here and here," Reggie says, using a stylus to show the critical spots.

"Do we have a positive ID on his being there?" I say, arms crossed over my chest as I survey the entire layout.

The photographs are blown up, and like a puzzle, we've arranged all the prints to show the house, the grounds, the driveway—even the road leading to his compound.

"I've captured his image going in and out on more than one occasion," Freddie says. He's sitting at his laptop. "He's definitely there."

Logan nods and straightens, stepping back from the table. "I'll go in and take him out."

Possessive anger tightens my chest. "I'll take him out."

Our eyes lock briefly before my brother enters the room, breaking our moment of conflict.

"What's going on here? Meeting already started?"

I move my angry gaze from Logan's to my brother. "Freddie has a positive ID on Wade Paxton. He's at this compound in Twatrington. I'm planning to dispose of him."

Rowan's blue eyes flash to mine. "I said we wait."

I can't stop the explosion. "I can't do that, Ro. He has to pay for what he did."

"And he will," my brother's voice is firm. "When the time is right. We're not going to be implicated in an act of aggression against a neighboring country."

"We have all the evidence we need to build a case—" I start, but Rowan cuts me off.

"Hampton is giving him asylum. We have to respect his authority and observe our borders."

I can't even speak I'm so livid. Throwing my hands in the air, I step to the window to look out at the emerald coast. Rowan steps behind me, placing a hand on my shoulder.

"I know how you feel, but we have to observe protocol."

Looking over my shoulder I meet his blue gaze. "And if he starts recruiting?"

"We'll know."

I don't like this. It feels dangerous. It feels like we're playing with fire. Still I can't cross Rowan. I have to support him as king.

And I'm redoubling the watch on Wade Paxton.

Chapter 27: Paper Faces

Zelda

Fittings and flowers and teas and lunches fill Ava's days leading up to the royal wedding. She's met more royal ladies and debutantes than I can count, and my head is swimming with all the names and titles. We've tasted cake after cake until I don't think I can eat another bite—something I can't believe I'm thinking. The masquerade ball is tonight, and it's the final event as we lock into the countdown leading to the big day.

I've checked in with Ximena and Selena, and they are thriving at our villa in Tortola. I miss being there. I miss the ease and the relaxed atmosphere of the place. The frenzy of wedding preparation has me exhausted, but the baby is well. I'm able to spend time with my sister, and we're almost finished. Sustaining thoughts.

Cal waits at the bottom of the stairs in a dark blue waistcoat and white satin breeches. A long white cravat is around his neck, and he's wearing a simple black mask over his eyes.

I'm trying to navigate an enormous Louis XIV style gown with a giant hoop skirt. The bodice is off the shoulder blue velvet with silver accents that cuts low across my breasts, pushing them up and making them look even rounder than usual. My hair is styled in an elaborate updo, but I opted for a small silver mask that sits right across my eyes.

"This is insane," I whisper, moving the skirt around. "I'm going to fall on my face in this thing."

"You look amazing," Cal smiles, his eyes lingering over my décolletage a moment before he gives me a light kiss. "The girls are blowing my mind."

"It's the dress," I tease.

"Not entirely." The way he says it causes a humming beneath my skin.

"Behave," I whisper. "It took me twenty minutes to get into this thing."

"I'll do my best to beat that time getting you out of it."

My hand is in the crook of his arm, and I'm thankful we don't have to walk too far. The ball is across the palace in the enormous grand ballroom behind the lavish grand staircase. Guests are being led in from outside, presented, and then they descend to join the party.

"At least we don't have to walk down those stairs," I say, going with him through the double doors and across the black and white tiled floor of the grand foyer.

Ava is across the room at the head of the line with Rowan. She's dressed in an elaborate gold lamé gown in an Egyptian theme. It's form-fitted with an enormous mermaid-style skirt. A turquoise line leads up the center of her body to a brass loop between her breasts holding the top together. Around her neck is a collar necklace made of hundreds of tiny turquoise plaques. Her dark hair is parted in the center and two chains drape down the sides from the crown of her head. A shining gold mask covers her eyes.

"She's Claudette Colbert!" I say to Cal. "No wonder she wanted to surprise me."

"Exotic," he says with a nod. "It's perfect for her."

Rowan stands beside her in a matching costume. His tan, lined torso is bare, and he's wearing a knee-length tunic with alternating gold and leather strips. A small collar of tiny gold rectangles is around his neck and on both biceps are gold and beaded cuffs. He looks amazing.

"Sexiest couple alive?" I glance up at my escort.

He winks and kisses my cheek just beside my ear. "They've got nothing on us. Just wait til I find you under all those petticoats."

"I'm not wearing panties," I say wrinkling my nose, and he groans.

"Can I start searching now?"

That makes me laugh more, and he leads me to the dance floor as the music plays. I'm in his arms, our bodies pressed together as we sway. I watch my sister from across the room of maskers, and I figure she'll be swamped with guests all night. I'm so happy she's blissed out with her king, but I wouldn't trade all her social obligations for anything.

My chin rests against Cal's shoulder as I study the guests dressed in every type of costume imaginable, from elaborate Venetian-style carnival to simple tuxedo and evening gowns with Zorro masks. I can't stop looking at the dazzling display surrounding us.

"I thought it would be more *To Catch a Thief*," I whisper, "But it's more anything goes."

"The only rule was to have your face covered." The song ends, and Cal takes my hand.

A woman in an elaborate lavender costume composed of a vast network of beads and lace with a matching facemask and enormous headdress steps to us.

"MacCallum?" I recognized that voice. "Is that you?"

He turns and takes a step back. "Mother. You look... Startling."

"It's an Antonio Baroque original," she scolds, but Cal is right. Her white mask with dark eyeholes is nightmarish. "Your brother made a bold choice."

"I think he looks great," Cal says. "Very intimidating."

"I'm sure it's the influence he's under—" She's going after Ava, and I'm about to snap back a reply when Cal wraps an arm around my waist.

"Have a lovely night, Mother," he says, curtailing my knee-jerk, mother-hen response.

"They look incredible," I grumble, feeling the heat under my skin. "She's just an old stick in the mud."

"She *is* old," he says with a grin. "And you're going to have to stop letting her get to you."

"Never!" I pretend-shout. It wins me another little kiss.

"I'm going to get us champagne." He steps back and lifts my hand, kissing each of my knuckles. "Stay right here until I get back."

"Shirley Temple for me," I remind him.

Smokey hazel eyes move to my breasts. "I might have to get a head start on unwrapping you. Those perfect tits are causing a rise down below."

My eyes narrow as I trace a finger across the top of my cleavage. "Don't be too long."

He grins and shakes his head. "You're killing me."

Laughing, I look out over the crowd as he disappears in the direction of the bar. It's impossible to recognize anyone, and I can't stop a touch of anxiety filtering through my stomach. It would be the perfect opportunity for a criminal…

"You look amazing." A deep voice interrupts my thoughts.

I look up to see a tall, muscular male in a white pirate style shirt and black leather vest and pants standing beside me. His mask is simple black, and his head is uncovered.

"Logan?" I lean closer, examining his eyes.

"You guessed right," he teases gently. His smile reveals straight, white teeth. "You know me too well."

"I recognize your eyes." I point toward his face then glance around us. "Is Freddie with you? Is he a pirate as well?"

"I haven't seen Freddie tonight," the handsome guard says. "Would you like to dance?"

For a moment, I hesitate. Cal asked me to wait here, and in this mob of masked dancers, it might be hard to find each other again. At the same time, I'm sure he wouldn't care if I had an innocent dance with Logan.

"Can we stay in this general vicinity?" I move my white-satin gloved hand in a little circle toward the floor.

"Of course." His arms go around me, and in that moment, I'm not sure it's such an innocent dance for Logan. "You're almost never alone," he says, his lips just brushing the top of my ear.

My hand is on his large bicep, and I clear my throat wishing the song would hurry up and end. "I guess Ava and I are pretty inseparable. And Cal is usually —"

"It will be your life if you move here to live in the palace."

Leaning away, I meet his blue eyes. They're heated and serious. "You're right," I say with a friendly smile. "But we're not planning to move here."

His body tenses, and his dark brow lowers. "Where will you go?"

I don't know why I feel guilty all of a sudden. "We're staying in Tortola. Cal... bought the villa we were renting. It's where we want to live."

He's quiet, and his face turns away, toward the crowd. The muscle in his square jaw moves. "You deserve better than that," he says quietly. "He's putting you in danger again."

My insides tighten, but I manage to laugh. "You do remember I'm a con artist and a thief, right? I think I'm getting a better deal than I've ever deserved."

Blue eyes return to mine, and the emotion I see there puts a knot in my throat. "You can't see yourself like I do." I start to pull away, but his arms tighten around me. "I'm sorry," he says quickly, recovering. "I shouldn't have spoken so plainly. It's just that — we spent a lot of time searching for you. I don't want to feel like it was in vain."

In vain... I think about Tortola. I think about the beach club and Logan bringing us food. I remember the night Cal rescued me, and how Logan was there as well. We're not moving, and I'm pretty sure the song has ended.

"I'm so sorry, Logan," I say quietly. "I never thanked you for all you did to help Cal find me."

His arms lower, and he steps back. "You never have to thank me. No one could have kept me from helping find you."

"Still, I never expressed my personal gratitude. You sacrificed time, and I'm sure it was very dangerous."

This time when our eyes meet, his flash with something like frustration. "I only want to be sure you're safe before... Before I turn in my resignation."

"What?" My eyes widen. "But you're Cal's best man! You and Freddie have been with him since —"

"I need a change of scenery." His voice lowers. "It's difficult to keep watch over you like I did before, without..."

His voice trails off, and embarrassment clenches my chest. I remember how the guards are always with us, no matter where we are or what we're doing. What Cal and I are always doing.

"I understand." Nodding, I feel the burn in my cheeks. At the same time, I hate to be the reason Cal's special unit is divided. "What if you requested another role? A reassignment?" I'm not sure what I'm talking about. "It would be better than your leaving —"

"Leaving?" Cal is with us, handing me a glass of sparkling pink soda with a cherry. I move to his side, holding his arm and avoiding Logan's gaze. "Where are you going?"

Logan's voice is all business. "I was thinking France... Italy, perhaps."

"What?" All joking is gone from Cal's voice as well. "Why would you do that? We need you here.

Does Rowan know about this?"

"I haven't discussed it with anyone yet," Logan says, and I step away, moving closer to the dancers so they can talk in private.

The awkwardness of the situation, realizing he's probably seen Cal and me making love, is a bit overwhelming, especially in view of Cal's tease that Logan might have feelings for me. I don't want to believe he does. I don't like reading meaning into situations...

"Such a troubled face on such a beautiful lady." An older voice addresses me, and when I look up, a little yelp squeaks from my throat.

A man in a sinister golden skull mask with black holes at the eyes and nose looms over me. On the forehead is a strange, round symbol, and the straight teeth are yellowed and awful.

"I'm sorry. Did I startle you?" His voice is low, and he's wearing a gold damask suit with a black cape.

My heart is flying in my chest, but I clear my throat. "No—not at all." I do a little bow, trying to regain my composure. "I'm not troubled, thank you."

I start to move away, but he steps forward, pulling me to his chest roughly. "Let's share a dance, and you can tell me why you're sad. I have powers. I can make the bastard pay."

His words are a growly hiss, and the creepy skull moves closer to my face. Small words are painted around the temples and over the brow bones in a rust color like blood.

"Who are you supposed to be?" I don't miss the tremor in my voice.

"I'm the Triskel skull. I can see inside your mind." His eyes widen in the dark sockets, and I can't tell if he's trying to tease me or terrify me. He's succeeding at the latter.

"It's very... unusual," I manage.

We move side to side, and his eyes hold mine in a steely, angry gaze. I swallow forcefully, ready to pull away when he speaks again.

"You think you've beaten me." The voice is no longer disguised, and with a jerk, I know who it is. "You're wrong. I always win."

"Wade Paxton!" All I can think is protect myself, protect the baby! I struggle against him. I'm breathing too fast, and I can't get away.

"That little finger cut was only a tease. Have they told you what was done to Mr. Hines?" My entire body is shaking, and I'm afraid I might throw up. "You are never safe from me, Zelda Wilder."

"Let me GO!" I scream, but my words are lost in the blast of the music.

He holds me a beat longer before dropping his arms and backing into the crowd. Revelers close around him like a sea, and I realize what's happening. He's getting away! Wade Paxton is in Monagasco, and we have to capture him before he disappears again!

"STOP!" I scream. "Stop that man!"

The music is too loud, and only the people around us have bothered to look. I'm in these stupid fourteenth-century shoes, and my head doesn't reach the shoulders of many of the guests. I try to push through them. I have to stop him.

"Zelda! What's going on?" With a little cry, I turn to see Reggie standing beside me. He's wearing a long, satin tunic and pants. A turban is on his head, and his mask is off. His skin is bronzed, and he has an Aladdin-style beard attached to his chin.

"Paxton is here!" I grab his shirtfront. "He was just here threatening me! He disappeared into the crowd that way!"

I'm pointing and gasping, and Cal returns to my side. "Zee!" He holds my arm. "Breathe, Zee, tell me what happened."

His words are in my head, and tears coat my cheeks. I'm trembling and weak, and I feel like I'm right back in that little camp on that hellish island.

"Paxton is here," Reggie speaks low in Cal's ear. "We need to spread out and find him."

Cal's eyes widen and he looks quickly from me to his uncle. "It's going to be like finding a needle in a haystack. How is he dressed?"

"Skull!" I manage to gasp. "Triskel skull! He's in a gold suit with a black cape."

"Get Rowan inside," Reggie snaps. "He's completely exposed. Anyone could take a shot at him."

I feel like the world has tilted sideways. "Ava! I have to get to Ava!" I gasp, gripping Cal's arm.

"Logan!" he shouts over the guests surrounding us. At once the beefy security guard is with us. "Take Zee to her room and stay there. Message Freddie. We need all guards to be on alert. Paxton is here."

"What?" His voice is a shout. "I'm going with you."

"I need you to stay with Zee. Protect her. I'm going to finish that bastard tonight."

"I'm going to finish him," Logan argues.

"You're wasting time!" I gasp, wiping away the tears. "Somebody get to Ava!"

Reggie is already gone, headed in the direction of the royal couple. Cal's eyes meet mine, and I see the fierce determination burning there.

"I won't let him get away this time. I promise you."

Chapter 28: Double Strike

Cal

Reggie takes off in the direction of Rowan. I signal Freddie. He's across the room in a plain black tuxedo and no mask, but he's hampered by the multitude of guests. We're not alerting the crowd of what's happening in the hopes of avoiding a panic.

I scan the four exits searching for a skull mask, gold damask, and a black cape. So many masqueraders are in the ballroom, and the legion of headdresses and Venetian costumes makes it almost impossible to find him.

"Like a needle in a haystack," I growl, pushing through the dancers.

Frustration tightens in my chest. I promised Zee. I promised myself—I will not let Wade Paxton slip away this time. A thump at my wrist, and I pull my sleeve up to check my smart watch. It's a text from Freddie. *Southeast corridor.*

Turning quickly, I catch a glimpse of a man in a black cape moving quickly and steadily through the dancers toward the south door leading out, and I immediately spring into action.

Grabbing arms and waists, I gently but firmly move the party guests aside, keeping my eyes on that black cape. He's ahead of me. He'll be out into the courtyard before I make it to the exit, but he'll still have to cross to the palace gates before he'll be able to hail a cab or get in his car. For security reasons, the courtyard is completely cleared of all vehicles during royal events.

Sure enough, he's gone, but I'm making better time. I'm right after him in mere seconds. He's moving slower to avoid drawing attention. *Too late, you bastard, you've already got my attention.*

Out in the courtyard, he's walking fast in a straight line to the black wrought-iron gates. Mask gone, I pull off the white tie at my neck and break into a run. The noise of my shoes echoing on the cobblestones alerts him, and he breaks into a run as well. My only hope is that he'd planned to hail a cab and doesn't have a car waiting. Would he be that stupid?

Paxton is through the gates, but just as it slams, I'm pushing it open. He doesn't stop at the line of cars, rather plunging into the crowd of spectators instead. His skull mask is still over his face, but I'm exposed. Smart motherfucker. He knew the crowd would stop me.

I see him ahead, slowing to a stroll now. He pauses at the corner and turns back to face me, doing a little salute in my direction before resuming his casual walk into the night. The sight of his audacity flashes my chest. *NO! He will NOT get away this time.*

Instead of diving into the crowd, I run to the first Towncar. "I need you to drive me one block north — just on the other side of this crowd! Quick!"

The driver answers in the affirmative and pulls the black vehicle out of the circular drive. The spectators part, leaning forward to see who is leaving early. I look away from the flashbulbs popping in the windows and strain toward the edge of the crowd. It's like the shore of a great sea.

Once we're close, I pat the man on the shoulder, toss him a fiver, and dive for the door. "Thanks, old man. You're a life saver."

I'm out the door and running full speed in the direction Paxton was headed. It's possible he had a car waiting for him around the block, but I have to hope he didn't. I have to believe he's cocky enough to think he won again.

I'm right.

My breath is coming in heavy pants when I skid around the beige stone building, and looking up the winding alley decorated in colorful lights and little tables at the cafés, I see a man in a gold suit slowly walking away. He must have ditched the cape.

I break into a run, dodging pedestrians and casual diners until I'm almost to him. My wrist catches on a wrought-iron grate, momentarily stopping me. He takes a left off the main route, and I snatch my arm free. When I reach the point where he turned, I see it's a narrow, dark alley. With only a moment's hesitation, my military training kicks in.

I'm defensive, stepping slowly into the potentially deadly space. My eyes are dazzled from the lights of the street. We're behind the shops, where the garbage cans and back doors meet in a dingy corridor.

Looking ahead, I see it's a dead end. Either he's still here or he was able to escape through the back door of a restaurant. I take careful steps. My arms are up as I turn quickly around every dumpster and box where he could be lurking.

"Don't know when to quit, do you, MacCallum." I jump back at the sound of his voice, loud behind a stack of crates. We're facing each other, and I do a quick blink to ensure it's only us.

We're alone here.

"I'll quit when I've finished you," I say, my voice hoarse from running.

"Murdering a prime minister is a capital offense. You'll hang for it."

"Yes, and attempted murder of a king is punishable by death. It evens out."

He reaches up to remove the skull mask. His dark hair is greased back, and the thin moustache quirks over his lips. "Let's see what you've got, boy."

His fists rise, and while I know Freddie will use the GPS on my smart watch to find us, I'm happy to spend the time it takes them to get here beating his ass.

A lunge forward, and he attempts a swipe at my jaw. I dodge and plant a solid right jab in his mouth. A satisfying crunch and a grunt of pain from Paxton gives me more pleasure than I expected it would.

"What did you think would happen coming here tonight?" I say, circling him, watching the line of blood slowly trickle down his chin.

"Just reminding your fiancée who holds the cards in this town." His dark eyes glitter, and my throat tightens.

"Don't you ever speak to Zelda. Don't you ever go near her." I'm breathing fast, rage clouding my judgment.

"I don't have to," he says with a sinister grin. "My men are in every part of this country."

Which is why we won't be living here, I think. "They'll scatter without a leader," I say, moving closer. I want another shot at this asshole.

"Perhaps," he says, not taking his eyes off me. "Still, I have other ways of inspiring your cooperation. A royal baby is an incredibly powerful chess piece."

The snarl rips through my throat as I lunge at him. I'm not in control at this point, and I'm finished reasoning with a thug. Zelda's battered face, her tears, and her severed finger are in my mind. Seth's mutilated body… our baby girl.

My arms are around his neck, and I grip his face in my hands. In one swift move, I'm ready to finish him, but he lunges hard, throwing his body weight against me. I have him in my grip. His arm moves, punching me strong in the torso just as I make the twist, snapping his neck, ending his life.

He drops to the pavement in a dead heap, but I stagger back, falling heavy against the brick wall. Pain rips through my side, forcing a loud curse from my throat. When I look down, I see the twisted handle of a knife extending from my side at the level of my waist.

With every breath the pain slices deeper. A river of dark red blood soaks my white breeches. I'm bleeding fast.

"Fuck!" I groan as my knees give way, and I slide to sitting against the wall.

I'm hidden behind the stack of crates, and I'm gasping for breath. Fatigue sweeps over me as with every heartbeat another gush of blood pumps from my body.

I fumble with my sleeve, doing my best to pull the cuff back. I've got to text Freddie. I've got to tell them where I am. I can't wait for them to find me. I'm running out of time. Searching with my fingers, a flash of panic grips me. My smart watch is gone. I must have lost it when my arm caught on that grate.

They'll track the GPS, but it's not near enough to this alley.

Blackness closes in, starting from the edges of my vision. I'm cold, and my fingers aren't following my brain's instructions. I try to shout when the noise of voices echoes at the mouth of the corridor, but all I get out is a whispered "Freddie..."

I look across the way to Wade Paxton's dead body. Fighting with everything in me I try to hold on.

But I'm not stronger than this.

The clock is counting down faster.

My eyes won't stay open.

I'm bleeding out.

After everything we've survived, all we've been through, with my last conscious breath I call to her. *Zelda...*

Chapter 29: Backup

Zelda

Being stuck waiting in my suite is torture of an entirely different kind. I have my phone at least, so I'm able to text Ava and know she's okay. She's in her suite with guards stationed all around. She and I are under lockdown on Rowan's orders until the palace is secured.

Logan alternates between pacing the balcony and standing in the hallway just outside my door. I run my fingers over the heavy blue velvet of my costume, thinking with a sigh how Cal was supposed to help me out of it. *Damn Wade Paxton.*

"I'm going to change out of this costume," I call in the direction of the balcony where Logan currently stands watch.

He doesn't reply, and I leave the sitting area to go into the bedroom to slowly remove the elaborate getup. It's heavy, and I could use some help with the buttons in the back, but I'll figure it out.

After a series of twists and stretches that would make a contortionist proud, I'm out of the heavy thing. I toss it on the small sofa and walk over to the closet. It's a warm night, and I take out a filmy cotton dress with crisscross spaghetti straps. It's loose around my middle, and I don't bother with shoes. Standing in front of the mirror, I start the process of removing pin after pin as my hair drops around my shoulders in large curls.

"So much for the masquerade," I say mostly to myself.

"We checked every guest as they came in." Logan answers, causing me to do a little jump. "Sorry," he says quickly. I thought you knew I was here.

"I guess I did," I say, trying to keep my hands from trembling. "I-I wasn't really sure where you were."

It's stupid to act awkward around Logan. He's been with Cal and me for so long, and he helped to save me. We're friends for chrissake.

He takes one step from the balcony into my sitting room. "I wanted to apologize." Looking down, he clears his throat. "If I made you uncomfortable earlier. I guess I expected you to stay in the palace."

For a moment, I pass my eyes over this fellow. He's very tall and only a bit bulkier than Cal. He has short dark hair and a light scruff on his jaw. A dark brow pulls severely over blue eyes. He's very handsome. He should stay here and find a lady of his own.

"You don't have to apologize," I say, giving him a kind smile. "And I hope you change your mind about resigning. Cal needs you. You and Freddie and Cal are a team."

Clearing his throat, he runs a hand over his mouth. "We were a team. Lately... I've had trouble engaging."

I'm still not quite sure I understand. "Maybe you need a little break?"

He only does a half-smile and turns to face outside. I look over to the wet bar and think how if Cal were here we'd share a nightcap, discuss the evening, tease each other and fall in bed to have sex or search for a movie to watch... or both.

"It's difficult not to be angry with him," Logan quietly confesses. "I would never have let you be taken."

"Excuse me?" My sharp tone causes him to look back at me. "Cal gives me my freedom. He knows I don't like feeling trapped."

"Sometimes decisions must be made for your own protection. Like right now. You have to stay in this room until we're sure it's safe."

My lips press together. "Look, I appreciate what you've done for me, your part in my rescue..." An edge is in my voice. "But you will not criticize Cal to me or blame him for what happened."

"I'm sorry," he says quietly. "I didn't mean to make you angry."

"Logan," I exhale and walk to where he stands at the edge of the balcony. "We've all been through a hideous ordeal. Perhaps a little time away... perhaps you could meet someone to share your time with—outside your official duties here."

"Right." His smile is bitter, and I get the distinct feeling my encouragement backfired.

"I hope I didn't overstep or invade your privacy by saying that."

"Please don't patronize me."

"I would never!"

"You are more than an official duty." His eyes burn with something new... and just as fast the shutters close. His tone returns to formal. "Forgive me. I take my position here very seriously. It's impossible not to feel I would have handled things differently."

My bottom lip goes between my teeth. I don't know if I should say thanks or apologize. I decide to simply nod and say, "Okay."

I go to the wet bar and pour a ginger ale for me. No champagne with the little princess onboard. Tracing my finger along the edge of the glass, I think about Cal, and his team and my idea at the ball before everything blew up.

"You should stay in Monagasco," I say. "It's your home, and you love it here. We're leaving anyway."

"Right," he says, that tightness returning. "You're leaving the security of the palace and the guards."

Weariness rolls over me in waves, and I can't retread this argument. "Either way, I hope you find happiness. I am grateful to you for all you've done. Now I'll say goodnight."

"Sleep well." His voice is quiet. "I'll be here."

As exhausted as I am, however, sleep never comes. I lay in our enormous, king-sized bed staring at the ceiling and listening to the sounds of the palace after dark. I think about Cal out there somewhere, and freaky Wade Paxton and his horrifying mask. The sight of it still makes me shudder.

The ball was cut short and all the lords and ladies and dignitaries returned to their houses or castles. Ava and I were sent to our rooms like children.

"No, that isn't fair," I sigh, turning again in my bed. "We were sent heavily guarded to our secure rooms."

My window is open, and I listen to the noise of night birds. I hear cicadas screeching. I miss Cal. I want to be in Tortola, or at the very least, I wish we were at Occitan so I could go down to the shore. I wonder what Ximena and Selena are doing...

Hours drag by, and Cal doesn't return. Logan's footsteps as he walks from my sitting room out to the balcony echo in my quiet suite. The baby isn't big enough to disturb me, but I can't seem to get comfortable around my belly.

I'm about to throw back the blankets, grab a robe, and demand he play a round of blackjack with me when my phone lights up, buzzing and vibrating. A soft tap on my bedroom door follows next, and I hear shouts and the scuffling of feet in the courtyard below.

Logan appears in my room, and the expression on his face shoots dread through my veins.

"What's wrong?" I demand.

Scooping up my phone, I see Ava is calling me. I haven't heard from Cal. In one fluid movement, I'm out of the bed, grabbing my robe and holding it in front of me as I approach Logan.

"We need to go to the hospital," he says. "There's isn't much time."

My heart is breaking, and I can't seem to breathe. Ava sits beside me clutching my hand, and I can't stop shaking. My entire world is crumbling, and I'm on the edge of a cliff, facing the end of everything.

Wade Paxton is dead, but before he went down, he used that same fucking knife—the one he threatened me with when I was trapped in the bathroom during the Grand Prix—and jammed it into Cal.

269

My Cal...

He's in a room far from us fighting for his life. Fear claws at my throat as a fresh wave of tears fills my eyes. Rowan's face is ashen. His mother sits stoic, staring at the floor in front of her, and all we can do is wait.

Wait and wait.

Minute after minute.

One second, two seconds.

Fifty seconds, one million...

We're waiting for any change, for a word from the doctor. For Cal to come out of the coma.

"Paxton was aiming for his heart," Freddie says to Rowan.

They speak softly to avoid alarming the queen.

Or me?

I don't know.

All I know is I'm leaning forward in my chair, straining every muscle in my body to hear their words.

Rowan's jaw is clenched, and anger permeates his tone. "Why did it take you so long to find him? You had GPS! You should have gone directly to him."

"His watch was missing." Freddie's voice is strained. "It's a miracle we found him at all."

"It's a miracle he was so close to the hospital."

Guilt is heavy in the guard's voice. "There was so much blood. I thought we were too late..."

The door bursts open, and a small, female doctor emerges. It appears to be the same woman who treated Ava, and I briefly wonder if they have a royal physician. We're all on our feet.

"*Majesté,*" she begins in French, speaking to Rowan, but I've been here before.

I clutch his arm before she can say another word. "English, please!" I shout.

The doctor is taken aback, but she clears her throat and continues in English laced with a thick French accent.

"His majesty is in hypovolemic shock," she says. "We've given him platelets, plasma, dopamine, and now a steady supply of fluids and antibiotics. Still, he does not wake up."

White filters into my vision, and I'm going down. Strong arms surround me at once, and Logan carries me to a nearby chair. Ava is beside me, again holding my hand.

"He's going to be okay," she repeats like a mantra. "He's going to be okay."

I'm not sure she's right this time.

"What can we do?" Rowan asks, and all of us—the queen, Reggie, my sister, the guards, me—lean forward, hanging on the doctor's words.

Her voice is grave. "We are keeping him warm, and we are monitoring his kidneys and other vital organs for any sign of failure. If he is a religious man, we have a priest on standby."

Ava's mantra dissolves into a little cry. My stomach has relocated to my throat, and I lean forward in my chair until the tightness recedes.

"I'm so sorry," the doctor says, "All we can do is pray he responds to treatment."

"I need to be with him." Somehow I manage to stand. I grasp Rowan's forearm again. "Let me go back to him. I need to be there."

Three sets of eyes are on me, and it's Ava's voice that tips the scales. "If it were you," she says softly to the crown prince, and his eyes close as he nods.

271

"Zelda must go back. He would want her by his side."

"Of course, *Majesté*," the doctor nods.

She steps to the side, and motions for me to follow her. On shaking legs, I do so. We go through the double doors into a wide, white hall. Fluorescent lights coat everything in a clinical green hue. The air is cold, and a faint smell of disinfectant assaults my nose. We approach a pale wooden door, and the doctor slowly opens it, letting me inside.

When I see him, my heart drops. "Oh, Cal," I whimper.

He's so pale. Dark circles stain the skin beneath his eyes, and his full lips are blue. So many tubes run under the blankets to his body. My nose heats, and I carefully pick through the monitors and machines to his side, to where I can touch him. His hand is cold, and I wrap it in both of mine, holding it to my lips.

"He's receiving a steady supply of antibiotics and fluids," the doctor says.

A shiny silver stool is in the corner, and I step over to roll it to his bedside. My limbs are so heavy. My entire body feels heavy with despair, but I sit at his side, pressing our palms together, resting my cheek against the back of his hand.

No matter what happens, I won't leave him. Through the steady beeping of the monitors, the slow rise and fall of the respirator, I'll be here. I'll wait as long as it takes until I see his warm hazel eyes again.

An incoherent prayer slips from my mouth before I turn and press my lips to his skin. The doctor touches my shoulder, and a sad smile is on her face.

"I'll try to find a more comfortable chair. The nurse is available if you need anything. Otherwise..."

She goes to the door and leaves us alone. Carefully, I place my hand on his chest, just above his heart. I can't feel it beating, but I see it on the screen. Leaning my head against my arm, I blink back the tears.

"Don't leave me, MacCallum." My voice breaks. "I can't live without you."

No change.

"I love you, my playboy prince," I whisper, closing my eyes as more tears fall.

I'm alone in this dark room. The only sounds are the machines letting me know if he's still with us or if he has slipped away. This will be the room where my life ends.

I hold his hand to my cheek as grief overwhelms me.

Chapter 30: A Wedding

Zelda

Sunlight streams through the blinds waking me, and I want to throw open the French doors to see what kind of a day my little sister gets for her wedding. Instead, I lay on my side for a moment, thinking about all that has happened in the past weeks and how much has changed.

I run my hands over my growing stomach, thankful for my little princess. She appeared at the most traumatic time of my life, and she has given me so much strength. She's a treasured part of her daddy I will always have.

Closing my eyes, I wonder if she'll have his warm hazel eyes. I wonder if she'll love movies and pizza…

I'm pretty sure she'll love pizza.

Tears appear in my eyes. I've gone from being a strong survivor who never cries to a weepy fount of pregnant-lady emotions. I suppose it's warranted, but I'm still getting used to my heart spilling onto my cheeks at a moment's notice.

With a sigh, I reach up to touch them away. My breath hiccups, and I don't mean to shake the bed. Still, I'm busted. A strong arm goes around my waist, and warm lips move through my hair to the back of my neck, kissing down to my shoulder.

"Tears so soon?" Cal's voice sends warm love filtering through my veins.

"You should save them for the wedding."

"Pregnancy hormones," I say, turning to smile up at him.

His arms tighten around me, and he presses a light kiss to my lips, to the side of my jaw, to the base of my throat. "As long as they're happy tears," he says, giving me a smile.

"I'm so much more than happy. I guess that's why it keeps running down my face."

My hands are on his shoulders, and I can't help loving the way the morning sun casts a warm glow over his skin. I trace my fingers lightly over the muscles in his arms. Lifting my head, I bury my nose in his chest, inhaling deeply his luscious cedar and citrus and Cal scent.

He's here. He's okay, and I'm so deeply grateful. The weeks of his slow but steady recovery were so difficult. I'll never forget my dark night of the soul when we didn't know if he would live or die.

"Go back to sleep." He moves down to rest his cheek against my breast.

"I'm too excited to sleep!" I squirm under the weight of his body against mine.

"Our little princess needs you to sleep," he says, turning and pulling my back to his chest to spoon. Instead it presses his morning wood right against my ass.

"Somebody else is ready to party."

That makes him laugh, and his hand slides down my stomach, catching the edge of my sleep shirt and moving under it.

"We will have very mellow sex then go back to sleep." As he speaks, his lips graze my neck right behind my ear and chills scatter down my body, pooling desire low in my belly.

Reaching behind me, I thread my fingers into the side of his hair. "You don't know the meaning of the phrase *mellow sex*."

"You're right. I want you to ride me like a bull in one of those Western rodeos."

Laughter explodes through my lips. "It's too soon for that much crazy. I might hurt you!"

He kisses my neck again. "I can't think of a better way to go."

"Don't say that!" Squirming out of his arms, I push him onto his back to examine his side. "You're getting better."

He props on his elbows and looks down at the ugly wound where Wade Paxton stuck that horrible knife into his side and almost killed him. Thank God it lodged in a rib instead of puncturing his lung. He lost so much blood. Freddie and his team searched for almost an hour before finding him.

"I thought losing a finger was the worst pain I'd ever felt." I recline beside him, looking deep in his warm hazel eyes. "I can't live without you, MacCallum Lockwood Tate."

My throat aches, and he rolls toward me, into a kiss. It's long and slow, just lips, pulling, chasing.

"Shh," he says against my cheek. "Those days are behind us. It's all good things now."

It's true. Wade Paxton had been found guilty of conspiracy to assassinate Rowan, of ordering Blix Ratcliffe to shoot Ava, kill Seth, and kidnap me. Cal wasn't even questioned in his death. It had been dismissed as self-defense.

The bad blood between Totrington and Monagasco will likely continue, but the imminent threats appear to be gone. Except for Blix, who has disappeared. Logan and Freddie are determined to find him.

Rowan's coronation ceremony was last week, and today, my little sister will become his wife, the Queen Consort.

"Ava will be the most amazing queen," I say with a little smile as his lips trace a path down my neck. "I'm so proud of her."

"We can finally go home." He lifts my shirt to kiss one breast then the other before moving down to my stomach. "Ready to go home, princess?"

I exhale a delighted laugh, threading my fingers into his hair. He continues his trail of kisses, moving downward, and I arch back, closing my eyes as we spend the next several minutes waking up my favorite way.

Ava's hands shake so hard, she can't put on her eyeliner. "Give me that," I say, stepping around in front of her.

"I am freaking out," she says in a low voice, glancing around the room at the laughing and chatting ladies in waiting. "Everyone in the world is going to be watching us today—and if they don't, it'll be on the Internet, and they'll watch it over and over for the rest of eternity!"

"Now that is one sure way to make yourself crazy." I'm holding the liner-pen, drawing a dramatic swoosh over her striking emerald eyes. "You are going to be fine. Your dress is gorgeous, *you* are gorgeous, and all you have to do is walk down there and say 'I do.'"

"I have to say a little more than that." She steps back to face the mirror, and I straighten the front of her long, flowing skirt. The lace across her bodice is so delicate, and the spaghetti straps are perfectly fitted to her elegant shoulders.

I'm wearing a sky blue dress made in a similar design as Ava's. It's mid-thigh length with a swishy, flowing skirt. The cut is empire waist to allow for my growing baby bump, and it has a sweetheart neckline and delicate, cap sleeves.

"It's all a bunch of repeat after me stuff," I say.

"Help me with this tiara."

The unique headpiece is in the shape of a large flower at her temple and covered in dozens of sparkling diamonds. It extends over her head like a headband, and her long hair hangs in flowing waves down her back.

"You look amazing." I can't help it. Tears heat my eyes.

"Oh!" she cries. "Don't cry! You'll make me cry!" I rush to the window and snatch up the tissue box.

"Quick—look up at the ceiling and do math in your head." Her brow wrinkles.

"Does that work?"

That makes me laugh. "Even if it doesn't, you're not crying now."

"I'm too nervous to cry."

The queen enters the room at that point, and everyone stops chattering and bows. Ava and I do a brief curtsey, and she waves dismissively. She's dressed in a blue one-piece sheath with a long, matching coat on top. A small blue hat with a matching netted veil is on her head, and that ever-present, three-stranded pearl necklace is beneath her collar.

"That's enough. Are you ready to go out, Ava?"

"Ready as I'll ever be," my sister says softly, reaching for my hand.

I give hers a firm squeeze, and as maid of honor, I step around to help with her dress and flowers.

"You don't need much help with your dress," I say.

"You look very beautiful," the queen says in her stern voice, startling us.

I step behind Her Majesty and make big, teasing eyes at Ava. *A compliment!* I mouth, and she blinks away, doing her best not to laugh.

"Thank you," Ava says.

"You look like Bridgette Bardot," the queen says, turning to me.

"Wow! Really? Thanks." I feel truly complimented, whether she meant it that way or not. It's hard to know with this woman.

My hair is styled in a barrette at the back with a jeweled flower clipped over it. The rest is down my back in waves like my sister's. I give it a quick check in the mirror, and we step out into the large foyer, where ironically, Reggie waits to escort my sister into the car that will take us to Saint Augustine's, the enormous old church where the wedding will take place.

"And here you thought this would be me," I can't help teasing.

Reggie cuts his blue eyes at me. "Or so you think."

I hesitate a moment, wondering if he knew it would turn out this way all along. We don't have time to discuss it. A car is waiting for us under the covered back patio, where a tent has been set up around the door to prevent early photographs of Ava in her dress.

"Paparazzi again," I tease her as we settle into the car. "I forgot how much I hate those guys."

"Perhaps they've succeeded in blinding me," she quips. "I hardly even see them anymore."

"They're a menace," the queen grumbles, looking out the window from where she sits beside her brother. "Willing to kill us for a simple photograph."

I don't like that sentiment. Ava nervously plays with her bouquet, and I put my hand on her forearm reassuringly. She takes mine and smiles.

"You're going to be fine," I whisper. "Hajib is with us."

It's a short drive to the church. Our trusted driver stops the car at the end of an intimidatingly long red carpet. Reggie steps out to escort the queen into the enormous edifice, leaving just the two of us in the car. Ava turns to me and grips both my hands in hers.

"We've come a long way since that rainy night in the ditch," I say, smiling through the tears.

"I'd never be here without you." Her voice is soft and tears glisten in her eyes.

I dig in my hidden pocket for the tissue. "Here." I touch her eyes gently. "No more tears. It's your fairytale."

She leans forward, and we hug each other a long moment. I think about my mom and I hope she can see us from above. I know she'd be so proud of her Ava-bug. She might not think I've done too bad myself. The thought makes me smile.

We hear the noise of a throat clearing, and I look up. "The rumor mill is starting over this delay," Hajib teases.

"Tell them to keep their shirts on." I scoot toward the door. "You got this, Ava-bug. I'm right behind you."

She nods, and we step out of the limo into the next chapter of our lives.

An endless stream of ups and downs and vows and songs and sermons and pictures, and I'm finally in Cal's arms on the dance floor.

"I'm going to send Ava a personal thank you note for this dress," he says, with that naughty grin. Your legs stole the show."

"You're not too shabby yourself," I reply, running my finger over the epaulet on his military coat. "Hot."

"It's a chick magnet."

"Oh, really?" My eyes narrow.

He laughs lightly. "No."

"Come now, MacCallum," I tease. "Don't be modest. I'm sure the Captain of the Caribiniers bags lots of babes."

"The number is way down as of late," he says, playfully serious. "It's actually been stuck at *one* for quite some time now."

"One very happy babe." I stretch up and kiss his cheek before placing my temple against his square jaw. We're still dancing, and I curl my fingers in his soft brown hair. "Sir Sexy Cal."

"What's that?" He pulls back, grinning.

"The first night we met you were wearing this coat." I think about the charity ball, him knocking me off balance from the start. "I'd never been attracted to a man in uniform. I'm usually ready to run when I see one."

"No worries. I'm usually ready to run after you."

That makes me laugh. We're interrupted by the announcement of the King and Queen of Monagasco. Ava and Rowan arrive in all their pomp and circumstance, and a sad twinge tightens my stomach. Cal doesn't miss a thing. The music resumes, and I'm back in his arms.

"What's wrong?" he asks softly.

"She seems so far away from me now," I say. "Like she's moved to another world, and I'm left behind."

He slides his thumb over my hand. "Everyone's excited about the coronation and the wedding. Give it a week or two. It'll die down, and you'll be just the same. Look at Ro and me."

My voice is quiet. "I hope so."

"Anyway, you'll be the Duchess of Dumaldi, wife of the heir presumptive... You'll be as snotty as the rest of those titled biddies."

"I can't do all this again," I say with a sigh. "I'm exhausted... and I miss our villa."

He holds me close. "I'm taking you home first thing tomorrow."

Our eyes meet, and relief washes over me. "You make me so happy."

"I plan to keep on making you happy for a long, long time."

I lean in against his shoulder, and a naughty idea makes me smile. "I know what will make you happy." My voice is low and sultry and right at his ear. "I'm not wearing panties."

"Time to go." He stops dancing and steps back, gripping my hand to escort me off the floor.

I'm laughing when I notice the crowd has

parted. A tall woman in a crown and a flowing white dress is making her way quickly toward us. I look up, and tears heat my eyes. It's Ava.

"Zee?" She hurries straight to me, pulling me into a hug. "I kept looking around the room, and I couldn't find you."

"I'm here, Ava-bug." I reach up to move a dark wave off her cheek. "Did you need something?"

"I just wanted to say thank you. I wanted to hug you. We're leaving for our honeymoon tomorrow, and Cal said you were going back to Tortola." Her green eyes are round, and I recognize that look. "It feels like everything is changing."

"Only logistically," I say, squeezing her hand. "You'll come and visit us, won't you?"

"Of course!" Her voice is high, and I pull her close for another, longer hug.

"You were born for this," I say with conviction. "You're going to be fine. And Rowan makes you happy, right?"

"Yes," she says, and a little smile touches her lips. "Very happy."

"That's the most important thing. Everything else will fall into place."

She blinks a few times, and I know she's hearing me. Nothing has changed. She'll trust whatever I tell her, and I take that responsibility very seriously.

I watch as she's pulled away from me, into the crowd of dignitaries and debutants, and warm arms surround me from behind. Cal is at my back, his arms around my waist. I'm not the princess in this story. I'm no Cinderella. The good news is, it doesn't matter. We've both found our happily ever after.

The end.

Epilogue

Cal

Zelda's head is on my shoulder, and our beautiful baby girl is in her arms. Her little head is a halo of blonde hair, and my chest is so fucking full as I hold them both in my arms.

I sit beside Zelda in the hospital bed. Our newborn daughter, Her Royal Highness Princess Isabella Scott Livinia Wilder Tate of Dumaldi, is cleaned, fed, and sleeping, and I'm still trying to get my head around how we started this morning like any other day and ended it as parents.

After the royal wedding, we didn't waste any time returning to Tortola and our villa. Ximena and Selena were so excited to see Zee. They had a little party with bouquets of hibiscus flowers and the most delicious, savory meal.

Ximena made cornbread cakes and a type of stew with shrimp and peppers, tomatoes and water chestnuts, and what appeared to be okra.

"Callaloo," she called it.

Zelda had told me about the simple, yet incredibly delicious meals her friend would make for them every night in that wretched camp, but it was my first time experiencing one. Needless to say, she is now our official cook.

The three of them had stayed up chatting late into the night, catching up, while I'd retired early.

I'm now officially Monagasco's ambassador to the West Indies and pretty much all the Caribbean islands, and as such, my time is spent meeting with local officials. I listen to and observe what is going on around the islands, analyze it, and discuss weekly with my brother.

It would sound like a cushy, made-up job, but after Zelda's ordeal and the extended search, we decided it doesn't hurt to have a network of friends in the area. Especially since it appears Totrington is ahead of us in that regard.

Zelda is enrolled in college — when she's not accompanying me to dinners, charity events, and banquets around the islands. She has always tried to get Ava to get her degree, but I convinced her with her brains and nerves of steel, she should be a CEO somewhere.

She laughed, but I was only half joking.

So our days have fallen into the happy routine of me charming the pants off the dignitaries who've been duped into thinking Totrington is the better of our two countries, and Zelda is quietly learning how to conquer the business world.

Naturally, our evenings are spent with loads of hot sex, crack pizza, and our favorite movies. Why, just last night I'd been showing Zee how if she lay on her side and I got behind her at just the right angle, we didn't even notice how giant our little princess had become as I fucked her sexy mother's brains out.

Yes, the sex has been a challenge these last few weeks, but now look at us. We're here in this executive hospital suite with our precious little life-changer in our arms.

"What are you thinking?" Zelda's voice pulls me from my reflections.

I reach over and touch those pillow lips. "Just wow, look what you did," I say softly.

She smiles, her blue eyes softening. "You had something to do with it."

"Hell, I simply laid back and enjoyed the view." I'm not kidding. Zelda is gorgeous when she's getting off on me.

"She's really beautiful, isn't she?" Zee cuddles our sleeping princess closer against her, and I cover her tiny head with my palm.

"She has your hair. She seems to have your eyes. I can only pray to god she has your sexy lips..." As the words are leaving my mouth, something strange happens in my stomach.

"No," I say, feeling suddenly angry at the little dick who might dare try to kiss my Belle. "Actually, I hope she looks like *my* mother. Right now. As in, the way my mother looks today."

"MacCallum Lockwood Tate!" Zee's voice is sharp, but when she sees my face she bursts into laughter.

"What?" I say, not finding the humor in this situation.

"Oh my god!" She laughs more, and I'm getting a little pissed.

"What's so funny?"

"Does the over-protective daddy thing kick in that fast?" She's looking up at me with those sexy blue eyes, and I lean down and cover her mouth with mine, sweeping my tongue inside to silence her sass.

"I guess it does, and I don't give a shit."

"She's going to have to date, Cal."

A frown pulls my lips. "We can discuss it when she's thirty."

"Beautiful Belle," she smiles, cuddling her closer.

"You went with Belle," I say, remembering the endless names crossed off and added and crossed off her list.

"She was always my favorite princess," Zee whispers. "She likes to read."

"She's smart," I agree. "For example, that spot right there on your breast? It's very comfortable. I've slept there a few times myself."

"Belle also has the sexiest prince."

"Zelda Scott." My voice is stern.

"MacCallum Lockwood." Hers is a tease.

"Thirty," I say, kissing her again as she giggles.

The arrival of our bundle of joy increased the pressure on Zelda and me to tie the knot. Honestly, I've been ready to make her mine since the day I met her more than a year ago.

Finally, once Belle passed the three-month mark, Zee relented to Ava's constant badgering and my mother's not so subtle hints about how having a princess out of wedlock is not the Monagasco way...

The queen has no idea the reason we left Monagasco was so we could live as far as possible from my royal baggage. It's the only reason Zee agreed to marry me in the first place.

God, I love this woman.

Now we're bracing for the arrival of my family and a weekend of celebration and wedded bliss. Zee's ready to climb back into her sexy saddle of love, and I've been impatiently waiting to have her beautiful body all over me again. Her long curls just grazing her dark, tight nipples...

Sorry. Distracted.

The big day is here. Zelda says it's bad luck for me to see her before the wedding, so she has spent the last two days with her sister. I only shake my head — we're so far past such things.

Still, it means Rowan and I have been able to catch up in a way we don't normally get. We'd spent last night drinking and talking married life. Today, as we're preparing for the ceremony, he's more serious.

"I need to discuss something with you," he says as I stand in front of the mirror, fiddling with the khaki tie Zelda picked out for us to wear.

"Linen wrinkles so fast," I say looking down at my slacks.

"During the reception, let's talk."

I look over my shoulder at him. He's wearing the same beige linen vest over shirtsleeves as me. But his steel blue eyes are worried.

"Definitely," I say, giving him a nod.

We head out to the driftwood canopy strewn with white tulle and hibiscus flowers. A local pastor waits in the center, Ro is at my side, and I see Ximena in the front row dotting her eyes and holding our Belle. I give her a wink and she smiles.

The soft sounds of a local steel-drum band indicate it's time to begin, and my stomach tightens. I haven't seen my girl in two days, and I can't imagine what she's cooked up for me.

Ava precedes her down the aisle. She's wearing a filmy green dress, strapless and short, and her dark hair swirls in the breeze. She's very beautiful, and I give Rowan a glance. Yep, he's transfixed. I do a little chuckle. Good to know.

The song changes, and I feel tightness in my throat. Shit, I'd better not cry like a fucking pussy. Still, I've wanted this woman to be mine for so damn long.

It's sunset. The world is striped in pink, purple, blue, and gold, and Zelda appears at the top of the aisle. Her dress is made out of some kind of filmy material. I don't even look at it. All I can see is her beautiful hair moving around her face. She has a little headband around her head. Her lips are that soft pink color, and her sexy legs are on full display. She's a fucking goddess, and I feel like the luckiest guy in the world.

"Shit," I whisper, and the pastor laughs.

It's the only thing that breaks my focus. "Sorry," I say, giving him a quick glance.

"No worries," he says with a laugh.

And she's beside me. She's standing here barefoot, and she seems so small. I don't know how it's possible, because Zelda Wilder has always been larger than life to me. She's looking up at me, and I see the most amazing thing. Her blue eyes are glistening. They're huge and warm, and so much love is spilling out to me from them. I want to skip all these words we're supposed to say and pull her to me and kiss her long and hard.

But I control myself.

The friendly island pastor leads us through all the traditional vows. My mother, whom I've barely noticed sitting next to Ximena, is satisfied. We exchange our rings. I laugh as I slide the rose-gold wedding band over her prosthetic wooden finger. My pirate wife, Margo Tenenbaum. The band sits perfectly atop the engagement ring I gave her last year.

Finally, he gets to the part where he announces us as husband and wife, and I can kiss my beautiful bride. I hold her for a moment, looking over her face as the wind pushes her hair all around us. My eyes move from that slightly off-center line in her chin to her fuller upper lip I love to bite to those flashing blue eyes. Good god, how did this happen to me?

Holding her cheeks, I kiss her with all the love in my soul. The crowd erupts into applause around us, and we turn to face them. It's time to party. Ximena has Belle for the night, and I want to love my woman until dawn.

The steel drum band plays "Waiting in Vain," and I think of our reunion night at Bomba's, her cute little buzzy self. She's singing softly in my ear, and I love the sound of her voice. My hands slide over her smooth skin, and I close my eyes, holding her small body, a perfect fit to mine.

The song ends, and she smiles up at me. "You've made me so happy, MacCallum."

"That's all I've ever wanted to hear, beautiful." I touch her cheek, and the song changes. It's another island favorite, and we laugh as our guests surround us to dance. Ava grabs Zee's waist, and the two of them dance together. I step away to watch the show, and my brother catches my elbow.

"I'm sorry to bother you with this on your wedding day." His voice is grave, and my military past instinctively triggers.

"What's happening?"

"Let's walk," he says.

Together we stroll down to the enormous pit dug in the sand. A fire glows orange over embers, and several chairs and a canvass-covered sofa are positioned around it.

"I'm pleased with the job you've done establishing our position here," he says. "Wade Paxton spent a lot of time cultivating ways to disappear in this area. I like knowing we've exposed all his secrets."

"We've exposed a lot of them," I correct, thinking of the one Paxton operative who continues to evade discovery.

"This appeared with my mail last week." He hands a crude scrap of paper to me.

I unroll it, and it's an old-school style message made up of letters cut from a magazine. It's unsettling.

Wade Paxton owed me twenty million pounds sterling. I want my money. Instructions for delivery are pending. Don't make me move on your family again. –B.

My stomach grows tighter the more I read. "What the fuck?" I hiss. My muscles tweak, and I'm ready to fight. "Who else knows about this?"

"I've shown it to Reggie, Logan, and Freddie." He looks back over his shoulder, and I follow his gaze. He's thinking of Ava. "I will not let her be hurt."

I watch the glowing orange flames dancing over the embers as I think. "Ava is stronger than you realize." I remember how she found the rat at Occitan. "I'll find this fucker, and I'll take care of him. I'll be sure he remembers every finger he's ever cut."

Rowan turns to me and smiles. "I knew you'd want to do the honors. Still, I'd be happy to have a few moments alone with him before you do your worst."

"Done," I say. "We'll get on it tomorrow."

His large hand covers my shoulder. "Enjoy your honeymoon first. Ava is safe at the palace for now. I just wanted you in the loop."

I nod. "Have a Presidente—on me."

He exhales a laugh. "You're living the charmed life here. Sometimes I envy you."

"It's pretty fucking awesome."

We walk slowly back toward the party. The band is taking a break and the music has changed to a techno dance number. Ava and Zee are holding hands and moving their hips, and they're without a doubt the hottest sex kittens on the beach. Zee has Belle on her chest, and our little princess is blissfully sleeping through her mother's celebrations.

The task before us notwithstanding, I'm warmed and happy with the way our story has unfolded. As leaders of a country, there will always be some fucker needing to be handled. So long as I've got the most beautiful woman in the world and my little angel at home, I'll be good.

My player and my princess have made me the luckiest guy in the world.

* * *

Logan Hunt returns to Monagasco to assume his role as bodyguard to Queen Regent Ava Westringham Tate.

Love is not in his plans until he reunites with a sexy blonde hiding a dangerous secret.

Dirty Dealers **is the all-new stand-alone romance in the Dirty Players world.**

Get your copy now wherever eBooks are sold.
Also available in print format.

Keep turning for an Exclusive Sneak Peek!

Your opinion counts!

If you enjoyed *A Player for A Princess*, please leave a short, sweet review wherever you purchased your copy.

Reviews help your favorite authors more than you know.

Thank you so much!

* * *

Get Exclusive Text Alerts and never miss a SALE or NEW RELEASE:

Text "TiaLouise" to 64600 Now!

(Max 6 messages per month; **HELP for help; STOP to cancel**; Text and Data rates may apply. Privacy policy available, allnightreads@gmail.com)

* * *

BOOKS BY TIA LOUISE

Signed Copies *of all books can be found online at:*
http://smarturl.it/SignedPBs

THE ONE TO HOLD SERIES

NOTE: All are stand-alone novels. Adult Contemporary/Erotic Romance: Due to strong language and sexual content, books are not intended for readers under the age of 18.

One to Hold

Derek Alexander is a retired Marine, ex-cop, and the top investigator in his field. Melissa Jones is a small-town girl trying to escape her troubled past.

When the two intersect in a bar in Arizona, their sexual chemistry is off the charts. But what is revealed during their "one week stand" only complicates matters.

Because she'll do everything in her power to get away from the past, but he'll do everything he can to hold her.

* * *

One to Protect

When Sloan Reynolds beats criminal charges, Melissa Jones stops believing her wealthy, connected ex-husband will ever pay for what he did to her.

Derek Alexander can't accept that—a tiny silver scar won't let him forget, and as a leader in the security business, he is determined to get the man who hurt his fiancée.

Then the body of a former call girl turns up dead. She's the breakthrough Derek's been waiting for, the link to Sloan's sordid past he needs. But as usual, legal paths to justice have been covered up or erased.

Derek's ready to do whatever it takes to protect his family when his partner Patrick Knight devises a plan that changes everything.

It's a plan that involves breaking rules and taking a walk on the dark side. It goes against everything on which Alexander-Knight, LLC, is based.

And it's a plan Derek's more than ready to follow.

* * *

One to Keep

There's a new guy in town...

"Patrick Knight, single, retired Guard-turned private investigator. I was a closer. A deal maker. I looked clients

in the eye and told them I'd get their shit done. And I did..."

Patrick doesn't do "nice."

At least, not anymore.

After his fiancée cheats, he follows up with a one-night stand and a disastrous office hook-up. His business partner (Derek Alexander) sends him to the desert to get his head straight--and clean up the mess.

While there, Patrick meets Elaine, and blistering sparks fly, but she's not looking for any guy. Or a long-distance relationship.

Patrick's ready to do anything to keep her, but just when it seems he's changed her mind, the skeletons from his past life start coming back.

* * *

One to Love

Tattoos, bad boys, love...
Boxing, fame, fortune...
Loss.

It's the one thing Kenny and Slayde have in common. Until the night Fate throws them together and everything changes.

It's a story about fighting. It's about falling in love. And it's about losing everything only to find it again in the least likely place.

* * *

One to Leave

Stuart Knight is a wounded Marine turned Sexy Cowboy.
Mariska Heron is the gypsy girl who stole his heart.

Some demons can't be shaken off.
Some wounds won't heal.

Until a pair of hazel eyes knocks you on your ass, and you realize it's time to stop running.

* * *

One to Save

"I lost myself in the darkness of trying to protect you…"

Some threats come at you as friendly fire.
Some threats take away everything.
Family won't let you go down without a fight.
The Secret isn't as secure as Derek's team originally thought it was, and a person on the inside of Alexander-Knight is set on exposing him, breaking him, and taking away all he holds dear.
Refusing to let anyone suffer for his crimes, Derek takes matters into his own hands. He's exposed, he's defenseless, but his friends are determined to save him.

* * *

One to Chase

Paris fashions,
Chicago nightlife,

Secrets and lies…
Welcome to the North Side.

Marcus Merritt doesn't chase women. He doesn't have to. But when the spirited and sexy blonde who left him wanting more shows up in his office looking for work, little things like the rules seem ready to be rewritten.

Amy Knight is smart, ambitious, and back home in Chicago to care for her mother. A courtesy meeting with one of the top lawyers in the city should be a boost to her career...

Until the polished green-eyed player turns out to be the same irresistible "random" she hooked up with at a friend's wedding in Wilmington. Bonus: He's the brother of her older brother's new wife. What the hell?!

Who's chasing whom? It all depends on the day. *Or the night.*

* * *

One to Take

Stuart Knight is a wounded Marine turned Sexy Cowboy. Mariska Heron is the gypsy girl who stole his heart. Now they're fighting for their Happily Ever After...

Life is never simple.
Even perfect couples face storms.
The question is whether our love is strong enough to survive.
I believe it is.

She told me to leave.
If I leave, I take her with me.
~*Stuart Knight*

* * *

PARANORMAL ROMANCES

One Immortal

Melissa is a vampire; Derek is a vampire hunter.

When beautiful, sad Melissa Jones flees to New Orleans with her telepathic best friend, she is looking for a cure — not an erotic encounter with a sexy former Marine.

Derek Alexander left the military intending to become a private investigator, but with two powerful shifters as partners and an immunity to vampire glamour, he instead rose to the top in paranormal justice.

At a bar on Bourbon Street, Derek and Melissa cross paths, and their sexual chemistry is off the charts. Acting on their feelings, they are pulled deeper into an affair, but Melissa is hiding, hoping to escape her cruel maker.

It doesn't take long before the shifters uncover her secret. Still, Derek is determined to confront the Old One and reclaim her mortality — even at the risk of losing his.

* * *

One Insatiable

(Loosely based on the Hades & Persephone myth.)

One wounded panther, one restless lynx: One insatiable hunger.

Mercy Quinlan is a whip-smart lynx and the youngest in her shifter clan. She's tough and independent and dreams of escaping her alpha sister's control and living life on her own terms.

When a lone black panther shows up in her hometown, Mercy is intrigued. He's just passing through, which makes him perfect... Along with his broad shoulders, defined muscles, and sexy fighter moves.

Koa "Stitch" Raiden is picking up what's left of his broken life. Exiled from his black panther clan, he's running from Princeton to Seattle when he's drawn to Woodland Creek.

He's aware Mercy is watching him. What he doesn't know is the sexy little vixen who sneaks through his window each night is both the trouble he doesn't need and the hope he can't live without.

* * *

THE DIRTY PLAYERS

Cinderella meets *Ocean's Eleven* in this **CONTEMPORARY ROMANCE DUET featuring secrets, lies, royal high jinks, scams and double-crosses; breathless, swooning lust, cocky princes, dominant alpha future-kings, and crafty courtiers, who are not always what they seem.**

The Prince & The Player (#1)

Let the games begin...
Runaway Zelda Wilder will do whatever it takes to secure a better life for her and her sister Ava. Crown Prince Rowan Westringham Tate will do

whatever it takes to preserve his small country.

When Zee is blackmailed into helping a vengeful statesman take down Rowan, she never expects she'll be pulled into a web of lies and international intrigue--much less that she'll find herself falling for Cal, Rowan's "playboy" younger brother.

Ava's no help, as she finds quiet walks in the moonlight discussing poetry and leadership with the brooding future king irresistible. Even more irresistible is kissing his luscious lips.

They're in over their heads, and the more time passes, the more danger the sisters are in. Shots are fired, and it's soon clear even a prince might not be able to rescue these players.

* * *

A Player for A Princess (#2)

From the Mediterranean to the Caribbean, the game continues...

Zelda Wilder is on the run, this time from the ruthless assassins who've decided she knows too much to live.

"Playboy Prince" MacCallum Lockwood Tate isn't about to let the beautiful player who stole his heart get away — if only he could decide whether he wants to save her or strangle her for her dangerous choices.

After tracking her down to a casino in St. Croix, Cal follows Zee back to Tortola where he intends to keep her safe. One problem: Zelda's criminal liaisons are two steps ahead of her.

Lives are threatened, and all of the players' skills are tested in this plot to capture a killer and save a princess.

* * *

Dirty Dealers

My job is to protect.
I'm the best, the king's elite.
She's the only thing strong enough to make me look away...

Logan Hunt is a guard. He's constantly aware of his surroundings; he knows every angle. He'll take a bullet.

His new assignment is to protect the queen regent, keep his eyes on her at all times. He's more than up to the task...

Until a face from his past returns, and the one mission he's sworn to complete becomes his biggest liability.

* * *

Dirty Thief

Ava Wilder is beautiful, she lives in a pink castle, and she's a thief.

Crown Prince Rowan Westringham Tate craves speed, commands armies, and is devoted to Ava.

Their romance is straight out of an erotic Cinderella story, until the one man Ava is running from shows up to claim what she stole — or to claim her.

Now Ava may have to steal one more thing to protect Rowan: *A life.*

ACKNOWLEDGMENTS

Writing this duet has been one of the most fun adventures I've had as an author. I've been a fan of sexy, high-stakes, globe-trotting stories since I was a kid, and getting to write one is a dream come true.

I have so many people to thank for helping me bring this story to life, so let me start with the usual suspects...

Mr. TL as always is my sounding board, my brainstorming partner, my best editor, and my rock. Ilona Townsel is my constant cheerleader from the very beginning, and joining her squad are the amazing Helene Cuji and Elle Ramsey. You ladies are my support team.

My organization and marketing efforts were boosted so much by my PR brain and right arm Heather Roberts, and special thanks to my eagle-eye Candice Royer for your proofreading help!

Enormous thanks to Steven Novak for the sexy new cover design (and to Joseph Cannata for being the perfect Prince Cal!).

I am eternally grateful to my BABES for their excitement and support, for telling your friends, and being an all-around fantastic group of reader-friends. To my A-Team and my early eARC readers, thank you so much for your enthusiasm and mad teaser-making skillz. You ladies make me strong.

Last but never least, to all the readers who message me saying you love my books, who buy my books and leave reviews, who come to see me at author events, and who cherish my characters as much as I do, you mean more to me than I can ever possibly say.

Let's get on to the next adventure!

Lots of love,
<3 *Tia*

Exclusive Sneak Peek

Dirty Dealers
(Logan and Kass)
© TLM Productions LLC, 2017

Chapter 1: Assignment

Kass

The sound of rain.
Metal scraping.
Fast breathing; accelerated heartbeat...

"It's empty." Blix's voice is jagged glass, and my nerves fly to red-alert.

We're in a warehouse where dim lighting casts black-and-blue shadows, and the smell of rain grows stronger.

Petrichor, the scent of rain on dry earth.

Lunging forward, I reach inside, frantically feeling around, raking my fingers through layers of what feels like crimped strips of paper. "I don't understand." My voice is a cracked whisper. My life is on the line.

"You're a liability," he says.

"No..."

My shoulders try to shudder, but I take deep breaths, doing everything in my power to stay calm. Fear is a sign of weakness, and weakness is like fine wine to my cruel boss. If I beg, he'll shut down, and then I'll be lost.

Control. "Last year I made you a million—"

"And you lost it all in one night."

Calm. "He betrayed us both."

"You fell in love with him."

My stomach roils as I reject that accusation. I've only been in love one time in my life, and it wasn't with some lowlife Miami drug dealer.

"He was a dirty dealer," I counter. "He made us believe we could trust him. We let him get too close, and he betrayed our trust."

"You let him get too close." He hits the *you* hard. "Now you owe me even more. And you will pay."

Ice filters through my stomach. He takes a slow step away, turning his back to me. I hold my breath, listening to his heels click on the damp concrete. Raindrops begin a staccato thrumming on the roof. The rhythm grows faster, and the metallic smell of damp asphalt floods my nose. The pungent sting of tobacco cuts it as he lights a cigarette.

A cloud of blue smoke surrounds me. "What am I going to do with you, Kass?"

An ironic smile is in his voice, and my throat closes. I've never been in the room when it happened, but I've heard what Blix does to people who disappoint him. I've cowered away from the noise of grown men screaming like girls, and I've smelled the fetid mix of vomit and urine as their bodies fight his torture. Certain sounds stay with you forever. The dull snap of Blix's wire cutters as he removes his victim's fingertips is one of them.

My response is fast, breathless. "I know where he's staying. I can take you to him."

"And how are you going to do that?" Another cold smile. "In your car?"

Vile, evil, villain. The words appear in my mind

like flashes on a touch screen. None of them are strong enough. A bead of sweat rolls down the center of my back, and it takes everything in my power to hold still as he steps closer, so close, I feel his warm breath on the tiny hairs at my temple.

I fix my gaze straight ahead, mentally seeing his pale blonde hair, his flat white-blue eyes as I answer. "Call Taz. Tell him to go to Port Everglades. There's a motel across the street, a Crown Inn."

He raises his hand, and I wince, bracing for the blow. Instead, I hear the grinding of his thumb over the metal wheel, and a burst of orange fire shoots from his lighter, straight up in front of my eye.

"No!" I jerk back, whimpering.

It only makes him laugh. "He'd better be there."

I pray he is, although I know what it will mean when they find him.

"Taz will bring him here, and we'll have a short lesson on stealing from the boss." He's still beside me, exhaling cigarette smoke around my hunched shoulders, evaluating me.

I have to turn this around. Clenching my jaw, I force the knot in my throat to relax. I force my shoulders down. "I don't need that lesson," I say in a low, steady voice. "You left me in charge because I've never let you down."

A sharp pinch on my upper arm makes me cry out in pain. "Never is a long time. Running this unit is a man's job. They steal from you because you're weak."

Swallowing, I control my voice. "I am not weak."

"He's been slipping an empty box into every shipment for the past six months. I've got suppliers all over the Caribbean demanding blood. I'm about to give it to them."

I still focus straight ahead. I won't let him see the fear in my eyes. "So you'll kill Davis. Then what? Send them my head as a peace offering?"

"Not your head..." The tip of a knife blade bites the top of my cheekbone. "But perhaps your blue eyes."

My will slips, and I shriek. "NO!" My hands fly up, cupping around my face.

He only laughs again. The click of his heels echoes in the large warehouse as he walks away from me. The noise of the rain has quieted. "Apparently, I have to use my own eyes," he mutters.

"Or eyes you own," I say still holding my face in my hands.

"They're worthless, but at least the color is nice."

I can't stop shaking. Constant shudders rack my body. I hate being alone with him. I hate when he treats me this way. I hate the power he has over me — the power I gave him when I made that first deal so many years ago, all those years ago when I was desperate and had no other choice. That day I was so low, I hoped this job would kill me. I have so many regrets.

Blix's buzzing phone distracts him from his game of torture. "Blix." The voice on the line is unintelligible, but I know it's Taz, his right hand. His sergeant at arms. His capo. "Yes... At the warehouse... Bring him here... I have everything I need."

He finishes the cigarette. Stomping it out, he moves quickly to the back of the warehouse, and I know he's lost interest in me. I know the way his features are changing, and the dead focus entering his eyes as he prepares to deal with a traitor. He's detaching from whatever human feeling is left in his black heart.

Drawers and cabinet doors open and close, and he lifts out tools, dropping them each with a sharp *Bang!* on the metal countertop. I'm not going to die, at least night tonight, but dread still twists my stomach. I know what's coming when Taz arrives with Davis.

"What brought you back here?" My voice is demure, not challenging.

When Blix left six months ago, I'd heard he was running from some government job gone wrong, and all I could hope was never to see him again. I was wrong. The worst ones never die.

He doesn't even look up. When he answers, he's under the cabinet moving heavy objects. "I came for you."

His voice emerges just before the sharp *Zee!* of a power drill slices through the air. I flinch sharply both from his answer and the noise.

"Me?" My eyebrows pull in a frown.

I've been in Miami five years overseeing this arm of his drug smuggling operation. I tell myself I'm not as bad. I'm not a dealer, and I never even touch the merchandise. We're not supposed to touch it. We receive shipments of poppy and opium from cargo ships out of Turkey. Then we ensure they get onto cargo ships headed to South America and the Caribbean. That's it. No further involvement.

Davis got greedy. He saw the rise in prescription drug addicts and thought he'd line his own pockets by stealing just a little here and there.

Davis is a fool.

I'm a bigger fool.

When these guys go down, I'm going right along with them.

"Since your eyes have failed me, I'm going to see if your body is still worth anything."

My stomach turns at the suggestion. "I don't do that. I've never done that..."

"Now you do." He pushes past me, but I follow right behind.

"You promised — "

All at once he's in my face again, seething with fury. "I promised not to take the boy. You promised to guard my lines. Which check are we going to cash?"

My chest is tight with fear. My little brother Cameron isn't as little as he was when I started working for Blix. Back then he was only thirteen, but now, at eighteen, he's old enough to be one of Blix's foot soldiers. Men who are always one screw up away from a cruel and horrifying death. I won't let that happen to him.

"What do I have to do?" I'm quiet, resigned.

He touches my cheek with the tip of his finger, tracing a line to my ear and into my hair. "So easy to control." He twists a lock of my pale blonde hair around his finger. "So beautiful. Your assets are wasted here."

"It's where I want to be." Far from my past, I don't say out loud.

"Too bad." That flicker of gentleness is gone and I hear a car pulling up outside. "We'll discuss your new assignment tomorrow."

Ice is back in my stomach. I don't want to be here when the torture starts. I don't want to hear it, but I don't have a way to leave. Doors open and slam shut, and I hear Davis's fast-talking pleading. Soon they'll turn into high-pitched screams for mercy.

He won't find it.

"I will say," Blix pauses, giving me one last bit of his time. "It's a job you might enjoy."

I will not. I don't say the words out loud. I barely have time to think them before Davis's voice enters the back room. He's still laughing nervously, trying to buy time.

"Blix, it's me! Your right hand. Your pal! I wouldn't—AHH!" His voice breaks, and I know Taz has jerked his arms back, looping them behind his back and tying them with yellow, nylon rope, as per usual. "Blix! Wait!"

He's still pleading when the deafening *Zee!* of the power drill cuts through the night.

Blix's voice is loud, flat. "Thirteen suppliers across the Caribbean have been shorted in the last six months. They will each receive a piece of you as retribution, and to show I have zero tolerance for theft."

"It wasn't theft!" Davis's voice is hoarse as he tries to shout over the power drill. "I got you a better price here in town. In South Beach!"

"I'm going to start by removing the kneecaps."

The noise of the drill goes louder. Taz's meaty chuckle is cut off by Davis's raving screams. I run for the back door, pushing through to the outside and sliding down the wall until my ass hits damp grass. My knees are bent, my face slick with tears, and I wrap both my arms over my head, trying to block out the screams.

It's not enough. It's never enough to kill that sound. I can only pray one day the one screaming isn't me.

* * *

Dirty Dealers is available on all eBook retailers and in print format.

* * *

Are you on Facebook?

Join the Dirty Players Discussion Group and chat all about the story with fellow readers:

www.facebook.com/groups/DirtyPlayersTLM

* * *

Never miss a new release!

Sign up for my New Release newsletter, and get a **FREE Subscriber-only Bonus Scene** from *One to Love*! (**http://smarturl.it/TLMnews**

ABOUT THE AUTHOR

The "Queen of Hot Romance," Tia Louise is the Award-Winning, International Bestselling author of the One to Hold series.

From "Readers' Choice" nominations, to *USA Today* "Happily Ever After" nods, to winning the 2015 "Favorite Erotica Author" and the 2014 "Lady Boner Award" (LOL!), nothing makes her happier than communicating with fans and weaving new tales into the Alexander-Knight world of stories.

A former journalist, Louise lives in the center of the USA with her lovely family and one grumpy cat.

Books by Tia Louise:
One to Hold (Derek & Melissa), 2013
One to Keep (Patrick & Elaine), 2014
One to Protect (Derek & Melissa), 2014
One to Love (Kenny & Slayde), 2014
One to Leave (Stuart & Mariska), 2014
One to Save (Derek & Melissa), 2015
One to Chase (Amy & Marcus), 2015
One to Take (Stuart & Mariska), 2016

The Prince & The Player, 2016
A Player for a Princess, 2016
Dirty Dealers, 2017
Dirty Thief, 2017

Paranormal Romances (all stand-alones):
One Immortal (Derek & Melissa, #SexyVampires), 2015
One Insatiable (Koa & Mercy, #SexyShifters), 2015

Connect with Tia:
Website: http://www.AuthorTiaLouise.com
Sign up for Tia's Book News:*http://smarturl.it/TLMnews*

Made in the USA
Lexington, KY
04 May 2017